ELYON'S BARRIERS

ELYON'S BARRIERS

THE CHRONICLES OF THE ZAUPHRII
BOOK I

BOBBY WAYNE

Bobby Wayne Fiction

THE CHRONICLES OF THE ZAUPHRII
BOOK ONE
ELYON'S BARRIERS

Author: Bobby Wayne
Published by: Bobby Wayne Fiction
www.bobbywaynefiction.com
Copyright © 2025 by Bobby Wayne
Copyright © 2012 by Bobby Wayne Draft Version 1-728726621
ISBN: 979-8-9853475-4-8 (Paperback)
ISBN: 979-8-9906619-3-6 (Hardcover)
ISBN: 979-8-9853475-6-2 (eBook)

This book was printed in the United States of America.

CONTENTS

ACKNOWLEDGEMENTS

I want to thank my family, friends, and the many gracious acquaintances who let me bounce ideas for *The Chronicles of the Zauphrii* off them over the years. Your patience and feedback have meant the world.

A special thanks to my daughter Ashlee, for stepping in with fresh ideas whenever I found myself stuck, and my daughter Aspyn, for helping me bring this world to life with her gift of visualization and imagery.

I'm also deeply grateful to my editor, Steve Rzasa, for his skill and insight in helping shape this story into something stronger and more refined.

And to you, the reader, thank you for choosing to experience this journey with me. So, sit back, get comfortable, and enjoy.

Welcome to Elyon's Barriers.

PRONUNCIATION GUIDE & MAP

Hooni'i   (Hoon-eye)

Zauphrii   (Zah-free)

Rauthlin   (Roth-lyn)

<u>Rauthlin sects:</u>

Shawktee   (Shawk-tee)

Awutanee   (Awoo-taw-nee)

Wyunaktee (Wi-un-awk-tee)

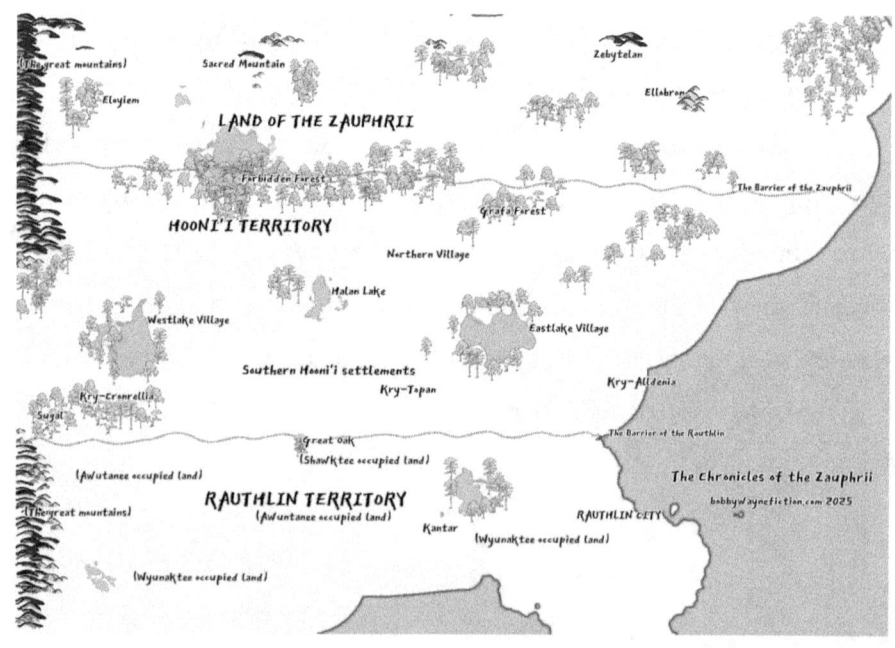

THE CHRONICLES OF THE ZAUPHRII

BOOK ONE

ELYON'S BARRIERS

By Bobby Wayne

There were they whose eyes were opened so that they see, yet they were blind, and those who were made blind, yet their sight remained. But do any really see when they share the same common element? It was the very reason for Elyon's barriers.

Hatred......

AT THE GREAT OAK

Nightfall loomed over the land as three Hooni'i crept closer to the giant oak tree elevated on a small hill. They had long passed the southern villages' self-imposed boundary and were having second thoughts on their plan for village fame and fortune. They were unaware exactly where the boundary was, but they knew the Great Oak was in Rauthlin territory.

Bracket was just a few years out of his youth. He was a dark complected Hooni'i with short black hair and a slight, but fit, build. He had never actually seen a Rauthlin before, and he didn't plan on seeing one now. From what he was told, the Rauthlin looked sort of like them, the Hooni'i, the distinction being that the Rauthlin were, for the most part, larger than the Hooni'i and had black feathers instead of hair. It was said they also had completely black eyeballs, the kind of soulless eyes that would grip one's heart and crush it with fear. He had heard that despite the terror of their abnormal eyes, they were deceptively pleasant looking.

Nonetheless, the thought of seeing a Rauthlin up close was too frightening to consider. But there he was, sneaking into their land in the middle of the night with his friends, Han and Jehbo.

The moon illuminated their shadowy silhouettes in the cool night air. They crept along, trying to be as covert as possible. The Great Oak loomed eerily in front of them.

Bracket paused for a moment beside Jehbo and Han, who had stopped. Bracket stood mesmerized by the tree before him.

Han hunkered down, his tall lanky frame folding, and looked around. "Both of you stay down," He whispered. His brown hair hung shoulders length. Han was older than the other two. As such, the others often deferred to him.

"Shhhhh," Jehbo hissed back. Jehbo was short with a muscular stout physique. His skin was light and his brown hair curly.

"I'm starting to think this is not a good idea," Bracket said. "I'm having a bad feeling about this."

"Well, it's too late now," Jehbo said.

"Tomorrow, we'll be famous," Han replied. "The southern village mark will be on the tree for proof. You can't get cold feet now."

"Yes, I can." Bracket shook his head. "This is dumb. We shouldn't be doing this."

"Shhhhh," Jehbo whispered again.

The evening breeze stilled. Silence took over. The three slumped down and listened.

Jehbo pointed to the shadowy outline of a thick rod several feet away. "What's that?"

"A branch or a stick or something?" Han shrugged.

Jehbo gestured to the others. "It's sticking out the ground with nothing around it."

"It's too straight to be just a stick," Bracket said.

"Maybe it's a plant," Han said.

"That doesn't look like plant life," Bracket muttered. He looked at his friends' faces, wondering if he looked as scared as they did. This new unknown didn't put his nerves at ease.

"This is silly." Han crawled over in the dirt. His body shuffled along toward the object. The others watched. Han appeared to examine it for a few moments, then tapped it with his sword. The impact made a metallic *clink*.

"It's some sort of metal object, a thick metal rod," Han said with an exaggerated whisper "It's jammed in the ground good, too."

Bracket watched as he looked around and pointed. "Look. I think that's another one over there. Maybe they are some sort of markers." Han then scooted his way back to the others.

"How do you think they got there?" Bracket asked.

"Someone put them there, stupid," Han snapped. "What do you think?"

"Do you think a Rauthlin put them there?" Jehbo asked.

"I can't figure why a Hooni'i would put something like that way out here," Han said.

"But why would the Rauthlin?" Jehbo asked.

"To tell us to get the heck out of here," Bracket replied. "And that's what we should do. Let's go back."

"Oh, stop being such a wimp." Han scowled at him. "We came this far. If I were trying to scare Hooni'i away, I wouldn't do it with metal rods.

Bracket glowered back. He wasn't a wimp by any means. *I'm just trying to be cautious..*

"But Bracket is right," Jehbo said. "Why are metal markers sticking out of the ground in the middle of nowhere?"

"I don't know, but let's do what we came here to do. Then we can get out of here," Han said.

Bracket looked at Jehbo. The two nodded reluctantly.

"Okay, just as we planned," Han told Bracket. "We'll go on both sides beyond the oak to look out while you start carving. You got the blade ready?"

"Yeah." Bracket gripped his knife.

Han drew his sword. He signaled to Jehbo to do the same. "Let's go."

Bracket watched them both run up past the opposite sides of the oak. They looked around. They both gave the okay sign to Bracket that all was clear.

Bracket clenched his teeth and ran to the center of the Great Oak. He began carving the southern village symbol into the tree's thick bark.

He wasn't sure how he got stuck with the job of carving. Like his father before him, he was handy with the sword. However, Han wanted him to do it. Han could have done it himself, but Han wanted to carry his sword and usually got his way amongst the three of them.

Bracket tried to focus on the job at hand. He had practiced many times. The carving had to be large and deep enough to be seen from a distance. He was also to carve in their initials, but with his present fear, which was no longer a consideration. *Be done already.*

The knife scraped away at the bark. He could almost feel the Great Oak's scowl in protest at such degradation by the sound the bark made under his blade. The scraping seemed so loud he thought they might as well have shouted the announcement of their presence over the entire plain. Sweat poured from his head as he whittled away at the bark. Every second weighed heavy on him. The pace of his breathing increased.

Jehbo returned and came up next to him. "Bracket. Are you almost done?"

"Almost halfway…"

"Hurry up."

"I'm going as fast as I can."

"We saw lights a way off. There must be Rauthlin over there."

"Then what are you doing here talking to me for? Go keep watch."

Jehbo shook his head and trotted back toward his original position.

Bracket continued to carve. *Hurry up, he says. I am going as fast as I can.* He then paused as he thought he heard what sounded like a tussle and Han's voice shout out something.

He stood and stepped around to see what was going on. When he did, he saw Jehbo standing there rigid.

Han's body lay on the ground with a large figure over him. "He came out of the ground!" he yelled, with the terror trembling in his voice.

The large figure stabbed Han's abdomen with a large blade and gutted him up to his chest. Han convulsed and made a horrible choking sound, then fell limp.

Bracket stood frozen several feet behind Jehbo and began to shake uncontrollably.

The large figure got up and shook the dirt from what appeared to be its hair of feathers. It turned and looked at them. Bracket could see his completely black eyeballs glaring at them in the moonlight. *It's a Rauthlin. He just killed Han.*

The large figure yanked its blade free from Han and with his other hand, picked up Han's sword on the ground next to him. A dark pool spread from underneath Han's back, and he stared at the sky, unblinking.

The Rauthlin stood and ran toward them.

Jehbo turned to flee in Bracket's direction. "Run, Bracket!"

Bracket didn't need any more encouragement. He fled down the hill, and when he looked back, he saw the blade sever Jehbo's head from his neck. Bracket stumbled on the slight downgrade and lost his footing. He hit the ground in a cloud of dust.

I'm going to die. He thought of his parents and his little brother. *Why did I leave my parents' home in the Northern Village and live in the south again? Was my need for independence worth it? Just one act of stupidity was enough. I was trying to be famous, but in the end, it was all folly: Folly leading to death; the death of my friends; the death of my dreams; my death.*

Bracket Doyle was going to be murdered by a bloodthirsty Rauthlin, and there was nothing he could do about it.

However, when Bracket rolled forward, he got up and kept moving. He was surprised to still be alive. Looking back again, he expected the inevitable blow from the sword. Instead, he saw the shadowy image of the Rauthlin standing a few feet in front of the Great Oak.

The Rauthlin peered out at him in silence, unmoving. Next to him lay the shadowy image of Jehbo's severed head.

It's not chasing me.

Bracket wasn't going to wait around and ask it why. He ran as fast as he could, worried he would stumble again as he stumbled across the landscape.

He took another chance and dared to look back again. The Rauthlin was at a distance now, but his dark silhouette could still be seen in the moonlight standing in the same place. Bracket felt the Rauthlin's hatred, seemingly trying to "will: him to death. *Is this Rauthlin just playing with me and giving me a sporting head start?* The Rauthlin then kicked Jehbo's head, and it tumbled away from him. He then grabbed the head by its hair and stormed off.

Gasping in horror, Bracket just turned around and kept running. The more distance he put between him and the Rauthlin, the more he felt that maybe he had passed the unknown boundary, the barrier, Elyon's barrier. As he thought about it, the only other possible explanation was that the actual boundary had to be not too far from the oak tree.

Winded, Bracket slowed to a jog. *It's the boundary. The Rauthlin can't pursue me. Praise Elyon.* Of course, Bracket was not into the deity of Elyon like his parents, and those of the Northern Village and the lake communities. But if he was going to be thankful to Elyon, now was the time.

He stopped to catch his breath. His panting deepened into anguished groans. He could not stop shaking. It was then Bracket noticed he was still holding the carving knife. His hand convulsed. He was barely able to loosen his grip.

How am I going to explain this? He would have a story to tell, sure. But unlike before, he no longer wanted the attention. He only wanted to get away. *Yes, far away.*

Bracket began running again, as fast as he could manage in his exhausted state. He was going to get as far away as possible from that Rauthlin, even past the southern village. He would go all the way north to his parents' house, to the comfort of his mother's forgiving and loving arms, to the home of his father's strength and care.

He had wanted to leave home and make his own way, but now he was running back.

Bracket wondered what the great Bumpus, the Northern Village icon, would say about this. He knew what his father would say. Yes, his father told him stories about these creatures beyond the barriers and why they were not to venture near them. Now he could say to him he had seen one. Not one of those so-called, white-feathered evil creatures who were supposedly beyond his Northern Village home, but this bloodthirsty killer was more frightening than anything he'd ever encountered.

A Rauthlin.

The Hooni'i depiction of them did not do the terror of them justice. A Rauthlin. *It's real, it kills, and it hates.*

Bracket picked up his pace to a full sprint. He put his head down and swung his arms with reckless abandon. Yes, Bracket Doyle was going home.

THE HOONI'I
THE NORTHERN
VILLAGE

(Months Later)

The mid-morning sunlight filtered through the trees as Bumpus closed the door of his modest home. He inhaled deeply, savoring the fragrant breeze that carried hints of wildflowers from the hills beyond the village.

Bumpus was a middle-aged Hooni'i with olive skin. His wavy brown hair was streaked with silver and his warm brown eyes radiated a quiet kindness. Though his build was unremarkable, neither particularly tall nor broad, he was a well-regarded figure in the Northern Village.

He had earned respect not only for his skill as an archer in his youth but also for his unassuming generosity and keen mind. He had long ago traded the chaos of battles for a quieter life of tinkering and helping his neighbors.

Today, his path led him to Grandel's house. It was a visit he always approached with a mix of duty and anticipation. The old widow, once a mentor to his late mother, had become something of a guiding light for Bumpus. Her wisdom had a way of peeling back the layers of his worries, often leaving him with a clarity he hadn't even known he needed.

He adjusted the leather strap of the pack on his back. Its contents were carefully arranged: tools for repairing the widow's wobbly table and chairs, a loaf of fresh bread, and a bowl of stew prepared by his daughter, Lana, who had insisted on contributing to Grandel's well-being. She too would often check on her and spend time with her. This morning, Bumpus had gladly carried her offering.

As he began his walk, the village pathway buzzed with activity. This wasn't an ordinary morning. The Northern Village was to host visitors from the West and East Lake Communities. It was part of an annual two-day celebration of Elyon. The villages would rotate this event every year. However, the villages to the far south of them did not worship Elyon and did not participate.

At this time, some Hooni'i were beginning to line up in the path for the annual Race of the Warriors. The event was marked in long tradition and was a symbol of pride to the victorious village. The participants would overcome obstacles that tested their archery and horse-riding skills. It would be the main event that kicked off the celebration.

As Bumpus walked along, Elder Frencrest walked toward him in the opposite direction. Frencrest was one of the three elders of the Northern Village. He was a tall slender Hooni'i with greying hair. With his lanky build, his stride was long and deliberate. He was in good shape, generally, and would normally have his morning walk along the pathway almost every day. He would say that during these times he would spend time in prayer and that his walks were therapeutic. He would feel one with Elyon's glory.

"Good morning, Bumpus," the elder called out, his long strides unhurried.

"And to you, Elder Frencrest," Bumpus replied, inclining his head respectfully.

"A glorious day to celebrate Elyon's blessings, wouldn't you say?"

"Indeed," Bumpus agreed, shifting the bowl in his hands. "May His glory shine brightly over all of us."

Frencrest nodded as they both continued to walk by one another.

As Bumpus continued, he looked out toward workers building a platform and placing wooden targets as part of the archery portion of the competition. Noticing Bumpus, the workers waved at him, and he nodded back.

Further along, he began walking off the pathway across the grassy hill that let out onto another trail. While doing so, he passed by some kids at play frolicking past him.

"Hi, Bumpus!" one of them shouted, her voice high-pitched with excitement.

"Hi, Bumpus!" another echoed, waving as she dashed by.

He smiled to himself at the innocent childlike freedom they had absent the burdens of an adult. It was an innocence that he had forfeited long ago. "Good morning," Bumpus said. "Good morning." Bumpus then stepped onto another pathway that led away from the bustling village center and walked up a gentle hill where, nestled among scattering trees, Grandel's cabin came into view.

As he neared Grandel's cabin, he was struck again by its humble charm. The widow had lived there as long as he could remember. Her home was a constant in a world that often felt in flux. He set the bowl of stew on a barrel by the door and knocked lightly.

"Grandel? It's Bumpus."

A familiar shuffle and soft voice answered. "Bumpus, my dear, come in! The door is not locked."

He pushed the door open and stepped inside. He was greeted by the comforting scent of herbs and the faint crackle of the small fire in the fireplace. Besides the fire, the room was shadowy, being lit with a beam of light coming from the window. Grandel sat in her favorite chair by the window. She was knitting a small blanket that Bumpus knew she had been working on for quite some time. To one side was a bed, and to the other side of the room, was a table and two chairs. Behind the table and chairs was a partition where she kept food and prepared meals.

Her grey hair was thin but brushed back neatly. The gentle wrinkles of time wore on her brown face. Upon seeing him, a twinkle of warmth shone in her eyes. "Bumpus. It's wonderful to see you," she greeted him, as she always did, as if she had not seen him in a while. "Forgive me for not greeting you properly. I've grown too fond of this chair," she chuckled.

He laughed. "No forgiveness needed, Grandel. You've earned the right to stay comfortable. I've come to see what I can do to fix your table and chairs."

"I appreciate you. You are always so thoughtful."

Bumpus held up the bowl in his hands. "I've also brought over some stew that Lana made. It's a very tasty batch, if I should say so myself. Have you eaten this morning?"

"Yes, thank you." She cleared her throat. "You must thank your beautiful daughter for always spoiling me." She then pointed toward the partition. "If you can put it over there, I will enjoy it later."

He nodded and walked behind the partition and set the bowl down on the ledge of the pantry. He then took off his backpack and opened it pulling out the wrapped bread. "Ah," he said. "I almost forgot." He walked back around and held it out to her. "Fresh bread."

"You know my weakness," she waved her hand loosely. "I will eat well today." She nodded back to the pantry. "I also have some cider if you want some."

"Maybe after a while," Bumpus replied. "I'll put the bread over with the bowl." Bumpus did so and then carried his backpack out to the table and chairs.

He shook one of the chairs and acknowledged that one of the legs was loose. He examined the other which was less stable than the first. He flipped it over and noted a crack in the wood connecting the seat to one of its legs. "Oh my, you could have hurt yourself on these chairs. You are fortunate that you do not carry much weight. But I can reinforce them and tighten the nails in the legs. They will be as good as new."

She laughed. "Well, the way you and Lana continue to feed me, you'd better reinforce it really good!"

Bumpus smiled and examined the table. It was not as bad as he thought. Again, he would reinforce a couple of the legs that were loose.

Bumpus spread his tools out and began working on one of the chairs first. He edged one of the nails out, paying special attention to limit breakage of the wood. He considered if he should just replace the whole leg but decided to remove it and reinforce the wood and nail it back on anew.

Grandel sat back in her chair and continued to knit.

Bumpus successfully removed the nail and wiggled the leg free. He looked up toward Grandel who smiled at him in return. He then took his hammer and began tapping the other nail out of the leg. "There will be a lot of Hooni'i crowding the village over the next few days. Do you intend on going to any of the events?"

"I will go to the feast tomorrow. Elder Doyle and his wife said they would pick me up and take me. I am too old to be around bustling crowds to see a race. The feast is enough. How about you and Lana?"

"Well, they are setting up for the race on the pathway right in front of my house!" He shook his head. "So, I suppose I am forced to be there for the race." He then tapped a smaller nail into a piece of wood that would be used to reinforce the dislodged leg. "I know Lana will be attending everything, especially the race. She appears to be very fond of one of the participants, you know."

"Ah, yes. Giron, I believe his name is."

Bumpus stopped and looked back up to her. "So, she has told you about him?"

"Yes, every time she visits me lately," she smiled.

Bumpus raised a brow. *I knew she liked him, but she doesn't talk about it to me all the time. What could Lana possibly be telling her that she is not telling me?*

"Ah, Bumpus, don't be disturbed that she talks to me about such things," she said seemingly reading his thoughts. "Such conversations are not easily shared between fathers of daughters."

"I see," he said as he fastened the leg and hammered it back into the chair. "I suppose I should be grateful that she reached out to someone as wise as you. It's only been her and I since her mother died when she was but a child. I miss Donia very much. I wish she was here during times like these."

"Donia was special. She would have been proud of how you raised her. I too miss my husband being around and wish he were here now to be with me in my old age. We both have a similar experience of loss, Bumpus. But we have a community to help each other. In that I am grateful."

"Yes, a community," he smiled warmly. Bumpus reached for another nail and held it in place. "Well, what else should I know about this love interest?"

Grandel laughed. "What you already know, Bumpus. Yes, she is very fond of this Giron, and she believes he has the same interest in her."

Bumpus sighed. He then returned to tapping the nail in. "Well, I knew this day would come sooner or later, I suppose."

"It's easy to keep them as children in our minds rather than recognize that they have grown and are of age to marry and start their own families. You should get to know him. She wants you to. She told me so."

"Thanks for being direct with me," he chuckled sarcastically. Bumpus wiggled the leg to confirm it was sturdy. He flipped it over and sat in it. He then stood and reached for the other chair. "What else did she tell you?"

"Lana has a good heart, like her father," Grandel said, her tone firm but kind. "She also worries about you, Bumpus. She told me you've seemed troubled lately."

Bumpus paused, his hand resting on the chair. "She noticed?"

"She loves you. Of course, she noticed," Grandel replied, setting her knitting aside. "You've been carrying something heavy. Tell me, what's on your heart?"

Bumpus did not respond but tapped another nail into the leg of the chair and wiggled it. *I didn't know it was so obvious.* Neither did Grandel speak further, nor did she turn her eyes away from him. Bumpus turned the second chair over to confirm its sturdiness. *Why am I hesitating? She knows something is wrong and there is no denying it now. Next to the elders, she has the closest relationship to Elyon that I know.* He slowly flipped the table over with its legs upward. As he examined one of its legs, he glanced back at Grandel. She still patently stared at him waiting for a response. Bumpus sighed. "Yes, Grandel. It's true. I have been distracted lately. I was not aware that Lana had noticed."

"She knows you better than anyone, even when you do not confide in her."

Bumpus sat down in one of the chairs facing Grandel. He folded his hands. "How do you know if Elyon's trying to tell you something? I mean, I don't expect a loud voice to say something or anything."

She nodded.

"Have you heard what happened to Bracket at the southern boundary?"

"Everyone knows, I suppose. Word even reached an old Hooni'i like me."

"I don't know how to explain it. It's... a sense of unease." He turned his head and looked away trying to form the words that were on his mind. Bumpus then looked back up into the widows attentive and loving eyes. "Grandel... I've felt it growing ever since Bracket returned from the southern boundary. The barriers, Elyon's barriers. I feel like they may not be as secure as they once were. I know it sounds foolish."

"Come," Grandel waved her hand for him to approach her. Bumpus picked up the chair and moved it next to her. She then reached out and took his hands in hers. "It doesn't sound foolish. It sounds like Elyon is stirring something within you."

"I've been feeling uneasy about the barriers for some time now. I cannot shake it. It's not just a passing thought or a temporary feeling. I cannot explain it. It's like a strong impression that I am supposed to do something. This impression has increased after hearing of Bracket's near-death experience at the hands of a Rauthlin. I didn't even have these feelings years ago when I inspected the northern barriers of the Zauphrii."

"Elyon's barriers have protected us all our lives, and for thousands of years before that. What is it about the barriers that concerns you?"

"I know it's ridiculous to think, maybe even sacrilegious. I feel that the time of the barriers is coming to an end. It's like everyone is living their lives and only I see the danger that is coming upon us." Bumpus put his head down. "I cannot shake it. I feel as strong about it as me seeing you are sitting here in front of me."

Grandel sighed. "It seems that you are carrying a heavy burden, Bumpus. Burdens are not meant to be carried alone. You should talk to the elders?"

"The elders, bah!" he gestured with the wave of his hand. "I dare not say anything like that to the elders. Elyon's barriers will always protect us, they say. I know it goes against their teachings."

Well, then, you can always go directly to the source Himself. Have you asked Elyon? Elyon is a burning fire, but He is also gentle and loving."

Bumpus lowered his gaze. "The truth is, I am scared to. And even if he told me, how do I know it's Him and not just my feelings? What if I'm wrong?"

"I understand, but it's something you must do, nonetheless. You must face your fears. You know this already, Bumpus. You don't need me to tell you that." Grandel's grip tightened, her voice was steady. "Elyon doesn't choose perfect Hooni'i, Bumpus. He chooses willing ones. Pray. Ask Him for guidance. You have a good heart, and He will lead you."

Bumpus sighed and nodded to her certainty and assurance.

She then held her hands out toward him. "Let me pray over you." She grasped his hands in hers and they both bowed their heads. Grandel prayed a quick prayer. "Elyon, creator of all and lord of all. Our dear Bumpus is burdened. His heart is heavy. Open his ears. Speak to him of what Your will is and give him strength to walk in it." She then squeezed his hands. "May it be so."

"May it be so," Bumpus said.

"Have faith and believe, Bumpus."

"I have many flaws, Grandel. And my following of Elyon's way has been weak at best."

"If you are called for a task, your imperfections and weaknesses really don't matter. In your weakness, Elyon is shown to be strong in your life. Rely on Him." She squeezed his hands again and nodded. "You will be alright, Bumpus. But I do sense that your uneasiness is a nudging from Elyon. Be strong and do not fear in whatever you must do."

He smiled and returned to fixing the table. She sat back and picked up her knitting again. When he was done, he made sure Grandel was comfortable and bid her his farewell. He would return home and continue with his distraction. What he had not told Grandel was that he had already begun experiments to figure out Elyon's barriers. However, up to now, he did so by his own will and direction.

Grandel had challenged him to pray and seek Elyon's direction. He knew he had to open himself up. But that would also mean if Elyon did speak to him, he would have to act upon it. In this, he was privately afraid.

Bumpus later returned home and began tinkering with his experiments. After a while he sat back in his chair and gazed at the cluttered props on the table. The room was normally orderly. However, this excessive clutter was the result of the intense concentration from his experiments. The afternoon's light beamed through the window illuminating the room. He looked up at the large map hanging on the wall. It was a map that he created. The map detailed his travels. It showed the topography of all the Hooni'i villages, including the marked forbidden areas. On both edges of the map, lines were drawn to signify the unknown populations across those boundaries. These were boundaries Elyon had put up Himself, Elyon's barriers. Mounted next to the map was a decorative Northern Village sword to one side and two arrows crossed, like an X, on the other.

Meanwhile, he tried to ignore the annoyance of the bustling crowd of Hooni'i forming outside. This noise interrupted his desire to be left alone with his thoughts. He walked over and shut the window. Bumpus then came back to his props. He rubbed his chin and mockingly repeated his name to himself. "Glettlebottom, Bumpus Glettlebottom." He picked up a clear piece of glass and smeared a colored chemical solution on it. He held it up to the light and pondered. He then looked back up to the map and let out a sigh.

The commotion outside continued. Some Hooni'i were beginning to line up in the path for the annual Race of the Warriors between these three Hooni'i communities. Outside, Bumpus heard two Hooni'i begin taunting each other. The last of his attention span fled. He slammed his hand on the table. He thought about grabbing his bow and quiver so he could take out each of the noisemakers.

Focus, he told himself. Bumpus held up the smeared glass piece in his hand for another look. He bit his lower lip.

It was Elyon's barriers that kept him awake at night. It was the great divide to the North and to the South, the unknown parts of his map.

The Hooni'i land was vast enough, but they were boxed in, albeit for good reason. It was said the strange populations on both sides hated each other and desired to kill off the Hooni'i. But those populations were prevented by Elyon's barriers from coming across to fulfill that desire. *We know the barriers are there but why can't we see them?* Grandel told him to pray to Elyon for answers, but he still had not done so. *I will keep at it until I figure out the answers to my questions.* However, to his annoyance, the noise outside interrupted his thoughts as the bustle of excitement of the race came closer.

Bumpus sat back in his chair. Two Hooni'i voices could be heard arguing above the rest. Bumpus finally buried his face in his hands. He surmised the two Hooni'i were directly in front of his window. One apparently was from the Westlake Community. He recognized the other as Girard, one of his fellow Northern Village inhabitants. Bumpus plopped his glass piece on the table. He walked over and re-opened the window. "Can't you two save it until the race? It's enough that I must tolerate this madness in our village every three years. Can't you take it somewhere else?"

Both Hooni'i looked at Bumpus, amused. They apparently enjoyed their own bantering and looked at Bumpus' rant as merely an invitation to join in.

"Why are you so angry" the Westlake Hooni'i asked. "It's about to start soon. Come out and join us."

"He's been angry a lot lately," Girard said. "It normally not like him. He must be working on something important." He then made a mocking gesture with his hand, bowing to Bumpus. "May I present to you the great Bumpus Glettlebottom."

Bumpus snorted at Girard and rolled his eyes.

"Oh, come on, Bumpus. Where is your village pride?"

"Where is your Hooni'i pride?" Bumpus snapped. "You two sound like a couple of cackling Freenoos."

"Oh, great, Gilo. Now he thinks we look like giant birds." Girard laughed.

Gilo turned to Girard and spoke with a lower voice. "Is that really Bumpus Glettlebottom the inventor, the one who, uh?"

Girard responded loudly so that Bumpus could hear him. "Yes, he is Glettlebottom, the inventor and explorer. As you can see, he is ornerier than ever."

"Quite angry," Gilo said.

"And downright mean, too," Girard said.

"With a somewhat nasty demeanor," Gilo said.

"Yes, he's glum indeed," Girard said with a sigh.

"Indeed, he is."

Bumpus threw up his hands. "You got me. I am sorry for being… well, glum." Bumpus took a breath and exhaled. "What are you two arguing about?"

"Bumpus, tell this cackling Westlake Freenoo that not only is my brother going to win, but all three Northern Village riders are going to finish in front of Westlake."

"You're an idiot!" Gilo shook his head.

"Tell him, tell him, Bumpus!"

Bumpus smirked. *I should favor Giron, since Lana likes him.* "Well, your brother Giron has been practicing a lot. So, I guess he should do well enough."

"You're both crazy. And Girard, you have a big head!"

"Yeah, and I'm smarter than you. You have the head of an insect. And an insect has a bigger brain than you. Even the insect thinks Westlake will get whipped."

"Whipped? Not by Giron! Your brother has an even bigger head than you.

Girard laughed.

Gilo pounded his fist to his chest and nodded aggressively. "The Northern Village doesn't have anything on us. Sa has won this event two years in a row. He's strong and looks better than ever."

"Maybe, he looks good, but this is our soil!" said the very animated Girard. "We have won the past three times on our soil!" Girard delayed for effect and repeated himself. "Our soil!"

Bumpus shook his head and was sorry he even got drawn into the discussion. He slowly shut the window again, and walked back to the table, letting the two Hooni'i continue to argue with each other. "Where was I?"

Bumpus sat and resumed his work. His thoughts returned to what was before him--the map, the glass, the chemicals, the arrows, the sword, the barriers of Elyon. The Rauthlin resided across the invisible barrier to the far south. They had black feathers instead of hair with no whites to their eyes, only blackness. The Zauphrii resided to the far north. They had white feathers and only the whites of their eyes.

Both wanted each other dead. Both wanted the Hooni'i dead. It was mayhem all delicately held in balance by Elyon. Why did it seem he was the only one concerned about this? Everyone seemed to trust the barriers. Did he not trust Elyon?

Bumpus turned back to the glass before him. *Considering that looking through a piece of glass alters the way we see an image, maybe I could figure out the right glass color combination whereby the barrier could be seen. Then the make-up of the barrier could be further examined. That way, it would be easier to explore and observe the Zauphrii and the Rauthlin, from safe distances, without risking lives. Or maybe gain an advantage if something happens. Perhaps learn more about the Zauphrii, the Rauthlin, and even Elyon himself.*

Again, if something were to happen, Bumpus repeated in his mind. *What could happen? We have always been protected. Nobody really cares what those across the barrier are doing, as long as it doesn't disrupt our special lives.* Bumpus saw Grandel's face in his mind. *What does this all mean?*

Now Bumpus knew there were some Hooni'i who didn't really care to heed Elyon's warnings and ventured out to live closer to the edge. He experienced this firsthand during his ventures to the forbidden forest of the Northern region. He longed to have another such adventure soon.

"Father, Father!" That was his daughter, Lana. He heard a door slam and her shoes scraping across the floor as she searched the house for him. "Where are you?"

Now, what?

Lana came into the room. She wore a simple beige dress with a thin brown wrap around her waist. Her skin was olive like her father. Her long brown hair was braided down to the middle of her back. "It's going to start soon. I have a good spot saved for us."

"I'm working on something. I think I'll pass."

"You are always working on something."

"There are more important things in life than a stupid race."

Lana smirked. "That's not what you thought when you were younger, winning all those archery competitions. You must go, and you know it! You're the great Bumpus Glettlebottom!"

"The Great Bumpus Glettlebottom," he muttered under his breath.

Lana raised an eyebrow at her father's mocking response. "Come on. I'm sure you'll at least appreciate the archery part. Everybody in the village is out there." Lana held her hands out to her sides. "We have to root for our village. We do."

Despite not wanting to go, Bumpus knew he would give in. He might as well just concede. He let out a long sigh. "Well, I suppose I can take a break."

"Good. You'll have fun. I promise."

Bumpus slowly meandered around and put things away. Yes, he had complained about going to the race. He knew he really shouldn't have a problem supporting the village and joining in on the celebration. It really didn't matter that she was right about it either. He was just being prude, and he knew it. He just did not want to do it right now. But he loved his daughter, even though she often saw the world in a more carefree manner than he did, which was increasingly more serious and considering threats that had not manifested.

His research pressed him. He felt an urgency about the barriers, and he couldn't explain why. Nothing would stop him from seeking knowledge about them, not protest from his daughter, not the elders, nobody. Admittedly, he hadn't been zealous in his religious recognition of Elyon since his wife died. Yet he felt Elyon was drawing his attention to the barriers for some purpose he couldn't yet determine. Yet he was still scared to pray to Elyon about it. *Maybe I'm   just entering middle age insanity*, he reasoned.

As Bumpus continued to take his time, Lana tapped her foot, waiting. She smiled at him. "Well, are you ready?"

"Yes, all right, I'm coming." He put a few more things away before following her outside. But his mind was still on Elyon's barriers.

THE RACE OF THE WARRIORS

A bustling crowd had gathered around a slightly elevated platform waiting for the beginning of the festivities marked by the Race of the Warriors. The noise of chatter bristled with excitement in anticipation of the race. Bracket sat to the side, with his arms folded, appearing uninterested. His eyes then followed his father, Elder Rodin Doyle, who stepped onto the platform. Elder Dole was one of the Elders of the Northern Village. It was his turn to be the lead host and oversee the events.

Elder Doyle was dark complected with short black hair. His short beard was speckled grey. He was dressed in a burgundy robe. He was a considerably lean for an elder, by the look of his frame even beneath the robe. One could imagine him as a warrior in his younger days. As he stepped to the center of the platform, the crowd calmed down. Elder Doyle gave the ceremonial speech and prayer which marked the celebration of Elyon had begun. Afterward, the announcer introduced the nine participants who stood proudly with their village's colors.

Bumpus leaned against a wagon next to Lana, surrounded by fellow Northern Village Hooni'i.

"Rame Samon from the Eastlake Village!" shouted the announcer. Many in the crowd cheered. Bumpus glanced at Lana, who politely applauded.

"Tam Gasane from the Northern Village." Louder cheers went up. Lana screamed loudly into Bumpus' ears.

"Sa Lay from the Westlake Village," the announcer continued to more applause.

Bumpus took a moment to look out over the archery targets while other participants were being announced. He felt a sudden, unexpected adrenaline rush as memories of his competition days flooded his mind. *Those were good times. Days when we were not at war, but at peace as we are now.*

"Giron Sebron from the Northern Village." Loud cheers rose from the home crowd. Lana screamed and cheered even louder than before.

Giron raised his arm enough to show off a flexing muscular bicep. He seemed to look directly at Lana through the crowd. Lana beamed back at him with obvious adoration and approval.

Bumpus caught this exchange and laughed inwardly, amused by their obvious attraction to each other. *Lana is in love and it's obvious that Giron feels the same way. She is as beautiful as her mother was. I guess this was inevitable.*

The announcer had to pause a moment because Giron's brother, Girard, could be heard continuing his applause and shouting moments after everyone else had stopped.

Bumpus returned his attention to the targets. They seemed to be a few feet farther out from what he remembered of the competition. The participants would need to account for the extra distance.

He considered shooting at one of the targets. *How would I have done it?* He imagined narrowing his gaze and pulling the nock of the arrow to its full length under his right eye. *Keep your arm and wrist rigid. Use your strength to focus on releasing the arrow over your left hand to its target.*

Bumpus had been shooting most of his life. The techniques were natural to him. To him, it was as easy as handing the arrow to somebody standing just in front of him.

The contestants had lined up at the starting line. Hooni'i blew horns and beat drums. They clapped and cheered loud encouragements to their contestants. Lana pulled on Bumpus' arm. "Isn't this exciting?"

Bumpus had to raise his voice to respond louder than he wanted to because of the noise. "Yes, Lana, yes."

Finally, the designated official from the Northern Village dropped the red flag. The nine sprinted seventy-five yards to the archery line. Sa from the Westlake Village pulled out front and increased the separation from the rest. Another Westlake participant ran clearly second, followed by Rame, Giron, and Tam from the Northern Village.

The two Westlake leaders pulled out and readied their bows when they were still about ten yards from the archery line. Nocking their arrows while still running was clearly a technique they had practiced many times before to gain an advantage in the competition, Bumpus noticed. This put them ahead of the others because they were ready to shoot when they reached the archery line.

Sa was still in motion when he let loose his first shot. He fired on the run from behind the line and slid to a stop right up to it. His arrow hit the target. Sa's partner did not shoot on the run but got off his shot next. It too connected. Sa's second shot hit the mark as well. His partner's arrow missed. Both had gotten off two arrows before the others even shot their first.

"What a shot!" Bumpus exclaimed, referring to Sa. "That was impressive!"

Giron's first arrow fell short of the target. Lana gasped. Her grip on Bumpus' arm tightened.

"Higher, Giron, higher," Bumpus murmured, adding to himself *Before Lana blocks the circulation in my arm.*

Sa's third arrow was even better, hitting right in the center.

"Fantastic!" Bumpus said.

"You are supposed to be rooting for our guys, Glettlebottom!" yelled a scruffy-looking Northern Village Hooni'i.

"What can I say?" Bumpus shrugged. "He can shoot!"

Lana gave her father a brief look of contempt.

Bumpus smiled and turned back to the contestants.

Sa sprinted to the next station for his awaiting horse. Giron's next arrow hit the target, but barely. The other participants all missed their shots except for another Eastlake participant, who was slowest to the line but hit all his targets and got off the archery line next.

Giron's next two arrows connected, and he was off the line running to his horse with a pack of four others.

"Good shot, Giron!" Bumpus nudged Lana.

Lana smiled sarcastically toward her father. She then abruptly turned around. "Run, Giron, run!"

Giron boarded his horse, but Sa already had a substantial lead, galloping far ahead. Giron's horse was fast, though. Giron pulled away from the second group and quickly overtook the Eastlake Hooni'i, Rame, riding second. The home crowd cheered.

Sa approached the area where the small scarves of his village colors were. He slowed his horse down to retrieve them in order, stuffing them into his pouch. By the time Sa was done, Giron was retrieving his first scarf. Giron was followed by Rame from Eastlake. Sa sped up his horse to the next area and drew his sword.

Melons had been placed on staggered poles. Sa slowed his horse down to a fast trot to go through the melon-slicing maze.

Bumpus knew that it was here that Giron had to make up ground. Rame was also close behind him. Meanwhile, Sa split his third melon.

Giron had slowed. With his sword drawn in his right hand, he swung and obliterated the first melon. He quickly switched the sword to his left hand and hit the second. He again swung it back to his right hand and demolished the third and final melon.

The home crowd cheered at what they saw Giron do. Giron had made up a lot of ground on Sa. But Rame got through quickly as well.

The horses surged forward. It was now a horse's sprint back to the finish line. Sa was about fifteen yards in front of Giron, and Rame was less than twenty yards behind them. Sa, Giron, and Rame opened their horses into a full sprint. The contracting of the horses' muscles flexed as their hooves reached out and pounded the dirt below.

Sa's horse seemed to have less stamina and began to lose ground. Giron's horse was the fastest. However, it had exerted itself earlier. It strained but was gaining ground on Sa.

Rame's horse was making up ground faster than the other two. The excitement of the crowd reached a frenzy. Giron's horse pulled even with Sa with Rame a length behind. The finish line was fast approaching. The riders yelled at their horses and bore down hard.

At the finish line, Giron's horse finally edged a half of the horse's length in front of Sa, with Sa's horse half of distance in front of Rame.

The crowd screamed as the horses skidded to a halt. Joyous cries erupted throughout the throngs of onlookers. Northern Village Hooni'i stormed out to meet Giron. Lana joined her friends and the swarming crowd.

Bumpus smiled. He had to admit, it was an exciting finish, but it was more the way Giron won that was impressive. Giron appeared to be a leader that wasn't afraid to press to achieve his goal. He didn't avoid the melons, for example, even though failure in his attempt to get through them would have put him out of the race.

Bumpus knew Lana appreciated him, too, but for a different reason.

Bumpus slipped away through the crowd as they continued their joyful celebration and made his way back home to his lab. He had more important things to do. The mystery of the barriers remained.

Giron dismounted. He was immediately swarmed by Northern Villagers who hugged him and patted him on the back, cheering so loudly he could barely hear. He soaked up their praises but searched eagerly for Lana.

Giron turned back around, still searching for Lana, but another young Hooni'i nearly tackled him. His younger brother, Girard, laughed and hugged him tight. Giron grinned and clasped Girard on the shoulders. "Giron, you did it!" Girard laughed. "I knew you would do it!"

"Imperial ran like the wind today, brother."

"It didn't hurt that you threaded through those melons with such skill, either."

Elder Doyle made his way toward them and waved for Giron to come to the winner's circle. "Guess I need to go," Giron said. "We'll continue our celebration later."

His brother gave him a playful push. "Go on, then. Don't be late for your accolades!"

Giron weaved through the crowd but still couldn't find Lana. He finally spotted her smiling at him and clapping her hands.

His heart missed a beat, and he momentarily forgot what he was doing. All he could do was stare. However, others continued to push him along.

Lana's beauty always seemed to have had that effect on him. Today was no different. *She is so beautiful. I just melt inside every time she smiles. I can't wait until this ceremony ends so I can spend some time with her.*

Meanwhile, Elder Doyle waited for Giron in the winner's circle. He held up his hand to quiet the crowd. "Come on, Giron!" The crowd gradually quieted for the presentation of the trophy and the prayer of blessing. Elder Doyle stepped forward. "What a great race!" he said.

"It was one of the best I've seen and one that will be talked about for years to come. On behalf of the Northern Village, I want to extend our appreciation to the East and West Lake communities for coming to our Village to celebrate the blessings of Elyon. All participated well and did their villages and communities, a great honor. Most importantly, their participation was for the honor of Elyon. It's unfortunate there can only be one winner of the Race of the Warriors. Only one can be the winner." Elder Doyle retrieved the trophy and approached Giron. "This year, I am pleased to present the trophy to Giron Sebron of the Northern Village!"

Giron accepted the trophy and held it up in the air for all to see.

Elder Doyle held a hand up again to silence the crowd. "May I ask the attending elders and leaders of the three villages to come forward for the blessing?"

The elders approached, all wearing robes of assorted colors. Giron knelt before them with the trophy in hand. All joined in the prayer. Elder Doyle and all the elders held their hands over Giron. Elder Doyle prayed, "Elyon, we ask your blessing for this congregation. We celebrate the hard work and discipline these Hooni'i endured to honor you. We thank you for peace amongst the Hooni'i. We now present to you the victor of the race of the warriors as a symbol of the victory of all Hooni'i who put their trust and hope in you."

He held his hand out to Giron. "Giron, the congregation and the elders pray a blessing over you: that you would continue to trust in Elyon, that you would have integrity and keep away from evil, that you would be a strong leader and show courage in the time of trouble, that you would always do good and fight for peace. May Elyon protect you, show you favor and cover those under your command. Let it be so to you."

"Let it be so," Giron repeated.

"Let it be so," the entire congregation repeated after him.

"Arise, Giron Sebron, champion of the Race of the Warriors."

The crowd cheered once more. Many gathered around to congratulate him. Giron enjoyed the accolades but wanted more than anything just to be with Lana. She had made her way to the side of Elder Doyle's wife, Lesina, who others simply referred to as 'Ma Doyle.' Ma Doyle was a warm slightly plump Hooni'i with a full bosom. She had olive skin and black hair which was often braided halfway down her back. Ma Doyle was conversing with the Doyle's three-year-old son, Atu. Atu had olive skin and curly black hair. Giron watched as Atu clung to his mother's dress. Elder Doyle joined them. Giron saw an opportunity and walked over with his trophy. Atu's eyes got big as Giron approached.

"That was wonderful, Giron," Ma Doyle said.

"Yes, you've made us all very proud," Lana said smiling.

"Thank you," Giron said, smiling back at Lana. He momentarily lost himself in her eyes. He stood mesmerized for a couple of fluttering heartbeats when suddenly he felt a tugging on his clothing from Atu.

Giron leaned down and patted him on his head. "So, Atu, what do you think?"

"Ya caught um good and umperial's wlly wlly fass. Can I hold da tophy?"

"Sure," Giron happily replied. He handed the trophy to him. Atu held the trophy to his chest and showed it proudly to his mother as if it were his reward. They smiled at Atu's glow of triumph.

Giron turned to Lana and spoke softly. "I'm glad you came out to see the race."

"The whole village is out here to support our warriors," Lana replied. "But I wouldn't have missed any race you were in."

Giron smiled and immediately became shy. Meanwhile, Giron noticed Ma Doyle elbowing her husband. Elder Doyle outwardly rolled his eyes. Elder Doyle playfully whispered in his wife's ear. Afterward, he spoke aloud. "I need to go talk to Elder Frencrest." His wife nodded as Elder Doyle kissed her. He then hailed Frencrest and left them. Atu handed Giron back the trophy.

Ma Doyle smiled at Giron. We are inviting a few Hooni'i over to our orchard after this. We can use some help preparing for the celebration activities tomorrow. I'm also making dinner. Can you and Lana join us?

"Yes, I will be honored," Giron said. He looked over to Lana.

Lana smiled at Giron in return. "Yes, I would love too."

"Oh, can Girard come?" Atu asked.

"Sure, he can," Ma Doyle said.

"…and Bumpus too?"

"Can he, Lana?" Ma Doyle asked.

"I'm sure he can," Lana replied.

"By the way, where is your father?" Ma Doyle asked. "I thought I saw him with you earlier."

Lana started to search the crowd with her eyes. "I don't know where he is. He was standing with me during the whole race." She continued to look around.

"It would be an honor to talk to your father, Lana, being who he is and all," Giron said. "I hope he is pleased with the Northern Village's return of the trophy."

"He was very impressed with you, Giron." She seemed to force an assuring smile.

"Well, I better check on my brother to make sure he is not getting into a fight or something. I look forward to seeing you and your father later then."

"I look forward to seeing you too."

Giron gave her a subtle wink as he set off into the crowd.

Lana watched him disappear into the crowd. She sighed deeply. She had indeed fallen for Giron and knew he had affection for her as well.

She then contemplated her father's recent sour mood. Her face became flush. She wondered if she caused him offense or did anything inappropriate to make him leave. Now Giron wanted to see him. *Why does everyone want to talk to him? He can be so difficult sometimes.*

To Lana, Bumpus was just the familiar father who raised her and whom she had been with all her life. But to the Hooni'i, he was more. And it seemed that to Giron, he was much more. *Father must come to the orchard tonight and behave himself. After all, I love Giron.*

Lana let that warm thought linger.

She brushed back a piece of her hair behind her ear. *I should talk to him. Remind him he has responsibilities to our community and others. But it won't be easy.*

Lana took a deep breath and headed home.

Bumpus was home and back to the work at hand, the glass, the chemical solutions, the barriers. Outside, all was quiet, the crowd quickly dissipated at the end of the race.

Bumpus discovered there was a magnifying quality when glasses were put together. The vision changed with space and distance. This magnification could also create focused heat from the planet's star to start a fire when applied right. However, this took more time than the standard tools of friction currently used.

Bumpus had seventy-three different glass/substance variations completed and ready to test. All that remained was the real-world application. *I must go to the northern barrier, the Barrier of the Zauphrii.*

He decided he would go the day after next, as soon as the Elyon celebration was over. He would tell Lana and others he was going out to do some environmental studies. They had long given up questioning him over such things.

I might have to give Lana more information. She's far more inquisitive and always worries about me. In fact, she'd insisted on going with him herself when he'd tried to take previous excursions.

But when Bumpus finally allowed her, she did not enjoy the inconveniences that went with it. Still, he wouldn't put it past her to convince the elders to tell him not to go or maybe have someone go along with him to babysit.

He considered this possibility. It wasn't a bad idea. But he didn't think he could trust anybody with his current obsession with the barrier. *That won't stop me from going. They don't understand the importance of this research.*

While he was pondering these thoughts, a knock came at the door. *Why am I constantly being interrupted?*

"Father, are you all right?" Lana pounded on the door again. "Father, open the door. Why did you lock the door anyway? I'm the only other Hooni'i living here."

Exactly, Bumpus started to say. However, he resisted making the flippant response. He made his way to the door. "Hold on. I am coming. I'm not as young as I used to be, you know."

The knocks came harder.

"I am coming." Bumpus opened the door. Lana stood there with a perplexed expression on her face. It seemed to him she was making a poor attempt at controlling her emotions. *She is always emotional about something.* "What's all the fuss?"

"Well, you kind of disappeared on me. I didn't know if something happened. Anything could have happened to you."

Bumpus stood there and looked at her. He did not respond.

Lana lowered her head, apparently realizing she might have crossed some boundaries with her aggressiveness. "I was concerned."

Bumpus maintained his silence.

"Sorry," she continued in a lower voice. "I'm just excited about today."

"I see," Bumpus replied.

"It was an exciting race, wasn't it, Father?"

"Yes, it was very exciting." Bumpus turned back toward the table.

"The crowds were even larger than the last time. Don't you think?"

"Yes, they probably were."

"Well, um, Ma and Elder Doyle invited a bunch of us to help pick fruit and flowers out of their orchard for the celebration tomorrow. Ma Doyle said she'll prepare dinner for us. Can we go?" Lana didn't wait for an answer. "You know how well Ma Doyle can cook, and you have said how much you enjoy her meals. But we'll have to leave soon while there is still light outside unless you have already finished your lighting experiment. Then we could go well into the evening."

"You are telling me about all this now?"

"They just invited us. And Atu wants you there. He asked for you. You know how he fusses over you."

"I have a lot of work to do. You go ahead and have fun."

"I didn't prepare anything for dinner for you to eat."

"What am I, old and helpless? I've been preparing food most of your life until you became a slightly better cook than I, that is."

Lana put her hand on her hip and tilted her head to the side. "Slightly better?"

"I'll be fine." Bumpus chuckled. "I don't have as much energy as I used to when I was younger."

"You know that excuse doesn't work on me, Father. You know you can run circles around most of these young Hooni'i, and you are hardly old or helpless."

"Yes, and you need to remember that, too."

Lana grinned. She walked over to hug him. She kissed her father on the cheek. She spoke with a softer tone. "Please, I want you to go. I'm worried about you. You always have work to do. This is supposed to be the celebration of Elyon. Let's get out, enjoy the company, and laugh with others. Besides, when have you ever resisted Ma Doyle's cooking?" Lana stepped back and deliberately changed her expression. "Hmm… something is wrong. This is not like you. What are you up to here?" she said jokingly.

"Don't try to reverse this on me," Bumpus said, amused. He pointed his finger at her, "Such a swing of manipulation and so quickly, too." He then nodded and raised his finger in the air. "Ah-ha, I know what this is about. I presume a certain young Hooni'i has been invited as well, eh?"

Lana blushed. "Well, if we are celebrating his victory, he has to be there, Father."

Bumpus pointed again, "The glug will be there, huh?"

"Ma Doyle invited him," she pouted. "And he is not a glug."

"Ah-ha again. You are defending him now. The truth comes out."

"Okay, Father, okay. Please no more Ah has. I'm not going to hide that I'm fond of him, and he is very fond of me too. I was hoping maybe you could get to know him. He wants to meet you, and you are never available."

"Well, I don't like him. All warrior and no brains, I bet."

"That's not fair. How can you say that until you get to know him? You can't rise in leadership as young as he is and not be smart."

"Well, I guess you are right. He has enough brains to like you. So, I guess there might be some hope yet."

Lana smiled at the compliment. However, Bumpus then scrunched his face. "On second thought…" Lana playfully punched him in his arm. "Ouch. Now you're abusing your father?"

Lana laughed. She looked up to him with the pleading eyes of a daughter that fathers can't resist. "So, you'll go? Please."

Bumpus' demeanor softened. "Okay, okay, but don't expect me to get all chummy with the glug."

"Father!"

Bumpus held his hands up in surrender. "Okay, maybe after a few drinks get into my system, it will be fine." He chuckled. "A meal from Ma Doyle is inviting. I'll bring some instruments with me to show Atu. He seems to enjoy science. Just give me a few minutes."

Lana hugged him. "Thank you. I'm sure you and Giron will hit it off nicely."

Bumpus shook his head and mumbled under his breath. He washed his hands in the basin and dried his hands on the towel next to it. He then gathered his coat. Bumpus wondered to himself if this day, and all its interruptions, would ever end so he could get back to his work. It would be just as well to him that the next day would conclude swiftly also. He had a vital quest to take, a quest that he had not told Lana about.

Elyon's Northern barrier was sitting there waiting for him, and nothing was going to stop him.

FOR ELYON'S FEAST

A group of about a dozen visitors, including Bumpus and Lana, had gathered by invitation at the Doyle Orchard. Despite being the hero of the day, it seemed to Bumpus that Giron was eager to show himself helpful. They all had just finished picking, washing, and gathering enough fruit for Ma Doyle to do her magic. She would make various dishes to contribute to hundreds of Hooni'i in attendance for the next day's celebration. They had also gathered an array of beautiful flowers for decoration. The flowers were placed in baskets and covered. Elder Doyle, Giron and the males rested by a barrel and wagon, while the females began entering the house to make preparations.

Bumpus had knelt to Atu with a magnifying piece of glass. He held up a flower to it and beckoned Atu to take a look. "You see how the flower appears closer when you look through it?"

"Well, it's a lil fuzzy."

Bumpus then held the flower up to Atu's face without the glass. "Now look at it without the lens." He then put the lens in front of the flower. Then with it." Bumpus repeated it twice as Atu contemplated what he was seeing.

"I see. It's different?"

"Yes, the light that is reflecting from the sky for you to see the object changes as the light is intercepted by the glass. You now see it differently."

Atu nodded and began to yawn.

The females had begun to retire inside to continue the preparations. Ma Doyle approached them. "Ah, Bumpus," she laughed. You have shown him many wonders today. But it's time for you to settle in Atu. Tomorrow is going to be a big day, and we have a lot of work to do still." She held out her hand for Atu. "Tell Bumpus good night."

Bumpus expected Atu to protest, as a young child would normally do. However, he appeared tired and went to her willingly.

"Night," Atu replied, and grasped his mother's hand. He then turned to the others. "Night."

They return good nights. Elder Doyle kissed her and patted Atu on his head. "Good night little one." Atu hugged his leg. Ma Doyle and Atu continued inside.

This left the five Hooni'i males standing outside conversing with one another. In addition to Bumpus and Giron, there was Elder Doyle, Elder Doyle's aloof son Bracket, and Girard.

"I think this is a good time to break out my special cider," Elder Doyle said. "Care to join me?"

"Thought you would never ask." Girard laughed.

Bumpus and Giron smiled and nodded.

Elder Doyle turned to his son, "Bracket?" Bracket shook his head tentatively.

Elder Doyle strolled over to a nearby barrel where he produced mugs and a thick glass jug. Holding up the jug, he happily turned to Bumpus, "One of your creations, Bumpus."

"What the cider or the jug," Girard interjected.

"The cider is way more valuable," Bumpus said. "I'm glad the glass jug could be used to hold such an important drink."

Doyle nodded and began filling the mugs. "It's wonderful when collaborative efforts come together for the common good." The Hooni'i smiled and chuckled, except for Bracket. "A toast to The Celebration and to Elyon's Feast."

Others replied, "To the Celebration and to Elyon's Feast." They happily took sips. Brackett took more than a few deep gulps.

Bumpus sat on the ground and leaned against the barrel. Giron sat next to him. Bumpus' own smile faded. *Not him.* But his body was already committed to that location, and the cider was hitting the spot.

Girard held up his mug to make another toast. "To my brother Giron, who held up the pride of the Northern Village and made me much profit today."

"Yeah, the profit he'll never share with anybody, not even me," Giron said. The Hooni'i laughed. They held up their mugs. "And what would have happened if I lost the race, my dear brother?"

"You weren't going to lose," Girard replied. "You had that look in your eyes."

"He knows me too well." Giron sipped his cider.

Bumpus looked at Bracket who maintained his own solemness. Bumpus had known him since he was a baby. He had known him to be confident, and assertive. However, since he came back from the edge of the southern barrier, he had been reclusive. They all knew Bracket's story, but they never heard it from him directly. Doyle had said Bracket was haunted by the death of his friends and their folly. He had nightmares about the murderous Rauthlin he had encountered. He spoke to him warmly. "How are you doing, Bracket?"

Bracket shook his head and proceeded to take another large gulp to finish off his drink.

Girard nudged Bracket, "Hey. It's okay. Relax. You're home with your tribe. There is no judgment here."

Bumpus noticed the opening to delicately pry further. "You know, I've been to the edges a few times too, Bracket, but mainly the Northern edge of the Zauphrii. Although I've never seen a Rauthlin, I did see one of the Zauphrii at a distance."

"You've been to the Northern boundary?" Bracket asked.

"You really saw a Zauphrii?" Giron asked.

"Yes, from the vantage point of the Forbidden Forest," Elder Doyle responded sarcastically.

"I know it was a frightening experience for you, difficult indeed," Bumpus continued, ignoring Doyle's snide comment. "But please consider you may now possess knowledge of things which could help us in the future, knowledge that could protect the Hooni'i."

"Didn't protect my friends," Bracket muttered.

Elder Doyle glared at Bumpus. "Elyon's barriers protect us, if we stay within the boundaries that He has mapped out for us. Which is away from the southern boundary and the Forbidden Forest."

His opinion, not mine. Bumpus turned to the others. "Hypothetically, what if the populations on the other side figure out how to get through the barriers?"

"Then we would have to fight them," Giron responded with resolve. "We would be at war."

"If the Rauthlin somehow got through, we would all die," Bracket said.

Elder Doyle rolled his eyes. "Wait. What are you talking about? Bumpus, we've been through this before." He glared back and forth between Bumpus and Giron. "Elyon always has, and always will, protect us by the barriers. You all know the story. I'm going to tell it again tomorrow night."

Giron was listening to Doyle but didn't take his gaze off Bracket. "What really happened out there?" Giron asked.

"I really don't want to talk about it," Bracket said.

"It will be good for you to get it off your chest," Girard said.

"Your experience may be invaluable, especially when coupled with the information I have regarding the North," Bumpus said.

"You shouldn't push him, Bumpus," Elder Doyle said. "He's trying to put it all behind him, as he should."

"There really is nothing much to it." Bracket gazed into the distance. "We went over to their territory, beyond the Southern Village, at the Giant Oak. A Rauthlin killed Han, and as Jehbo and I ran away, it chopped off Jehbo's head with one swing of the sword. I didn't see how Han met his end, but I heard him. I still can't figure out where it came

from. There really wasn't anything around there but the tree. And uh…
metal rods."

"Metal rods?" Bumpus asked.

"He chopped off his head with one swing?" Giron asked.

"How terrible," Girard said. "Did you say metal rods?"

"Yes, metal rods. We saw a couple of metal rods. They were sticking
up from the ground, spread apart in front of the tree."

Bumpus stroked his chin. "Metal rods in the ground." *Curious. What
could they be?*

"Why would metal rods be sticking out of the ground?" Girard asked.

"We had no idea. All I know is when I ran away, it stopped chasing
me." Bracket began to tear up. "It just stood there, staring at me. I kept
running and looked back again. It had not moved. It just continued to
stare. It hated me. I could feel its hatred toward me."

Bracket let out a long deep sigh. He shook his head, his face contorted
by pain that Bumpus assumed stemmed from his memories. "It's hard
to explain. Even now, I still can feel the oppressive hate. It wanted to kill
me. No, not just kill me. It would not be satisfied with just killing me. It
lusted for more."

"I'm sorry, Bracket," Girard said.

"Very curious," Bumpus replied. He had heard every word Bracket
said but his attention veered back to the single item of interest for him.
"Very curious. Maybe they are using rods to mark the barrier for some
reason or maybe to measure something. Or maybe they hope the metal
rods will somehow diminish the barrier. But why use rods? Do you
suppose the Rauthlin did not chase after you because of the barrier?"

"The thought did cross my mind," Bracket said. "Can we talk about something else?"

"Yes, let's," Elder Doyle said. "Please."

The five of them, including Bracket, nodded and took more sips from their mugs.

"So, Bumpus, how is the night lighting experiment going?" Girard asked. "Think you can do it?"

Bumpus was still deep in thought about what Bracket had said. He looked back at Girard. "What did you say?"

"The night lighting experiment. Do you think you can do it?"

"Oh yes, the lighting experiment. Yes, just give me some time, and I'll figure it out."

"It would be nice to see where I'm going at nighttime," Doyle said.

"But on the other hand, I guess it means we would be without excuse to work longer into the night," Girard said laughingly. "Bumpus, maybe you should reconsider what you're doing."

They all laughed with him. The teasing even brought a smile to Bracket's face.

"But seriously, Bumpus," Giron said. "This is important. It also can illuminate areas to protect us from attack and ambush."

Doyle finished off his cider. "We have not been at war with any village for a decade now, not even a skirmish. And we want to keep it that way."

"Elder Doyle, in my early years of training you taught that we always had to be prepared," Giron said.

"That was a different time." Elder Doyle's eyes then met Bumpus'. "A much different time."

"Yes, we can always depend on the army to find a military purpose for every community invention," Bumpus said sourly.

"We evolve," Giron said. "We have to use what we have, or it will be used against us."

"Ah, yes. To kill or be killed."

"Peace, peace. Aye!" Elder Doyle cried.

Giron smiled and continued in a more serious tone. "Don't get me wrong, Elder Doyle, Bumpus' work is vital to Hooni'i advancement and survival, and he is to be highly respected. It's just those with bad motives who will use the very same progress to destroy us. We must always be one step ahead."

"The balance of power, so to speak," Bumpus said with a smirk.

"It's just like Bumpus said," Elder Doyle repeated, "the power to kill them before they kill us. I've seen enough of that in my lifetime. The bottom line is we still build a society based on killing."

"Maybe you're right, Elder Doyle," Giron said. "Maybe you're right."

Despite the truth of what Elder Doyle said, Bumpus thought there would always be the necessity of survival to always consider. To his surprise, Bumpus was starting to like Giron's thinking. *Giron's perspective was not far from mine. He is inquisitive and more thoughtful than I thought he would be. I probably shouldn't be so harsh with Giron. After all, he and Lana seem to be on a collision course of love.*

Elder Doyle noticed Bracket's empty mug. "More cider, anyone?"

"Yes, please," Girard said.

Bracket and the other Hooni'i also nodded.

Bumpus decided to redirect the conversation. "I really do need to focus on my work more than I have. I think I am on to something. I must collect some environmental samples to the North. I've been working with different chemicals on glass which may impact light at nighttime."

"Fascinating," Giron said stroking his chin with his fingers.

"Amazing," Doyle said with an affirming nod.

Bracket held his mug down and looked at Bumpus, as a beckon of light regarding something else to temporarily take him away from his own somberness.

"But enough of that," Bumpus said. "Right now, it's about Elyon's celebration." He raised his mug for another toast, "To the Feast!"

The other Hooni'i raised their mugs again. "To the Feast."

Elder Doyle raised his mug and said, "To Ma's pies, of which I shall indulge myself. To the pies!"

"To the pies!" They all cheered.

The five of them continued to talk into the night until they parted their ways. But Bumpus learned much about Giron. He perceived Giron's prowess and leadership. Giron's understanding of protecting their way of life from potential threats was similar to his. It spoke to the unexplained urgency Bumpus felt inside regarding the barriers. A new plan was forming in his mind. He considered Bracket's information regarding the Southern boundary, the metal rods, and the Rauthlin. He then felt that Giron could be helpful to him in the Northern frontier. He also wondered if Giron could keep a secret, especially from Lana.

It was the following day. The sun shone brightly over the Northern Village. Hooni'i had gathered far and near, from the three villages to the feast, in honor of Elyon. As the festivities commenced, the village square transformed into a tapestry of color and life. Musicians assembled beneath a lolling oak, their instruments gleaming in the sunlight. A harpist charmed lively notes from his instrument. A flutist filled the air with sweet, airy melodies that danced like tiny spirits amongst the crowd. The rhythm of drums echoed, inviting all to join in the merriment. Hooni'i laughed, villagers twirled and spun with infectious joy, while children ran between them.

The scent of roasting meat fanned through the square, mingling with the sweet aroma of honey cakes and spiced pies. Long tables were laden with an abundance of food: golden-brown loaves of bread, their crusts crackling and warm; platters piled high with succulent fowl seasoned with fragrant herbs, and colorful bowls of roasted vegetables. A bubbling cauldron of hearty stew sent wisps of steam into the air. There was a sampling of various beverages and ales, both strong and mild. The villagers gathered, plates in hand, eager to sample the feast before them.

Meanwhile, Giron sat patiently at one of the tables tapping his thumbs together. He resisted his normal inclination to pile up his plate, sit down and dig in. Lana had insisted on preparing a plate for him. He was delighted to let her. But he was also hungry. Even though he felt somewhat awkward waiting. He caught the eye of Grandel, who was seated across and a few seats down from him. She returned a smile and nodded, appearing to read his thoughts of love. *Is it obvious to everyone?* Giron wondered. He sighed and continued to tap his thumbs together.

Girard then plopped next to him, smiling with food piled on his own plate. Girard mockingly laughed at all of the special attention Lana was giving Giron. When Lana left the table, Girard laughed. "You noticed she didn't offer to make me a plate."

"Be quiet, Girard," Giron said. "You're too loud."

Girard then leaned back in his chair, throwing his head back with exaggerated laughter as if Lana's attention to Giron was the most absurd thing he'd ever seen. "I already have my food while you sit there and wait to be served like a pampered baby," he said, continuing to laugh.

Ma Doyle appeared at Girard's side with a stern expression, giving him a gentle but firm tap on the arm. Her gaze lingered on him. "Shush, leave him alone."

"I can't help it," Girard whispered back. "This is so funny."

Ma Doyle shook her head as Girard began to eat heartily.

Giron sat patiently. He smiled with his mouth closed. Others feasted around him. *What's taking her so long?* Giron clasped his hands tightly, his thumbs fidgeting against each other in a restless rhythm. His stomach growled.

Girard's grin widened between him chewing noisily. He then leaned over and shook a greasy piece of meat in front of Giron's face. "Want a bite?" he asked, his voice being muffled and teasing.

Giron shook his head.

Girard shrugged and theatrically crammed the meat into his own mouth.

Lana finally returned with two plates. She set one in front of Giron with care, her fingertips brushing the edge of the plate as she smiled at him softly.

"Thank you." Giron smiled.

"You're welcome." Lana glanced at Girard with a raised eyebrow. She nudged him. Girard got the message and scooted to make room for her to sit next to his brother.

Giron ate, being careful not to appear to Lana like the gluttonous slob he figured he was. In between mouthfuls, he took a moment to gaze at Lana's beauty. He sighed. "You look beautiful today, Lana," he blurted.

Lana blushed. She put her hand gently on Giron's arm. "Thank you, Giron. We are all proud of you."

Giron tried to control his emotions. He returned Lana's warm smile.

Elder Doyle came to the table to join his wife. Atu trailed behind his father, his small frame struggling under the weight of a plate piled high, way more than he could possibly eat. His eyes sparkled with glee as he plopped it onto the table, nearly toppling a cup of water in the process. They sat opposite Lana and Giron and next to Ma Doyle. Atu grinned from ear to ear, waiting to delve in.

Ma Doyle scoffed at her husband. "Rodin, he can't eat all of that! Why did you let him get so much?"

"Oh, he's fine. He's going to be big and strong like Giron," Elder Doyle said.

"Yeah, yike Giron," Atu said. He grabbed his fork and began stuffing his mouth.

Ma Doyle smirked. "Slow down. Don't eat so fast. You'll get a stomachache."

Atu looked up at his mother and nodded. He then chewed his food in slow motion.

Lana put her hand over her mouth and chuckled as everyone laughed. Everyone continued to eat and converse around the table, enjoying each other's company.

Giron stayed quiet. He was trying to plot how he would get Lana alone. He wanted to express his feelings toward her.

He wanted to ask her to marry him.

Giron tried to stir up his own courage. He was determined not to let another day go by without speaking to her about it. He rubbed his fingers together under the table, attempting to encourage himself. *Today's the day. I won't let another moment slip by.* But as quickly as that resolve came, doubt crept in. *What if she's just being kind? What if her smile is nothing more than politeness? And her father... he doesn't seem impressed with me. Would I impress me?*

As a group of Hooni'i musicians began another tune. Giron bounced his head slightly to the music. The drums held a steady rhythm while the flutist echoed levity and merriment. It was then that Elder Doyle's voice drew Giron's attention away from his thoughts. "Lana where is your father, anyway?" he asked.

"The last time I saw him, he was in an intense discussion with Elder Grier over the complex properties of a bean." She laughed. "I think he is eating with him somewhere over there," Lana said while pointing toward a crowd.

"Always an intense conversation." Elder Doyle chuckled.

Lana shrugged and held her hands out. "You know my father."

Yes, always an intense conversation, great, thought Giron, *and over a bean no less.*

After a while, the musicians turned to play slow ceremonial music that brought immediate smiles to many The beat slowed to a rolling flow of the harpist and echoing flute. Hooni'i gathered to dance one of the several ceremonial dances. Lana beamed and swayed to the music. She looked at Giron expectantly. "Oh, I love this song, Giron, don't you?"

Giron easily picked up on her hint. "Yes, very much," he said. He held out his hand. "Would you like to dance?"

Lana looked into his eyes with gentleness. "Yes. I would like that very much."

Giron received her hand and escorted her to the area where others were dancing. She smiled at him. Their bodies swayed to the music as Giron's heart melted. He was mesmerized by the sight of her. Her hair sparkled as it flowed against the backdrop of the afternoon light. Every movement she made was like a delightful dream. It was a dream he wished would never end.

When the music ceased, her eyes continued to dance. He stood there awestruck. Giron finally mustered up his courage. "Would you like to go for a walk with me, Lana?"

"Yes, I would be delighted."

The two walked away from the crowd. The sun hung low, casting rays of golden light through an array of trees to the side of the village square. A mix of pale yellow and deep blue wildflowers sprinkled the lush green meadow beneath them. The light touched softly on the gentle flow of water as they approached a small creek. They followed its banks.

"It seems we are given fair weather for the festival today," Giron said, his voice steady, but with a hint of a deeper meaning beneath the casual words.

She looked at him, a smile playing at the corner of her lips. "Elyon has blessed us with fair weather indeed. It has been a clear day. Perhaps Elyon will favor us with the presence of the stars tonight." She then looked away, her eyes following the line of the stream.

Giron noticed a gentle warmth in her gaze. He took the opportunity to reach for her hand. He was delighted when she received his in return. They continued in silence until they stopped by a small tree. The tree's green and gold leaves reached out with a loving desire to softly caress the couple under their presence.

Giron reached out and held Lana's other hand, then faced her. He gazed wantonly into her light brown eyes. "Lana, I really enjoy being with you."

She blushed. "I enjoy being with you too, Giron."

"Lana."

"Yes."

"I'm not good at expressing my feelings. All I know is when I'm with you, my world comes to a complete stop. You're so beautiful and special to me." Giron hesitated. She stared deeply into his eyes, as if waiting for something. He lowered his head. "I told you I wasn't good at expressing my feelings."

"Oh, you are expressing yourself just fine, Giron."

Giron looked back up to her and held her hands more tightly. "Lana. I love you, and I would like the honor of courting you to be my wife."

Tears formed in Lana's eyes. Her response was to hold him close and then kiss. She looked deeply into his eyes when they finally parted. "I love you, Giron. Yes, I will be your wife."

Giron grinned and embraced her tightly. His heart hammered inside his chest. The love of his life just kissed him and agreed to marry him.

On the final day of the celebration of Elyon, he had one more reason to celebrate. Elyon had blessed him beyond belief.

The celebration went on into the evening. Hooni'i ate, played games, danced, enjoyed music, and gave gifts, all in honor of Elyon. There was no shortage of food in the village, and Bumpus was guilty of over-indulging. Bumpus had a great time even though Giron was attached to Lana everywhere she went. Bumpus had separated from the others to rest a moment.

Bumpus felt something pulling him into a relationship with Giron too. He took a moment to look up to the sky, speaking directly to Elyon in his mind. *Relationship with Giron, and this obsession with your barriers… what's next? Maybe I shouldn't even ask.* He chuckled. *At least I ate plenty of good food today. All in your name, Elyon.* He raised his hands to the sky. *I appreciate and celebrate.*

He found a spot on a grassy area by a tree. He rested his back against it, and from there, he kind of slid down to a seated position. Bumpus let out a long sigh of satisfaction. He closed his eyes and folded his hands over his belly. *Yes, Elyon, peace at last. Silence, tranquility, metal rods... Calmness, relaxation, metal rods in the ground...*

The sound of a Hooni'i clearing his throat interrupted his solitude. Bumpus was tempted to ignore the intruder by pretending he was sleeping. But he did not. When he opened his eyes there stood Giron hovering over him, holding two drinks in his hands.

"Wonderful feast. Glory and honor to Elyon," Giron said.

"Glory and honor to Elyon." Bumpus frowned at him.

"Mind if I join you?"

Bumpus hesitated before answering. "Of course. Have a seat."

Giron handed one of the drinks to Bumpus and sat next to him. Bumpus accepted it more out of being polite rather than wanting to drink anything. "I've been trying to talk to you all day. It's been an eventful celebration."

Bumpus laughed. "What I want to know is how you got away from Lana for a few minutes."

Giron chuckled. "I guess you kind of know we are fond of each other."

"I know indeed." Bumpus rolled his eyes.

Giron smiled and looked at the ground. "Well, I just wanted to tell you I admire your work very much. I hope you didn't think I was too out of line with Elder Doyle in the orchard."

"No, Giron. You weren't. In fact, I do agree with some of your thoughts on the matter. It's puzzling how things change over time." Bumpus took a sip of his ale. "Despite Doyle's words of peace, he was quite the fierce warrior long ago, as you know."

"Yes, I've heard." Giron took a deep sip of his drink as well. He smacked his lips and turned his attention back to Bumpus. "I grew up as a child to be trained as a warrior. My father died a warrior, and I set my mind to learn and be skilled for battle. Although we have been at peace, I believe I am as prepared as anyone else. It's in my blood. It's part of our culture. But every time I hear you and Lana talk, I realize the Glettlebottoms have opened a world of possibilities in my mind. Sometimes I wish I could be more like you rather than, well, like me." Bumpus laughed and shook his head. "Like me? You must be real love struck. And I had no idea Lana was listening to me." He smiled and looked Giron in the eyes. "Balance, Giron, is what we all need. Do you think I don't know anything about being a warrior because I have a different gift of which I choose to emphasize?"

"I don't understand."

"Yes, being a warrior is part of our culture as it has been with all Hooni'i youth, me included. Do you think I could have survived in wartime as a youth without submitting to the ideals of a warrior?"

"I know you were an archer."

"Yes. I was decent with the sword, too. But yes, my specialty was with the bow. You know, I won several village competitions years ago." Bumpus sat back and blew in the air. "I've been in many battles, too. I fought at Kry-Cronrellia and Sugal and many other skirmishes around the southern villages. I survived them despite the mayhem of it all."

"I don't understand. If you were such a warrior, why haven't you offered your services in the training others?"

"Because as far as being a warrior, there are many who are good at those things. Not so many are good at science. What I'm doing is a special gift from Elyon."

Giron shook his head and raised his mug. "So, we celebrate."

Bumpus raised his cup. "We celebrate."

Both Hooni'i sipped their drinks. "You are more than just a warrior," Bumpus said. "I can see it. I believe that is what Lana sees in you as well. I didn't see it at first, but I do now."

As Bumpus sipped his drink he thought about his beloved wife. She used to enjoy these feasts. He remembered the times they sat and talked about the beauty of this world and the majesty of Elyon. When she was pregnant, they talked about a world of peace that offered hope and opportunity to their baby.

Donia. My dear Donia. I wish you were alive now to see how our daughter has grown. You would be proud of her. Bumpus looked down at his drink. "Has Lana ever mentioned to you how her mother died?"

"We'll, uh, I had heard something about she had died in an explosive fire of some sort. A lightning strike to your home, I've heard some say." After a long pause, Giron asked softly, "Do you think it was Elyon's will?"

"I don't know if it was Elyon's will or not, but I do know my relationship with Lana would have been different if it had not happened. Lana would have been different. Elyon will judge whether it would have been for the better or not. But I also may have continued with a dangerous experiment that may have negatively affected all Hooni'i."

"Destructive experiment? What do you mean?"

Bumpus turned and stared into space. He set his cup down on the grass. "There was indeed an explosive fire that killed my wife, but it wasn't lightning that caused it. It was a decision we Hooni'i made at the time. It was a decision I made because we let our hearts harden towards one another. We decided to fight and kill for greed and other useless disputes. I think it was our will. I don't think we can pin it on Elyon. But I suppose Elyon already knew what choices we were going to make. I don't know."

Why am I confiding in him? Maybe it was because, on the day of Elyon's celebration, his heart seemed ready to confess the burden he had been carrying all these years, the burden he and Lana shared.

"When I was about your age, there was war with the southern villages," Bumpus explained. "There was constant strife with the central areas as well."

"It's strange that now, at the games, we were all competing as brothers, no matter our village," Giron said.

"I hope it stays that way and that we continue to work for a better relationship with the southern villages. But in those days, we thought nothing of killing each other. I've been in battles and had many friends die around me. I always wanted to be better than my fellow warrior and strove to do so. However, I also was an intellect with a thirst for knowledge. I assisted the man then known as Captain Doyle in perfecting our weapons to have a better and more lethal effect. At Doyle's direction, and with the continual advancements in steel and usages of glass, I eventually began spending more time working with the production of weapons than fighting."

73

Bumpus shook his head. "Of course, even less time with my wife and the baby. One day, while observing a simple lantern, I pondered the combustible substance of the natural blue oil inside of it. I wondered how I could make the substance used in our lanterns into a weapon that could more effectively kill our Hooni'i enemies. I thought the southern Hooni'i didn't care about Elyon anyway. 'Their souls be damned!' is what I told myself."

Giron's eyes widened. He leaned forward.

"When I advised Captain Doyle of my thoughts, he allowed me time from my duties to experiment. My wife was against my drive to create anything that could be used to kill Hooni'i. This led to discord in our home and many arguments. But one day…" Bumpus looked back up to Giron, half smiling. "I did it."

"You, did it? You did what?"

"I found when I used a certain chemical with the blue oil in a tightly closed container made with particles of the dorlan rock, and then broke that container, it caused sparks that burst into flames. An explosion of sorts, fire with force, but not very potent initially. Doyle was pleased."

"An explosion?" Giron repeated.

"Yes, but the containers weren't stable. I worked day and night to try to figure it out. I even brought some samples home. One evening, Lana, who was then a toddler, wandered into my lab, being very disagreeable. She started to get into things which was dangerous with what I was working on. As it was a warm night, I decided to give my wife a break and take Lana on an evening stroll to visit my elderly mother. My wife appreciated the gesture. I remember while we were at my mother's, it began to rain, so we stayed a little longer to see if it would stop before heading back.

"Suddenly, we heard a loud explosion from the direction of our home. I immediately knew what it was. I left Lana with my mother and ran through the night, arriving at the house. The house was destroyed and in flames. Furniture was tossed away by force." Bumpus bit his lip as the painful image flooded his mind. "She was tossed and discarded with the furniture. She was dead, my love, my life." Bumpus lowered his head. "My fault. Nothing even close to that had ever happened with my experiments. To this day, I don't know what happened. For years, I could barely live with myself for bringing it into existence. Did I lock the room? Should I have? Did my wife do something inside? Did she introduce some unknown element to the room that caused this? I don't know."

Giron bowed his head and put his hand on Bumpus' shoulder. Both had tears in their eyes.

"Only Captain Doyle knew the truth. He agreed my experiment was too dangerous to proceed with. We planted the story that the house had been struck by lightning. When Lana was old enough, I told her the true story." Bumpus shuddered, remembering the look on his daughter's face. "I didn't want her to live with the secret about her mother's death. We both had a long cry. She has not mentioned it to anybody to this day. Strangely, it made our relationship even stronger. We bonded together with a common pain. All we had was each other. I love her very much.

"Since that time, I have focused my experiments on how to improve life rather than cause destruction, for things more practical, rather than defense in fear of an enemy." Bumpus looked up to Giron. "Until now. I trust you will not mention any of this to anybody or even that you know about it to Lana or the Doyles."

Giron placed his arm around Bumpus' shoulders. "Of course." He took another gulp of his drink. Bumpus did the same. "All this brings reflection on my own life. My father was killed in battle during the same warfare you speak of. My mother died giving birth to my younger brother. But the loss of your wife that way is a hard thing. I thank you for confiding in me."

Bumpus nodded solemnly, a faint, bittersweet smile crossing his lips. "It seems we both carry scars from losing those we love. Life has a cruel way of reminding us how fragile it all is."

For a moment, they both sat in silence, the weight of their shared grief between them. Then Bumpus took a deep breath and straightened, his expression softening. "But I suppose we can't spend the whole night brooding over the past, can we?" He gave a small chuckle, to lighten the mood. "You said you had been looking for me all day. Was there something you wanted to talk to me about?"

Giron hesitated, his drink swirling in his hand as he looked into the amber liquid. "This might not be the right moment. I can bring it up later if you'd prefer."

Bumpus tilted his head, his brow furrowing slightly. "Nonsense. You've been seeking me out for a reason. Go on, what's on your mind?"

"This is probably not a good time. I can talk to you later."

"You obviously have been seeking me out for something. "

"No, it's just…"

"Just what?"

"I'm trying to be sensitive about what you just told me."

"It's okay."

Giron took a deep breath. "You know I am very fond of Lana."

Bumpus nodded. Yes, I noticed that you are..

"And I… she is uhh… very fond of me as well. Well, I was hoping I could get your blessing to uh…, your blessing to marry your daughter."

"You want to marry Lana?"

"Yes."

Bumpus stroked his chin. "Hmm, I don't know if my daughter should marry someone who is only fond of her."

"No, I mean, I am more than fond of her. I really like her very much."

Bumpus frowned.

"I love her."

"Whoa, I get it," Bumpus chuckled holding his hand up. You love her." He smiled then took another sip. "But you two don't really need my approval."

"But your approval is important to her and to me as well. I hope I can earn your respect."

"You already have my respect, Giron, and I'm sure you have Lana's." Just then, Bumpus had a thought. He looked up at Giron and blinked. He then smiled. "Giron, I know how you can further build upon that respect and approval."

Giron leaned closer to him with curiosity.

"I need your help with something. I also need for you to keep this confidential as well, at least for a while."

"Anything, what is it?"

"I already mentioned the nature of some of my experiments these many years." Bumpus grinned and scooted closer to Giron. "I don't want you to think I'm crazier than I already am, but I am working on something. I feel the same urgency I felt years ago with the explosives. It's becoming an obsession. No, it is an obsession. But this time, I believe it's Elyon Himself that is drawing me for some reason."

"What is it?"

"The barriers. Elyon's barriers."

Giron looked at Bumpus with a puzzled expression. "The barriers? What about them?"

"I'm drawn to them. I know Elyon is keeping those populations back, but how? What is the barrier made of? Why is it we cannot see it, but apparently, they can? So, we think. Is their vision better than ours? What is in the Zauphrii and Rauthlin's make-up that they are repelled by the barriers, and we aren't? Can we use such knowledge to our advantage if…"

"If what?"

"I don't know. I just feel I must do what I can to answer some of these questions. I feel an urgency."

Giron took another deep breath and blew it out. He pointed at Bumpus with his drink in hand. "Now, Bumpus, Elder Doyle does have a point. The barriers have been up for thousands of years."

Bumpus sighed. "I know, I know. I can't explain it. We're at peace and dwell in safety with Elyon's barriers protecting us. But what if Elyon has had enough of us? Or what if they figure out how to get around it? What if they have thousands of scientists working on it right now? What if they get through?"

"But they haven't, Bumpus. If they could have gotten through, they would have already."

Bumpus held out his hand. "How do you know that to be true?"

Giron leaned against the tree and then turned away. "I guess if that were to happen, we would be defenseless. I see your point."

"Exactly. We need intelligence."

Giron turned back to him. "What is it you have been working on, and what do you want me to do?"

"What are you doing over the next few days?"

"Just my normal duties."

"Can you get permission to take some time off?"

"Yes, of course. I'm in charge of many, and I could delegate some of my responsibilities for a time."

"Great. I'm taking a little exploratory trip north, and I need a partner, somebody with your skills. I want you to come with me. We'll just tell everyone I am collecting samples and doing some environmental type studies. And that's true. That is what we are going to do. They'll think we are going to veer off to the Grafa Forest, but we will head due north straight to the Northern Forest."

"You mean the Forbidden Forest?"

"Yes, the Forbidden Northern Forest. I've been through there before and have maps. We can tell Lana I would like to spend some time with you to get to know you better."

Giron smirked. "Okay, I can arrange that."

"Good! And you will have my endearing appreciation and approval," Bumpus said jokingly. "We will have to pack extra supplies onto a third horse. It will be a three-day ride in total to get where we are going. I previously stumbled upon a few Hooni'i families who resided in the Forbidden Forest, despite being forbidden to do so. There, I found hospitality from a Hooni'i named Cleet and his family. We can seek that hospitality again."

"I will be ready," Giron said.

At that time, they turned to see a young Hooni'i walking past them at a distance. He noticed them and waved his hand. "Elder Doyle is about to present the Story of Elyon," he shouted. "We are gathering up everyone toward the tents."

Giron waved back in acknowledgement and the Hooni'i continued.

Bumpus patted Giron on his thigh. "Yes, okay then, that's good," Bumpus repeated as he stood. "I guess it's time to go." He brushed off his pant leg with his free hand. Giron stood with him. Bumpus began to walk away back in the direction of the crowd. He waved to Giron to follow. "Come on. Let's gather with the others." The two continued to join in with the other gathering Hooni'i.

When they met up with Lana, her eyes met theirs inquisitively. Giron smiled at her and nodded. She smiled back expectantly toward her father. "So, he told you about his proposal of marriage to me?"

"Yes, he did."

"And you approve?"

"Of course, Lana. How could I not?"

She reached and hugged her father tightly.

"You will make a fine wife, Lana," Bumpus said, his voice warm with pride. "I am truly blessed. Your mother would be proud of you."

Lana leaned in and kissed Bumpus on his cheek. She then turned, reaching for Giron's hand. As their fingers intertwined, they shared a lingering gaze, their smiles filled with unspoken emotion.

Bumpus watched the moment unfold, his thoughts swirling. *What am I supposed to do now?* He cleared his throat, breaking the silence that had grown between them. "Well," he said, his tone shifting slightly, "Lana, Giron has graciously agreed to accompany me on a trip to the Grafa Forest. I'll be conducting some experiments there, and his assistance will be invaluable."

"Yes, Lana, we leave tomorrow," Giron interjected following Bumpus' cue.

"We will have plenty of time to talk and learn all about each other," Bumpus continued.

"Oh, that's great," Lana said looking at Giron for some reassurance.

"I am looking forward to it," Giron replied.

Bumpus quickly changed the subject back to the celebration feast. "Well, come," he said, putting his hand on Lana's back and gently nudging the two forward. "Let's join the others. I've always enjoyed Elder Doyle's telling of the story of Elyon."

"Me to, father," Lana replied as she gripped Giron's hand and moved forward.

Giron nodded and they all proceeded ahead to join the gathering crowd.

Evening was now setting in. It was time for one of the elders to tell the story that was told every year. It was Elder Doyle's turn. As he prepared himself to speak, Lana, Giron and Bumpus took a seat up close, next to where Grandel was seated. Hooni'i had put the finishing touches to the fire pit that burned behind where Elder Doyle sat. Elder Doyle then stood, offered greetings and began to tell the story.

Bumpus had heard the story many times. He also knew the way Elder Doyle said it, with every emphasis and hanging word.

Giron and Lana smiled at each other. They looked at little Atu, who sat with starry-eyed anticipation for what was about to be told. As his father began to tell the story, Atu listened with awe and fascination.

Bumpus closed his eyes and let the vision of the story run through his mind. It was the story about when Elyon created the Hooni'i and other beings.

"The Zauphrii and Hooni'i lived in harmony and interacted with Elyon's beautiful and magnificent spiritual creature," Doyle said. "The Great White Lions roamed the land in those days as well. The Zauphrii were not of spirit, but flesh and blood like them. However, the Zauphrii were of a different make-up. They were more connected to these spiritual beings than the Hooni'i. The Zauphrii were both overseers and aides to the Hooni'i, as the spiritual beings were to them.

"The description of the spiritual beings varied, and they could travel back and forth from this world to Elyon's domain. But the reports of the Zauphrii were more specific. They were slightly larger than the Hooni'i, with smooth pale skin, silky feathers instead of hair, no body hair, and piercingly colorful eyes.

"One day, one of the high and mighty spiritual beings rebelled against Elyon. He was referred to as light and the Son of the Morning. He convinced other beings to join in the rebellion. There was a great battle in Elyon's realm between the rebellious beings and those that stayed loyal. As these spirit beings' hearts hardened in rebellion, so did the magnificence of their outward beauty. These beings transformed into the hideous. They changed and grew twisted and grotesque."

When Elder Doyle said this, he twisted his arms and hunched his body toward Atu.

Atu scooted up closer under his mother and clutched her garment.

The crowd listened as Elder Doyle continued. "While the battle was going on in Elyon's realm, up to half of the Zauphrii also chose to rebel against Elyon. These supported the counsel of the rebel light. Their hearts became as darkened, as did their eyes, fully and literally.

"These became the Rauthlin, and they sought the destruction of the Zauphrii, who decided to stay loyal to Elyon.

"They also sought to destroy Elyon's beloved creation, the Hooni'i. Only the Zauphrii, who had not rebelled, stood in the way of Hooni'i annihilation. Much blood was spilled in those days.

In the mayhem that followed, and because of their zeal for vengeance for Elyon, the Zauphrii also became blind to Elyon's will. They began to look upon the Hooni'i with disdain because of our imperfections and disobediences. They became harsh and unmerciful. As a sign of Elyon's displeasure, He touched their eyes. Their color disappeared. No irises, no pupils, just the whites of their eyes. They appeared blind, but Elyon allowed them to keep their sight.

"Elyon stopped the spiritual beings' rebellion and banished the leading rebel and his followers. As lightning flashes from one direction to another, so was the expulsion of the rebel creature and many of his followers, somewhere away from this world. However, our world was still contaminated by their rebellion. Elyon took His light from our world; the magnificent beings left our realm. The counsel of the Zauphrii was no more.

"Without Elyon's guidance, the Hooni'i did evil to each other. We hated, cheated, killed, and did wrong to one another. In the Zauphrii eyes, the Hooni'i had become a rebellious cancer in Elyon's presence, also needing to be exterminated with the Rauthlin.

"To protect the total annihilation of the Hooni'i, Elyon ordered back some mighty spiritual beings to separate us. He sent the Zauphrii to the far North and the Rauthlin to the far South. Then Elyon put in place barriers so the Zauphrii and Rauthlin could not cross. He also disrupted the sea and raised the back mountains, so that neither the Rauthlin nor the Zauphrii could leave their domains.

"Now under Elyon's protection, He instructs us to be kind to one another, to love, show mercy, do justice, and we will be protected." Elder Doyle looked in Bracket's direction. "As long as we stay within the boundaries that He set in motion to protect us."

Bracket gazed off into space as if he had expected the rebuff from his father's look.

Bumpus felt sorry for Bracket in a way. He knew Bracket's experience could help them somehow. However, Bracket was afraid, perhaps too afraid to be useful. Bumpus then caught Grandel's eye. He stepped up to her and squeezed her hand. She closed her eyes and nodded. "Elyon, reveal yourself," she whispered. "May it be so," Bumpus repeated. "May it be so."

After the story concluded, the elders prayed over the crowd. The celebration continued for some time. It was getting late, and the gathering was winding down. Attendees exchanged farewells, their voices mingling with the soft rustle of the evening breeze. Bumpus took his time moving through the thinning crowd, offering warm goodnights. Finally, he spotted Giron near the edge of the gathering, engrossed in conversation with a few lingering guests. Bumpus stepped up behind him and gave him a firm tap on the back. "Giron," he said with a smile.

Giron turned, his face lighting up with genuine glee. "Bumpus! This was a wonderful night, wasn't it? I had a great time and I'm looking forward to our trip tomorrow."

"It was a good evening," Bumpus agreed with a deliberate nod. "And speaking of tomorrow, can you be ready shortly after sunrise? I'd like to get an early start."

"Of course," Giron replied confidently. "I'll be ready to go."

Bumpus' eyes twinkled with a hint of a more complex adventure ahead of them. "Good," he said, then motioned for Giron to step aside with him, Giron following with curiosity evident on his face. *If he knew there was always the possibility of danger when venturing into the forbidden forest, he may be more hesitant. However, he loves Lana and does not seem like the type to shy away from danger. I can brief him along the way.*

"By the way, Giron," Bumpus began with a small grin. He paused just long enough to let the suspense build. "About the trip..."

"Yes?" Giron asked, his brows lifting slightly.

Bumpus leaned in, his voice deliberately calm but tinged with amusement. "When you come tomorrow, remember to arm yourself."

Giron blinked, the corners of his mouth twitching downward in confusion. "Arm myself?"

"And don't forget your shield," Bumpus added, his grin widening before giving Giron a firm pat on the shoulder. He straightened, watching as realization, or perhaps more questions, started to flicker in Giron's eyes.

"I'll see you in the morning," Bumpus said. Then without waiting for a reply, Bumpus turned and walked off, his smile lingering. He didn't need to look back to know Giron was standing there, puzzling over his words. *My future son. He'll understand soon enough,* Bumpus thought with a chuckle. He then headed home through the shadows of the dispersing crowd.

VENTURE TO THE
FORBIDDEN FOREST

Bumpus and Giron left about an hour after sunrise. They would have left earlier if Lana hadn't insisted, they eat a hardy breakfast. With all the food they'd filled themselves with the day before, Bumpus hardly thought they needed to. But for Lana's sake, they did.

They packed the extra supplies onto a third horse that was tied to Bumpus' horse. It was important that they get there before nightfall to avoid the nocturnal meat-eating barnocs and the gray wolves who traveled in packs and roamed the area at night. Both types of creatures were in great numbers in the Northern Forbidden Forest where fresh game was plentiful. These creatures were sparser in the Grafa Forest, especially the barnocs, who almost never wandered that far south. In fact, most Hooni'i in his village had never seen a barnoc.

The two of them rode side by side, their horses moving at a steady pace along the well-worn path. The rhythmic clopping of hooves mingled with the rustle of leaves overhead and the distant calls of unseen birds. They then reached the open plane, which they would ride all the way to Grafa. The grassy plane sloped upward ever so slightly. Majestic mountains towered as a distant shadow hovered to the east of them. Bumpus, sat tall in the saddle. He began to recount his travels to the North, his voice carrying easily over the steady sound of the horses' gait.

"You see, Giron," Bumpus said, keeping his eyes on the road ahead, "while some of the squatters up there are friendly enough, there are others who wouldn't hesitate to harm you if they saw the chance. We need to be alert. Cleet warned me that some folks wouldn't think twice about killing an unsuspecting traveler for what they carried. They wouldn't blink at leaving one of their own to fend for themselves if they were injured, calling it 'Elyon's will,' even though they don't give a hoot about Elyon."

"Convenient way to clear your conscience," Giron said dryly.

Bumpus nodded. "Exactly. It's twisted logic, but in their eyes, the blame falls on Elyon, not them. His name is just another curse word to them."

"Don't they realize that Elyon's barrier is what's keeping them safe from the Zauphrii, living so close to the edge?" Giron asked, frowning as he glanced back at Bumpus.

"You'd think they'd appreciate it," Bumpus replied. "But they see Elyon and His barriers differently. But then again, that is where we are headed," he smirked. "Right to the edge."

Giron adjusted his grip on the reins, curiosity pushing him further. "How did you manage to navigate those woods and map them out?"

"Cleet was my guide," Bumpus admitted, patting the saddlebag where his maps lay. "I relied on him more than I'd like to admit. I mapped everything, the trees, streams, the lake. Even marked spots where Cleet said ambushes were common, places those 'worthless' Hooni'i like to hide."

Giron shook his head as they rode on, the horses' hooves crunching softly over the uneven ground. "They're just not like us, are they?"

"No," Bumpus said. "They live by their own rules, far from what we'd consider normal. They're freer, more reckless, and they don't care much about modesty or tradition. They're not bound by the same things we are."

Giron tightened his grip on the reins, feeling the weight of Bumpus's words settle in his mind. "Well, I would say that some of our southern village friends aren't that much different from them."

Bumpus chuckled. "I suppose not." He spotted ground rodents scurrying out of the way as they rode by. "You will find that they also have a more varied diet than us. If it moves, be it a dog, bugs, roots, or a rodent, they'll eat it. Have you ever tasted a barnoc?"

"I've never even seen one." "Well, they are hairy creatures. They can get big, up to ten feet tall when they rear up on two legs. However, they aren't the fastest creatures, especially the larger ones. But you don't want to let one get too close. They will rip your head off, with no hesitation."

"Great," Giron said with a wry smile. "Sounds like pleasant creatures."

"They are an acquired taste, but their fur makes a great coat for cold weather." "I bet one of those can feed a large family for weeks."

"And then some," Bumpus agreed. "But the smaller ones are more tender. Easier to cook, too." They rode in silence for a few moments before Bumpus spoke again. "What about wolf meat, Giron? Ever tried it?"

"No, Bumpus. I'm not eating dog."

"Like I said, these Hooni'i are not too particular what kind of animal they eat."

Giron shifted in the saddle, a frown crossing his face. "I'll be polite if they offer me something unusual, but I don't know what I'll do if they hand me a plate of dog."

Bumpus laughed and waved dismissively. "Don't worry too much. As long as you don't think about what you're eating, you'll be fine. It's all in your head. Besides, most of those creatures would eat you if they had the chance."

"Not if I have any say in the matter," Giron muttered under his breath, tightening his grip on the reins once more.

They traveled through prairies, the landscape giving way to an increasing uphill slope as they made their way northward. The sky was a vast, endless blue, occasionally dotted with thin, wispy clouds. Eventually, the Grafa Forest appeared, a shadowed wall of forest trees standing silent and still. Not long after, a mountain began to rise on the horizon, at first only a faint outline against the sky. But as they drew closer, its massive snow-capped peak grew more defined, towering and vast. The peak sparkled in the sunlight, pristine and majestic. Its slopes were steep and sharp, carved by ancient glaciers. The mountain's beauty was awe-inspiring, evoking both admiration and reverence. Bumpus could feel the strength emanating from its lofty heights. Yet he was reminded of the dangers lurking beneath its shadows, where the creatures of Zauphrii lay in hostility. "That's Zauphrii country," Bumpus said quietly, nodding toward the mountain. "Our destination lies at its base, near a lake."

"It's very beautiful."

"It is," Bumpus said awestruck, even though he had seen this sight before.

The two continued forward. After a while further, they reached the place where they had to decide whether to camp for the night or push further to another location. They discussed the wisdom of pushing forward closer or venturing inside Grafa for the night. They were good on water, dried meat, fruit, and nuts. And according to Bumpus' map, there would be other locations where the horses could drink and graze along the way. They didn't have time to hunt and fish, but they could veer off and do so if they had to. They decided not to go into Grafa and push forward. They continued to push until arriving before nightfall at a designated location on Bumpus' map. They set up camp in a small clearing. After building a modest fire, they settled in for the night, their minds heavy with thoughts of what lay ahead.

Despite the warmth of the flames, a chill crept into Bumpus' bones. It was as if the forest itself was whispering warnings on the evening breeze. Bumpus was uneasy. He could hear Grandal's voice in his mind. *Pray to Elyon. Ask Him to lead you.* He looked over to Giron who was tending to his horse. *I have now brought someone else into my obsession. He is not even aware of the possible danger I'm putting him in.* He felt a tinge of remorse. *Elyon, please lead us and protect us.* Despite his thoughts, Bumpus said no more as they laid out their bed rolls and turned in for the night. Giron fell asleep soon after laying his head down. Bumpus pulled his blanket over his shoulders and turned around. He slept restlessly that night, his heart pounding with anticipation for the coming days and entering the Forbidden Forest. When they awakened, morning dawned in a haze, the pale light barely cutting through a heavy shroud of mist hanging low over the open surface. The fog crept along the ground, swirling around scattered trees. The air was thick and damp, each breath leaving cold wisps in the morning air. They moved quietly; horses' hooves muffled on the damp ground as they threaded their way across the open landscape.

Giron shivered, gripping his coat tighter as the chill seeped in. "I can barely see what's ahead," he murmured.

"Just keep moving," Bumpus replied. "Once the sun burns off the mist, we'll see clearer."

But the fog lingered for a few more hours before it lifted. By midday, they paused in a sheltered nook to rest and tend to their horses, checking each piece of cargo carefully. Bumpus stretched stiffly, his breath drifting into the cold air.

After a brief break, they remounted, resuming their silent march. A bone-chilling gust blew suddenly, ruffling their coats and stirring the horses. Giron pulled his collar tight, shivering as he glanced over at Bumpus with a nervous smile. "I hope this coat holds up when night falls."

"We have one more night to lodge in," Bumpus replied. "If all goes according to the plan, we won't be out here the evening after next. Hopefully they'll be a warm fireplace waiting, and a friendly face with a pot of stew on the boil."

"You mean at Cleet's house."

"Yes. I think you will like them very much."

"Well, I guess we better get a move on if we plan to make it there on time," Giron said.

Cleet's family had made Bumpus' previous venture a pleasant one. *What if Cleet is dead? What if the entire family is gone?*

He and Giron would have to take the chance.

As they approached the forbidden territory, the landscape changed drastically. Scattered trees appeared closer together. The temperature dipped again as if they had stepped over an invisible frigid wall.

They had only a few hours of daylight left, and Bumpus knew that stopping too long would make it tight to reach their goal. He urged them to press on until they reached the forest's edge.

By the time they arrived, dusk was settling, and they set up camp again for the night. The night was chilling, but thanks to Bumpus' experience, they were well-prepared for the cold. Bumpus sensed that Giron wasn't as comfortable, though he kept his discomfort to himself. He knew the bedrolls offered a bit of insulation from the chill creeping in.

Bumpus unpacked supplies and handed Giron an extra blanket, though Giron accepted it with only a silent nod, unwilling to show his discomfort. The night was biting cold, and frost clung to their gear. They huddled close to the fire, feeling the comforting warmth even as a biting wind blew through their encampment.

When morning dawned, it was not as foggy as the night before. A light mist covered the ground, and with the first light, they packed up in silence, ready to make their final push into the Forbidden Forest.

After a time, Giron broke the silence. "Do you think we'll see any Zauphrii?" he asked.

"We might, at a distance, of course," Bumpus said. "The spot where we are going to test the barrier is a narrow part of the lake. Zauphrii are on the other side. We know the barrier is somewhere in between. It is a perfect spot to set up and observe the area of the barrier safely."

He glanced at his map. "The next marker will be a large boulder with three smaller boulders off to its right. Once we reach it, we need to bear left at a ninety-degree angle and head into the forest."

After a few minutes, he spotted it. However, just then, Bumpus thought he noticed movement at the edge of the forest. *This could be an ambush.*

Bumpus cast a glance at Giron. "If there's anyone waiting to ambush us," he murmured, "they'll see us coming from a mile away with all this open ground."

Giron nodded, his eyes scanning the tree line. "Well, we can't turn back."

Bumpus shook his head. "Not a chance. But we'll move in ready, just in case."

They exchanged a look, neither eager to risk nightfall catching them out in the open. Bumpus swung down from his horse, unhooking his bow and settling it within easy reach on his side. He slid his sword back into its sheath and shot Giron a quick, almost playful grin.

"Make sure your sword's visible," he instructed, nodding toward Giron's weapon. "And, I don't know, try to look... mean. Maybe a little irritated. That might keep any curious eyes off us."

Giron smirked, loosening his sword with a practiced hand. "I think I can manage that."

Bumpus gave a satisfied nod, and, after a brief pause, motioned forward. Giron returned the nod, then narrowed his eyes and gripped his sword tightly. He looked intently toward the forest and tapped his heels into Imperial's sides. They pressed forward toward the forest's edge moving steadily, ready for whatever might come.

THE AMBUSH

As they proceeded forward, the shadows from the trees thickened around them. Bumpus' eyes scanned the path, if you could call it a path. It seemed more like a worn trail which was suffocated by low-hanging branches and moss-covered roots. Fallen leaves and brush blanketed the ground. Bumpus noticed how the sunlight struggled to pierce the shade above, casting chilling patches of light here and there. To the left, where he knew an attack could most easily be mounted, the land sloped upward, providing cover for anyone hoping to get a vantage point. Bumpus kept his horse to the far right, where he could react quickly if any movement broke through the curtain of green. *I wish I had better prepared Giron for this journey,* Bumpus thought as his gaze flicked from side to side. *This place is just as I knew it would be from my maps.*

His heart pounded. Bumpus listened for any sound that stood out of the norm. All he could hear were the horses' hooves on the pathway and the clanging of his instruments in their pouches.

They passed by a possible ambush area that Bumpus had recalled from his time with Cleet. He gripped his bow tightly. A rodent scampered past them, causing both Giron and Bumpus to jump in their saddles.

"That was our dinner," Bumpus said.

"Very funny. How can you be so unconcerned?"

"Shh," Bumpus whispered, thinking he had heard something

They listened to the silence. Bumpus scanned the area around them but didn't see or hear anything, so he nodded for them to proceed. However, his instincts were heightened.

They rounded a corner and approached the boulders and trees that Bumpus recognized. Something didn't feel right.

As Bumpus' peered into the trees, he spotted a glint of light shining off metal. It came from above about sixty feet away.

Bumpus snapped his bow free with his left hand and had his arrow in place, the string drawn, aimed directly at the appearing Hooni'i, with his own bow drawn. who apparently had another target in mind before reacting to Bumpus.

The two pointed at each other. Time slowed. Bumpus could hear the *twang* of the Hooni'i's bow snap just after his. The motion of letting the arrow fly dislodged Bumpus from his saddle and he slipped to the ground. The Hooni'i's arrow sliced the air near his head, a brush of wind against his skin. It kicked out a chunk of bark from the tree behind him.

Bumpus landed on his side. Pain lanced through his ribs. He saw a Hooni'i with thick curly hair fall from the tree and cry out.

Two other ambushers shouted and charged, one from behind the boulder and another from behind an adjacent tree. Giron shouted back and charged towards them on his horse.

The ambusher coming from the boulder met Giron first. Giron swung his sword into his midsection causing him to fold from force from the blow. Giron could not completely avoid the other, who grazed Giron across his arm with his blade. Giron staggered in his saddle. He then dismounted to take on the Hooni'i who had grazed him.

Bumpus had to make another quick choice on how to assist Giron. He could either string up another arrow and shoot while they were still apart or grab his own sword and run to Giron's aid. Bumpus chose the arrow. The Hooni'i and Giron charged at each other with their weapons raised.

Bumpus lined up with a direct shot. He made his arm rigid, narrowed his gaze, and let the arrow go. The arrow whizzed through the air and thudded into the Hooni'i's chest. The Hooni'i collapsed. Giron made sure it was finished and ran him through with his sword.

Meanwhile, the other injured Hooni'i, who Giron had struck in the midsection, had risen in a feeble attempt to engage Giron. Their swords met with a vicious clang.

The contact caused the Hooni'i's sword to be knocked out of his hand. He stumbled back.

Giron showed him no mercy, piercing him through his chest.

Bumpus strung another arrow and began checking the area where the Hooni'i with the curly hair fell from the tree.

Giron ran over to join Bumpus. They both were relieved when they found the Hooni'i writhing in pain in the brush. He was of a slender build, tan, had green eyes and thick brown curly hair. Bumpus' broken arrow was lodged into his thigh. His forearm appeared broken.

"Don't kill me," he cried.

Giron poked him with his still bloody sword. "Why shouldn't we? You tried to kill us."

"Please, please," the Hooni'i cried.

"Well, your friends didn't make it, and you don't look very good right now," Bumpus said.

"I'll be okay. Please get me out of here. I didn't like them much anyway. They only had me along because I was a good shot."

"Good shot? You missed," Giron said.

"I wouldn't have if your friend hadn't caught me by surprise. I was aiming for you at first. You posed more of a threat. Once you were out of the way, we figured it would be easy to overtake that one, but we were wrong."

"Maybe we should leave him here to die on his own then," Giron replied looking at Bumpus sarcastically. "Elyon's will, you know."

"The wolves will pick up the scent of his blood and have a feast," Bumpus said as he looked around. "Do you have horses, supplies?"

"Yes, over there, yes" The Hooni'i pointed.

"Didn't you tell me we had to find shelter before nightfall?" Giron asked Bumpus. "Do we have time for this?"

"I think we can throw him over a horse and still make it to Cleet's place."

"What about the other bodies? I'm not lugging him and the other two bodies around with us through the forest."

"Couldn't bury them right anyway," Bumpus said. "There wouldn't be time for that. They are fresh kills. The wolves and barnocs are aggressive here. They would only dig them back up if not buried deep enough. Squatters burn the dead in these parts or bury them deep."

"I know about Cleet," the Hooni'i said. "I can take you there and they can help me."

"Who said we care about anybody helping you?" Giron replied as he cleaned off the dagger from the fallen ambusher and placed it into his pouch.

"We already know how to get there from here," Bumpus said. "But you can go with us." Bumpus reached for the Hooni'i's broken arm, steadying it as best as he could, bracing for the reaction he knew was coming. "This is going to hurt," he murmured, though he knew it offered little comfort. The Hooni'i clenched his teeth, grunting as Bumpus set the arm as carefully as he could manage. Bumpus quickly splinted it with a sturdy branch and tied it off with a strip of cloth torn from his own cloak.

He then cast a wary glance at the arrow jutting from the Hooni'i's thigh. The wound around it was red and swollen, and Bumpus could tell it would bleed heavily if he attempted to pull it out there. "We'll leave this be for now," he said, more to himself, keeping his voice steady. He pressed a thick cloth around the wound to slow the bleeding as best he could. "We'll deal with it at Cleet's."

Bumpus then turned to look at Giron's wound. Giron continued to collect supplies and pack them, paying no attention to his injury. There was a jagged cut along his forearm, oozing blood that would need stitches sooner rather than later. Bumpus approached him with a cloth to wrap it. "For your arm."

Giron nodded and allowed Bumpus to bound it tightly.

Bumpus and Giron draped the Hooni'i over one of the horses and tied him to the saddle, so he wouldn't fall off.

"I don't get why you are helping him," Giron said. "He tried to kill us. He does not deserve to live. He'll hold us back. We should leave him."

"I don't want that on my conscience," Bumpus replied.

"I'm sorry," the Hooni'i said rather unconvincingly.

Bumpus shrugged. "And...he is sorry."

"How do we trust him?"

Bumpus shrugged again. "You don't sound like a Hooni'i from around here."

"I'm originally from the Westlake community."

"That explains it. I assume that's where you learned how to use the bow."

"Yes, it is."

"That was a brilliant move and shot," the Hooni'i said to Bumpus.

"Not too brilliant. In my younger days, you wouldn't be alive right now."

"If I survive, you have to show me how you did that."

"If you survive," Giron replied pointedly.

When they had everything loaded, Giron took another look at the fallen Hooni'i. "So, they're dog food, huh?"

"Yeah, let's search them and get what we can. It will add to the extra gifts to give to Cleet's family for their hospitality."

Giron searched the dead bodies. He retrieved a couple of blades and other items to go along with their swords, which he packed in his horse's saddlebags. He then reached over and tapped the Hooni'i to his side. "Although it doesn't really bother me in the least, I guess it would be a shame for you to die on us and us not know your name. In case we needed to say a prayer or something."

"Tassel, my name is Tassel."

"Okay Tassel, if we are even threatened by animals, we can still throw you to them and make a run for it."

Tassel raised his weary head. "Then my friend, I hope that doesn't happen."

TO CLEET'S HOUSE

Twilight settled in. The sky had begun to darken, casting long shadows between the towering trees. Bumpus and Giron moved at a steady but cautious pace, guiding their horses and the pack animals laden with supplies. The forest grew dense around them, the fading light adding a layer of tension that Giron could feel in his grip on the reins.

Bumpus remembered this forest well enough to respect it, especially at dusk. Giron rode beside him, silent and tense, one hand hovering close to his sword. Bumpus caught the occasional nervous glance Giron cast into the underbrush, as if expecting another ambush or an attack by a wild animal.

A wolf's howl echoed through the trees, distant but unsettling. Bumpus kept his gaze forward, senses sharp as he assessed the path. They were running out of daylight. Every minute counted now.

"Shouldn't we be close?" Giron murmured, breaking the silence. His eyes darted around; the tension clear in his voice. "Shouldn't we be seeing something by now?"

"We are headed in the right direction," Bumpus said. "It must be further up. Tassel, does this look familiar?"

Tassel did not respond.

"Why are you asking him? Don't you know? What do the maps say?"

"We should be there shortly," Bumpus said.

Tassel was bent forward being secured tightly to the saddle. He appeared to be unconscious. Giron pulled his horse next to him and shook him firmly. "Tassel, are you dead?"

Tassel did not respond.

"Bumpus, I think he died on us."

"Shake him again."

Giron shook Tassel again.

Tassel still did not respond, other than to snore.

"How can he be sleeping?" Giron said. "I knew we should have left him behind. He slowed us down."

Another howl could be heard crying out.

"Bumpus, are you sure we are headed right?"

"Keep calm. We just need to keep going."

"We guess we have no choice," Giron said.

For the next ten minutes, they continued silently. Scattered howls increased in frequency and volume as their horses plodded along.

"Hopefully, they will be preoccupied with the dinner we left them," Giron said.

Bumpus recognized a tree grouping that meant they were close. However, it was getting too dark to clearly see the path. "We could have used a lighting apparatus right about now. I should have spent more time on it. We could strike torches, but we shouldn't stop. We are pretty much there, maybe 300 to 400 feet or so." A series of lights twinkled between the trees ahead of them. "That's it. Not too far now."

A deep growl interrupted Giron's excitement. The horses jerked back.

Tassel awakened. "Oh! What's happening?"

"Pull the horses tighter together and keep moving," Bumpus said, his heart pounding.

Giron did so and readied his sword. "It's getting darker I can't see. What is that?"

"A barnoc," Bumpus responded.

"It's close but hasn't attacked us," Tassel said. "It must be preoccupied with something else, or it would have attacked us already."

"Let's keep moving and maybe it will stay preoccupied," Bumpus replied.

They could see enough through the darkness to identify the barnoc who was tearing into the flesh of the fresh kill of an animal. It was handling its prey and did not appreciate their intrusion. It growled at them once again.

"Keep moving," Bumpus repeated. The lights grew closer.

But a second growl came from just beyond the first one. Another barnoc lunged out of the shadows.

The horses, still tied together, jerked at each other's saddles. The barnoc leaped at one of the riderless horses, tearing into the side of its neck before falling off. The horses began to pull away.

Giron was the closest to the riderless horse. The rope chain was pulled back and Giron almost fell. He hung on and struggled to grab his sword.

The barnoc recovered and pounced again, clamping its jaws onto the same horse. Giron started to whack at it with his sword. One of his swings contacted the barnoc's eye, freeing the bloodied horse from its grasp. The barnoc writhed in pain and fell away. It ceased pursuit. However, the horses were now in a free run, pulling at the galloping blooded horse behind them.

Bumpus wrestled with the reins, feeling the wild tugging of the panicked horses as he maneuvered through the thick trees. The horses strained as his eyes darted back briefly toward Giron and Tassel, who clung on, narrowly dodging branches that whipped by. Bumpus worried one of the ropes could catch on a tree and bring them all down in a tangle.

At last, they broke through to a clearing. Cleet's residence loomed ahead—a sizable log-built structure that stood solid and impressive against the darkening sky. The building was made from thick, weathered timber, stacked tightly to form walls that merged into the surrounding landscape. The roof appeared steep, and a wide, covered porch stretched along the front, held up by massive beams. A thin trail of smoke rose from a stone chimney, giving a comforting sign of life in the cool evening air. Bumpus felt a hint of relief; Cleet's place had always struck him as a fortress against the wilderness, built to stand firm no matter what the forest threw at it.

Before they could get their bearings, more hoofbeats pounded from behind. A young Hooni'i with olive skin and dark and straight hair, rode up beside him. The Hooni'i skillfully maneuvered his horse alongside Bumpus, his eyes sharp with focus. Just behind him came a second rider, this one with shorter, close-cropped hair, who matched his companion's steady determination.

"Easy, there. Easy," the first rider called, his voice calm but commanding as he tried to soothe the horses.

"Easy, easy," the second echoed, his grip gentle but firm. The horses gradually slowed, their wild gallop easing to a controlled trot. The injured horse was the last to settle, its sides heaving as it shuddered, still gripped by fear. Bumpus finally let out a breath as the animals steadied.

"This way to the stable!" one of the young riders shouted, pointing to a low structure beside Cleet's main house. Bumpus nodded, urging his horse forward, grateful they had reached the safety of Cleet's place.

The second rider spurred his horse ahead, swinging down and heaving open the stable doors. The hinges gave way to a heavy screech revealing a dim, spacious interior lined with empty stalls and thick with the smell of hay and leather. Bumpus and Giron led the horses inside, and almost immediately the animals began to settle.

As soon as they stopped, however, the injured horse wobbled, and limped, its legs trembling before it collapsed onto the straw-covered floor. Its flanks heaved, the ragged breaths shallow, and its whole body shuddered with pain and exhaustion. The other horses shifted uneasily, their ears flicking back, but the two Hooni'i quickly secured them to posts, giving them soft reassurances as they worked.

Giron dismounted, Imperial, and approached the fallen animal. Kneeling beside it, running his fingers along its coat. His voice was low and soothing as he stroked the horse's side, trying to calm it.

Bumpus also dismounted. It was then that Bumpus had gotten a better look at the young Hooni'i with olive skin and straight hair. He recognized him as Cleet's son. "Clay? Is that you?" Bumpus asked.

"Glettlebottom?" Clay responded. "It's been a long time. Father always said you'd come back." He nodded to the second horseman. "That's Jaune over there. He stays with us."

"That's the guy who invents stuff?" Jaune asked.

"Yeah, that's him all right," Clay said.

Bumpus walked up to Clay and patted him on his back. "I didn't recognize you. The last I saw you were so little, but now you're a grown Hooni'i with longer hair and everything," Bumpus said. "This is Giron."

"Welcome," Clay said.

Jaune nodded.

"We just got in late when we heard the noise."

"Glad you were there," Giron replied, still petting the horse's coat.

Bumpus stepped over, assessing the wound. There was a deep gash along its shoulder that was still bleeding slowly. One of its legs was also bleeding. Juane had grabbed a bundle of hay, stuffing it under the horse's head to keep it from pressing down into the rough ground. He shook his head sadly toward Clay.

"Sorry, we're going to have to put down your horse," Clay said.

"It was supposed to be part of a gift to your family for hospitality," Bumpus said. "There are still two good ones left, though. We happened to acquire additional gifts for you along the way."

Clay pointed to the injured horse. "We should notify our neighbors in the morning. We can share the horse meat while it's still fresh. We're going to have a feast tomorrow. I'll get Father."

Tassel moaned.

Everyone turned to Tassel, who was still tied to his horse. He was partially hanging to one side, bandaged up and bleeding from his leg. "Can someone help me?" Tassel asked.

"I'm sure they'll take care of you," Giron said.

While Giron and Juane tended to the fallen horse, Clay trotted over to where Tassel hung, tangled but holding steady. Bumpus joined Clay, and together they worked to untie the knots binding Tassel to the pack saddle. With a few firm tugs, they loosened the ropes, carefully easing him down from his awkward perch. Tassel groaned, as they eased him to the ground.

Clay and Bumpus turned their attention back to the horses. They untied the reins, leading each animal to a clean stall. They then carried Tassel inside, while Juane and Giron stayed back to put down the injured horse.

Cleet was an older Hooni'i, of slight build, who was balding. However, he was as physically fit as Bumpus had remembered him. "Sama, his wife, was a pleasant looking and plump Hooni'i. Bumpus knew they had treated many injuries in their lifetimes and so they took over the setting of Tassel's arm. They sedated Tassel the best they could. They had applied numbing medicine to his leg wound, to get the arrow out, and prepared herbs to resist infection. This process was very painful, as evidenced by the loud cries heard from Tassel in the other room.

Cleet said that Tassel would probably walk with a slight limp for the rest of his life, but he deserved it. Bumpus knew for someone like Tassel, not having the strength to hold a bow for a while was going to hurt him more than a limp. They also were kind enough to stitch Giron's arm up. During the process, Giron did not so much as flinch. Bumpus and Giron cleaned up and then took their places by a fire. Tassel had eventually fallen asleep, still heavily sedated.

Meanwhile, the smell of roasting fowl roasting mingled with the scent of freshly baked bread. Giron's stomach rumbled, and he cast a weary glance at Bumpus. "That smells good, but I'm not sure how long I can wait to eat something. I've a mind to crack open my bread rations," he murmured, looking over to his pack on the side of the room.

Bumpus shook his head and raised a brow. "We must be patient, Giron. Remember what I told you? It's rude here to pull out your own rations when you're a guest."

Giron grimaced. "Yes, I know you are right, Bumpus. But it smells so good in there it reminded me that I had not eaten since early this morning."

"Well, it's been a stressful day, that's for sure.," Bumpus said.

"Yes, I never would have thought I would have had a day quite like this one."

Bumpus raised his head and sniffed in the air. "Yes, I'm sure of it. It smells like roasted fowl. Sama uses an array of spices in preparing food."

"That would be great, Giron replied. "I hope it's not the horse."

"No, it can't be the horse yet. They will get to that tomorrow."

"Are we going to the barrier tomorrow?" Giron seemed eager to change the subject. Bumpus couldn't blame him. "Or do we rest in a bit?"

"I'm tired, but I still want to go in the morning if you're able. Or you can stay back, rest, maybe help cut up and prepare the horse." Bumpus smiled.

Giron shook his head. "I'll be ready. I just want to try to get some sleep tonight."

Cleet walked into the room where the two were. Sorry about the delay. Dealing with Tassel took a little longer than expected. Looks like a late dinner. I hope you two are hungry. Ma is setting the table now."

"Yes, indeed," Bumpus replied. He got up and hit Giron's thigh, indicating he should follow. "We are very hungry. You are too good to us, Cleet. Thank you."

"What are we having?" Giron asked.

"Clay caught a big fowl yesterday. There will be plenty with all the fixings."

Giron grinned. "I love fowl. What are we waiting for?" Giron brushed past Bumpus on his way to the dining room. Bumpus shared a mischievous look with Cleet. The two men chuckled and followed in after him.

Sama came in and sat the last of the food down on the table. She reached over and hugged and kissed Bumpus on the cheek. "If I knew you were coming, I would have made sure we caught a barnoc. I know how much you enjoyed it last time you were here."

"Yes, you prepared it in such an amazing fashion. I've been telling Giron here all about it."

She turned to Giron and smiled. "You are always more than welcome."

"Thank you for your hospitality," Giron replied.

"And thank you for the horse," Cleet replied. "We'll eat on it for a good while."

She laughed. "He's always thinking about food. You would think he would be the fattest Hooni'i you'd ever seen by now."

"I move around a lot, my dear. I will always work up an appetite." Cleet chuckled. "But what can I say? You're a good cook."

They all laughed. Cleet's family dug in.

There was no prayer of blessing before the meal and no acknowledgment of Elyon. Bumpus and Giron both bowed their heads and privately said a quick prayer before partaking. Cleet's family did not miss a beat, nor did they pause, nor did they even comment on them praying.

The bread was especially delicious. The fowl was the best fowl Bumpus could remember tasting and he told her so. They had their fill. Before Cleet and Giron started on their third helping, Sama got up and started to clear the table.

Clay sat back in his chair. "So, Glettlebottom, what brings you back to us?"

"It's obvious from the last time he was here," Cleet said, sitting up straighter in his seat. "It's something about the Zauphrii and the barrier. Am I right?"

"Yes," Bumpus replied.

"I knew it," Cleet said. "There has been a lot more activity over the lake than the last time you were here. When you were here last, we rarely saw them. But now, they are down there all the time."

"And more Hooni'i have been taunting them from the shore," Jaune said.

"I'm trying to find a way to make the barriers visible," Bumpus said.

"Why would you want to do that?" Sama asked, coming back into the room. "Just stay away. Some stupid Hooni'i gets killed there almost every week now."

"Oh, not every week, Ma." Clay rolled his eyes.

"Well, it happens too much." She narrowed her eyes. "Those Zauphrii are evil, I tell you, pure evil. Their kids will chop you up in little pieces and gnaw on your intestines for breakfast."

"Come on, Ma, you don't know that," Clay said.

Cleet and Jaune smiled at each other, and seemingly amused by the conversation.

"You just stay away from there or you'll end up like Dok, I tell you." She made chopping motions into her hand toward Clay. "Chop you up in little pieces."

Clay looked to Cleet and made and held his hand out. "Father. Make her stop. Please."

"Now, Clay, haven't I told you to respect your mother?"

Clay put his head down and tried to hide his smile. He looked back at his mother.

She again made the chopping gesture. "Dok, Dok, Dok…"

"Ma!"

Everyone laughed.

"What happened to this Dok, anyway?" Giron asked.

"The Zauphrii chopped him into little pieces, threw his remains into his boat and sent him back, I tell you."

Clay rolled his eyes. "He died, and his boat washed up to shore. His body was eaten by wolves, Ma."

"He went over there. I tell you. They killed him dead, tore him up to feed their kids and sent his remains back as a message to us."

Cleet laughed and turned to Bumpus. "You see what I must deal with? I don't think he went over there, but he got too close. He was killed by a Zauphrii arrow on his boat and washed ashore. That's what I think."

"Then the wolves got him," Clay said.

"So, is there any proof he was killed by the Zauphrii?" Bumpus asked.

"Sure! There were a couple of big arrows right in his carcass. That's all!" Sama replied.

"Yeah, I got one of them back there somewhere," Cleet responded.

Giron's eyes widened. He stopped chewing the piece of bread in his mouth.

Bumpus raised his brow toward Cleet. "You have a Zauphrii arrow?"

"Well, it ain't like one I've seen from any Hooni'i," Cleet said. "This one has writing on it, too."

"Can I see it?" Bumpus asked, sitting up from his chair.

"It's just an arrow," Sama said. "And Dok deserved it because he was *stupid*."

"Just an arrow?" Giron asked. "We're talking about a real Zauphrii arrow?"

"Heck, if it means that much to you, I'll go get it and you can have it. She doesn't like that thing around anyway." Cleet held his finger up to his mouth and rose to go into another room.

Giron leaned over to Bumpus and whispered, "I can't believe this. They are acting like it's no big deal. Could it be true?"

"You know what this means, Giron?"

"Yes, we can tell a lot about them from the weapons they make, if in fact it is from the Zauphrii."

Cleet returned with a large arrow. Bumpus knew right away it wasn't Hooni'i. Cleet gave the arrow to Bumpus, who examined it. Giron stared over his shoulder. It was about a yard long, thicker, and somewhat heavier than a normal Hooni'i arrow. *What type of bow fired it? What type of strength did the shooter possess?*

On one side of the arrow was an unknown symbol with letters from the Hooni'i alphabet next to it. *Of course, they would have our alphabet. We were all together once; if the stories were true. They probably speak the same language, too.* Bumpus read the letters out loud. "K-R-O-N. Who or what is Kron?"

Cleet shrugged. "Search me."

On the other side with smaller letters was another inscription: Z-O-N. *Who or what is Zon? O-N, I wonder if there is any connection or if they have similar meaning? Maybe we can go out on the lake and get closer to where the barrier might be. Elyon, help me. Maybe I'll be able to see something."*

Bumpus handed the arrow to Giron to examine then turned his attention back to Cleet. "May I impose on you one more favor?"

"Sure, anything."

"Can we borrow one of your small boats tomorrow?"

"Sure. I can load it on the ground sleigh for you in the morning."

Bumpus and Giron nodded to each other. Bumpus broke out with a big smile as Giron handed him the arrow back. "Let's try to get some sleep. Tomorrow, we have much work to do."

It was difficult for them to rest after their day, but Giron dosed off first. Bumpus slowly faded, but as he did, his mind raced with anticipation of what the morning would bring. He hoped it would bring out the Zauphrii and bring them closer to understanding the barrier. *Elyon, I am close. Give me the wisdom to discover the mysteries of your barriers. Help me learn more about the Zauphrii.*

THE NORTHERN BARRIER OF THE ZAUPHRII

Cleet had the boat loaded on the ground sleigh before they had awakened. They ate some leftover fowl and bread for breakfast and headed out to the lake. It was about an hour's journey to its shore. "Why aren't we approaching on land?" Giron asked.

"The contrast in lighting will be clearer in the open areas of the lake rather than the shadowy patches of the forest," Bumpus said as the sleigh bounced along behind them. "It's also safer."

The cool, brisk air was invigorating as Bumpus and Giron made their way through the forest. The earthy scent of moss and damp leaves rose around them. Eventually, the trees thinned and gave way to an expansive view of the lake stretching out before them. Gentle waves caught the light, each ripple reflecting sparkles of silver. Bumpus felt a stirring appreciation for the beauty around him. *This beauty is only possible in a world shaped by Elyon's hand.*

After a moment, movement down the shoreline caught Bumpus's attention. Two Hooni'i men had pulled their boat onto the bank a few hundred feet away. The men were laughing raucously, their voices echoing across the water as they took turns drinking from leather pouches of hide, filled with what was likely ale. Their hoots and drunken jests interrupted what was a peaceful scene.

Bumpus observed them for a moment, noting their unsteady postures and the careless way they moved, as they passed the pouches back and forth. *Not exactly ideal company,* he thought, glancing at Giron. "Let's set up our tent away from shore," Bumpus said to Giron as he frowned in their direction. "And pull our boat back out of view."

"Good idea," Giron said. "No reason to draw attention to ourselves."

Bumpus laid out his mat with an array of glass pieces and small containers. He pulled out a metal cylinder shaped instrument with clear glass pieces on each end and handed it to Giron. "Here. Take a look through this."

Giron gazed through the larger side at his feet.

"No, no, the other way, and you must look out. Point it to the Hooni'i over there," Bumpus pointed.

Giron adjusted the device and did as he was instructed. He gasped. "I can see them closer. It's as if they're a few boat lengths away."

"Correct. I will change the front piece with these treated glasses and see if the view changes."

Bumpus set up his stand to point across the lake. He estimated their site was about seven-hundred feet across the lake. Somewhere in between was the barrier. He also knew that, based on the reports, the Zauphrii that had been seen had never ventured out more than a few feet from their shoreline.

The last time Bumpus was there, he was able to catch a glimpse of a female, with her little ones, wading in the water. Cleet had said that after Bumpus had left, some Hooni'i started to verbally harass them and throw things in the water in their direction. Some even hurled arrows across. The sightings of the females with children ceased. But bigger stronger males started showing up. Now these males could be seen more frequently. Cleet believed the Zauphrii set up guards across the lake, which was duplicated on some of the land portions.

Bumpus hoped he would see one of them today. However, he was concerned that the two drunken Hooni'i could somehow interfere with his plans.

While Bumpus was setting up, Giron was still having fun with the cylinder. "Those guys have a bunch of arrows loaded in their boat."

"The morning has barely started, and it sounds like they are already drunk," Bumpus muttered.

The attention Giron was giving them caught their attention, though. *Perhaps they saw a reflection from the lens,* Bumpus thought. "Hey!" one of them yelled. "What are you doing over there?"

Giron put the cylinder down and gave it to Bumpus. Giron pretended he didn't understand the question and simply waved his hand in greeting. The two Hooni'i nudged each other and began to walk over.

"Looks like we are going to have some unwanted company," Giron said with a sigh.

"Are they armed?"

"Not that I can see. They aren't carrying their bows with them. What do you want to do?"

"Nothing," Bumpus said. "We are here to do some tests today. But you might want to have your dagger handy and be able to get to your sword if you must."

"It's already done, Bumpus, already done."

"Hey, what are you all doing?" one of the Hooni'i again yelled out as they approached.

Giron walked out to meet them. "Greetings to you. Beautiful day we're having."

"Yes, a beautiful day," one of the Hooni'i said.

"It would be a more beautiful day on the other side of the lake," the other Hooni'i said gesturing over to Zauphrii territory.

"What are you two doing with all this stuff?" the first Hooni'i asked.

Bumpus walked over and greeted them. "I am Bumpus, and this is Giron. We are doing some environmental experiments. Hopefully we'll be able to observe a few of the Zauphrii today, also."

"You'll see Zauphrii, all right," the other Hooni'i said. "They are over there a lot, now."

"Environ… what?" the other asked.

"Environmental experiments," Bumpus repeated. "We are studying the land here and observing the barrier."

"What for?" the first Hooni'i asked.

"You can't even see it," the other said.

"That's the point, we can't see it, but we want to know more about it," Bumpus said.

"Well, that doesn't make sense to me. We need to get an army together and go kill us some of those pale feathered freaks," the Hooni'i said.

Giron gave an insincere snicker. "Now, now, you don't want to go over and get yourself killed, do you? And besides, you don't have an army here."

"Yes, my friend," Bumpus said. "For your protection, it might be better for you to stay on this side of Elyon's barrier."

"Elyon!" the first Hooni'i exclaimed. He spat on the ground and used some choice expletives. "If Elyon cared for the Hooni'i, he would have destroyed those puking freaks to begin with."

Bumpus didn't like how the conversation seemed to be spiraling downward. "You know my friends, we came all this way and brought food. But there is one thing we forgot."

The two Hooni'i looked at each other.

"Ale," Bumpus said. "You think you can spare a little? I could use a little drink this morning."

"Why sure thing, Bumple," one of the Hooni'i said.

"Bumpus, my name is Bumpus."

"Okay, Mr. Dumpus."

"What brings you two out here?" Giron asked.

At this question, the two Hooni'i became worked up again. "They killed Dok! So, we're going to kill us a Zauphrii! Yahhhhh!" The Hooni'i yelled directly into Giron's face. Giron squinted in the face of rancid breath and flying spittle.

"Yahhhhh!" the other yelled, raising a clenched fist.

Giron wiped his face with his hand. "Really, you plan on killing Zauphrii? I mean, today?"

"Yes, today is as good a time as any. Why not today?" the Hooni'i said. "Yahhhhh!"

"Yahhhhh!" the other yelled in response.

"So how do you plan on killing a Zauphrii?" Bumpus asked.

"When my buddy goes out in the boat, one of them pukes will come out and shoot at it. I'll fire from the shore while he shoots from the boat. We'll hook one for sure."

"Or they'll run scared," snickered the other. "We'll show them not to mess with us, Yahhhh!"

"Yahhhh!" the other yelled.

Bumpus resisted the urge to slap the two Hooni'i and tell them how stupid their plan was. *Fools will be fools,* he thought.

"You want to join us?" one of the Hooni'i asked.

"No thank you," Bumpus said. "We only have so much time to do what we have to do before we have to head back."

"Well, good luck with your "eeevironmeetal, Bimpy," he slurred.

"Bumpus. It is Bumpus."

The Hooni'i handed Bumpus an ale filled pouch. "Here, you can have my ale. We got more over there."

"Thank you. We appreciate your hospitality," Bumpus said hoping they would leave.

Finally, the two turned and proceeded to walk back to their boat. Giron shook his head. "So much for taking our boat out today with them here."

"We'll see. They may over drink and pass out, for all we know."

"Let's hope so."

Bumpus knelt down and arranged each piece of glass by tint and thickness, their edges glinting softly in the light. Alongside them, he placed his slender jars of chemical solutions. Each jar had a label, handwritten with details of the mixture inside.

Meanwhile, the Hooni'i seemed to become even more boisterous than before, shouting curses across the lake to no one. Giron continued to shake his head. He then turned to Bumpus and shrugged. "They are not thinking logically. Hooni'i like that die of their stupidity sooner or later."

"I'm afraid you are right, Giron." Bumpus meticulously opened a thick, weathered notebook, flipping through its ink-stained pages until he reached a clean one. He began jotting down notes and planning his observations. He then turned and placed the cylinder on a stand and began looking through it across the body of water. He noted the way the water's surface caught the light, rippling in patches, and wondered how the lake might look through the tinted lenses, at different angles and under varying filters. A touch of amber perhaps, or a slight refraction from the yellow solution to catch glints of hidden minerals in the rocks.

How often do we miss things that are hidden right in plain view? he pondered, pausing his writing to think. *With the right adjustments, the view of the world changes.*

Bumpus made some adjustments and jotted notes down in the book.

"What am I supposed to do?" Giron asked.

"Just relax and keep watch."

"Watch what?"

"How about looking out for Zauphrii? Maybe you can keep an eye too on those Hooni'i." Giron shrugged and looked for a place to sit. Finally, he just sat on the sparse grass where he was, glancing warily at the distant figures down the shoreline.

Bumpus continued his work, occasionally pausing to make minute adjustments to the lens. At last, he gestured to Giron. "Can you hand me the first piece of glass over there?"

Giron sprang up, handed him a glass piece with a light-blue tint, then sat back down, watching Bumpus carefully replace the lens in the cylinder.

As Bumpus scrutinized the lake through the lens, he mulled over his selection of seventy glass pieces, each offering a unique perspective, a different way of bending the light. With each new adjustment, his notes grew, filling the page with insights both scientific and curious.

Giron sighed.

After an hour had passed, the Hooni'i seemed to calm down. All was quiet except for Bumpus' periodic shuffling of instruments and scribbling in his book. After a while, Bumpus would glance toward Giron. Giron appeared bored. He had consumed some of the Hooni'i ale. Otherwise, he just sat. A few times he laid back and let his eyes close.

Bumpus began to see similarities with certain solutions, and he experimented on a hunch. However, after a while, Bumpus noticed he had not heard the two Hooni'i in a while. He looked over in their direction to see what they were doing.

One of the Hooni'i, bearing a shield, pushed their boat out into the water. The other Hooni'i stuck arrows at different spots in the ground at the water's edge.

"It seems our neighbors are launching their plan," Bumpus muttered.

Giron sat up and followed Bumpus' gaze. "It looks like they are on the move."

"Those stupid Hooni'i. And right when I might be onto something."

"You found something?"

"Can you look for a bottle with the letters E-C on it?"

Giron assisted Bumpus in going through his corked bottles and reading labels until he lifted one small bottle into the sunlight. "Is this it?"

"Yes, thanks." Bumpus took the bottle from him.

"What is it, Bumpus?"

"I noticed a pattern with this series. Hand me the clear piece of glass in the corner over there."

Giron reached for a piece of glass. "This one?"

"No Giron, the other one next to it."

Giron pointed to another piece of glass.

"Yes, that one. Does it have L 43 sketched into it?"

Giron held the glass up. "Yes, L 43." He handed it to Bumpus, who fastened it to the cylinder. After about a minute, Bumpus took off the lens and spread the solution of E-C over the lens. He set it out to dry for a moment. *There seems to be a pattern to this E-C solution on the L series lenses. I need to keep working at it.*

As they waited, they both looked over to the two Hooni'i. The one on the boat was rowing out in the lake being profanely cheered on by his buddy.

"Wonder if he'll go all the way across?" Giron asked.

"Suspense, suspense," Bumpus replied.

"What about L 43?"

Bumpus nodded and wrote L 43 E-C into his book. He held the glass toward the lake and raised his eyebrows. Bumpus then affixed L 43 EC to the cylinder and looked across. He then pointed it more to the left than the right. He could make out a distortion, like a faded line into the shadows.

"Well?" Giron asked.

Bumpus smiled. "Headed in the right direction. Come and look at this."

Giron looked through. "Okay, what am I looking at?"

"Look across the shore and then look at the water."

"What?"

"Look harder, Giron. Do you see the slight line of discoloration a little bit offshore?"

"Uh, no. What are you talking about? Yeah, I kind think, it's kind of darker, but couldn't it be a shadow or something?"

Bumpus moved it to the right. "See it following a consistent path over there?"

"Okay, yes, sort of."

Bumpus then moved it to the left. "And there?"

"Yes. But still couldn't it be a shadow or something?"

"I thought that, too, but the light from our star is coming from that direction." Bumpus pointed to the sky. "Now, look back without looking through the cylinder."

Giron lifted his head and looked over while Bumpus took a clear lens and affixed it back to the cylinder. "I just put back the clear lens," Bumpus said. "Look now."

Giron looked again. "You are right, I don't see anything now."

Bumpus took the cylinder back. "I need to narrow it down some more, but I think I need something stronger. It's just a matter of time until we will be able to see the barriers."

Just then, their attention moved to the Hooni'i on the shoreline. The Hooni'i jumped up and down and yelled with a bow in his hand. The Hooni'i in the boat was also flaying his arms.

"What the heck do you think they are doing?" Giron asked.

"Look over there," Bumpus pointed.

Giron looked. Riding up the opposite shore were three Zauphrii on horses. Even at that distance, Bumpus saw their streaming white hair or feathers as it was. Their tan leather outfits added to their allure.

"The Zauphrii," Giron said.

Bumpus stared for a few moments. He quickly turned the cylinder toward their direction and peered inside. The image startled him, especially of one of the riders and the horse she was riding.

Yes, she... By no means did she look any less intimidating than the other two. In fact, she was even more intimidating in appearance. She was leading the other two horsemen. However, her horse had a significant single horn protruding from the middle of its head.

"A unicorn," Bumpus said.

"Let me see," Giron insisted.

Bumpus gave the cylinder back to him to look. After a moment he slowly lowered and stared at Bumpus.

The Zauphrii riders stopped nearer to the shore. They looked over the area and out at the taunting Hooni'i. The two males dismounted and came up further to the shoreline. The female stayed on her unicorn. She sat high in her saddle.

Giron shook his head. "I hadn't believed that such an animal existed accept in the stories of old."

"Amazing," Bumpus said. *The horned horse of the old stories.*

Meanwhile, the two Hooni'i continued to hurl loud profanities at the Zauphrii.

"Wow," Giron said. "She has swords strapped across her back. They have…" he paused. "Bumpus, we need to move back away from the shoreline. The two big strong ones are readying their bows. I think they are preparing to shoot at us. Oh--"

"Wha…," Bumpus said, just before hearing a sharp whistle, followed by the unmistakable slicing sound of an arrow cutting through air. He shot his eyes up, just in time to see an arrow fly from the other side of the lake, aimed right in their direction. "Grab your shield, Giron! Get back!" Bumpus called, instinctively stepping backwards. He felt the thud of a large arrow landing precisely where he had been kneeling moments before. The large arrow quivered, its tip embedded deep in the earth, vibrating as if holding a warning.

They're attacking us, he realized, his mind racing as more arrows flew their way, each shot disturbingly precise. *Their range is further than I had imagined.*

Giron dashed to grab his shield. "Get back! Move side to side, Bumpus—back and forth!"

Bumpus threw a glance over his shoulder, noting Giron's urgency. Another arrow struck the ground a few feet ahead of him, spurring him to change direction without hesitation. The ground became a treacherous field of near misses, each step a gamble. He could feel his heart pounding, as ducked and wove, each glance ahead and behind a swift calculation of the arrows' range and trajectory.

"Further back! Keep moving!" Giron shouted.

Bumpus didn't need extra encouragement. They retreated further until they finally slowed, turning to assess the distance they'd managed to put between themselves and where his mat, notebook and lenses were. Giron lifted his shield, standing cautiously upright beside Bumpus, who peered across the lake, chest still heaving from the rush of adrenaline.

"You think we're out of their range, Bumpus?"

Bumpus measured the distance with his eyes, calculating. "I hope so. It appears their bows have an exceptionally long range." He took a breath, still tense. *Strange marksmen,* he mused, his mind still on the edges of their observations. *If their intention was to chase us off, they succeeded.*

However, it was then that they saw that the Zauphrii had turned their attention to the other two Hooni'i. The one Hooni'i on shore was moving back and forth grabbing arrows and hurling them high in direction of the Zauphrii. Despite the Hooni'i level of intoxication, the

Hooni'i on the shore was swift at avoiding a few oncoming arrows, while hurling his own.

The Hooni'i on the boat took a shot. But the rest of the time he hid behind his shield. Several arrows hit the shield. This caused him to fall back and his boat to rock.

Bumpus thought he had heard the female yell out something. The Zauphrii stopped shooting. However, the Zauphrii archers were moving back and forth.

The Hooni'i continued to grab arrows and shoot at them now without opposition. They fell short and were never a threat to the Zauphrii.

"Should we help them?" Giron asked.

"My range is not that far and I'm not going to get any closer than I am now."

"But they are drunk, Bumpus. This is not going to end well."

"I know, Giron. I know."

And it didn't. The Zauphrii archers fired in delayed succession at the Hooni'i on the boat. One time he raised his shield to block an arrow. However, when he raised his head back up again, it was too late. The impact knocked him right off the boat and into the lake.

The other Hooni'i stopped and cried out for his buddy. Unfortunately, he made the momentary mistake of not moving or running for cover. This was a fatal hesitation in the face of the Zauphrii archers' relentless aim. Then came a sharp thwack—a massive arrow struck him directly in the thigh. Bumpus winced as he saw the impact twist the man's leg unnaturally, the force appearing to snap bone. The Hooni'i crumpled to the ground with a howl, clutching his shattered leg, his face contorted in pain. The Zauphrii archers showed no mercy. Another arrow came whistling through the air, slamming into the man's shoulder, jerking his body backward as blood bloomed around the wound.

Bumpus watched, his stomach sinking, as the Hooni'i flailed on the ground, helpless and exposed, while arrow after arrow rained down on him. His cries grew weaker with each impact, until his body barely stirred marking a dull silence. All Bumpus and Giron could do was hunch down and wait for the gruesome onslaught to end.

The Zauphrii archers ceased fire. They stood tall and seemed to look directly at Bumpus and Giron. The female rode her unicorn closer to the shore in between the other two.

"What do you think they're doing now?" Giron asked.

"What can they do but wait for us to come out or just leave. I'm glad we tied our horses back here."

"Me too."

The Zauphrii stayed there for about five more minutes. They appeared to converse with one another. *I am glad right now that they can't cross the barrier. I think we are far enough back,* Bumpus thought. Finally, the Zauphrii mounted their horses and rode off the same way they came.

Bumpus let out a sigh as he watched them depart. He then turned to Giron. "More dead."

"That's two more Hooni'i bodies to deal within twenty-four hours. I'm not sure how much of this I can take, Bumpus."

"It's really quite sad." Bumpus knew those Hooni'i, in his estimation, had acted foolishly, but a lost life was tragic in and of itself. "I wish they had been more cautious."

"Well, I am not comfortable taking the risk and going into the lake to retrieve that body."

"No, I think I'm with you on that one. Come on. Let's gather our stuff and retrieve some of those arrows. We can retrieve the body from the shore. As Bumpus gathered his things, Giron took a deep breath and slowly made his way over to the arrow ridden body on the shoreline.

Bumpus and Giron were back at Cleet's residence for the evening. The evening meal was being prepared. The horse had already been cut up and shared with some of the locals. It would be the meal of choice for many places that night.

Meanwhile, Tassel sat quietly in his chair, intoxicated with much drink. Sprawled out on a table in the corner were the dozen Zauphriinian arrows that they had collected, included the one that killed Dok. Bumpus spoke excitedly of the day's events. Everyone listened with amusement. None seemed at all upset, or surprised, that two drunken Hooni'i were killed by the Zauphrii. Nor was anyone upset that one of the bodies was still out there floating in the lake.

"I told you! That's what they get!" Sama had said earlier, sharing her family's disregard for stupid Hooni'i. *After all that happened, I am glad we survived and bought back the boat in one piece,* Bumpus thought. *We also can deduce what their society is like from the arrows that we collected.*

As others became busy with the preparation of the evening meal, Giron stood next to the table of arrows. Bumpus walked over, picked up one of the arrows and turned it over in his hands. He couldn't help but feel a strange reverence for the weapon that had claimed Hooni'i life. Each was crafted with unmistakable intent. The symbols were carefully etched and each word leaving behind the riddle begging for discovery. On five of the arrows had the same markings as the one that had killed Dok. On one side had the same unknown Zauphriinian symbol next to the word K-R-O-N and the other side, in smaller writing, Z-O-N. However, the other arrows had the same symbol and KRON, but on the other side, T-A-U-L in smaller letters. That same nagging question lingered in Bumpus' mind, unspoken but understood between him and Giron. What did Kron mean to the Zauphrii? Who or what were Taul and Zon?

"They're more than just weapons, Giron. Look here. This one's got a deeper groove around the fletching, and it's the same on the other marked 'Zon.' The Taul arrows don't have it. Why?"

Giron looked over and shrugged, though his eyes held a glimmer of interest. "Could be a way to tell them apart in a hurry. Different marks for different kinds of fighters?"

"Maybe," Bumpus replied, but he didn't sound convinced. He squinted at the name "K-R-O-N" carved into each one. "If Kron's a name, then why's it on every single arrow? Even if these were made by different hands? Doesn't make sense."

"So maybe it's not a name," Giron offered, poking the campfire with a stick. "Could be a title, a rank."

Bumpus huffed. "Or a belief, something they swear by."

Giron let out a long breath. "And Zon and Taul?"

Bumpus paused, feeling the question circle back in his mind. "If I had to guess, different tribes or factions, maybe sects within the same order. Or…different leaders they fight for. Zon and Taul might even be different groups within the same creed. Maybe Kron binds them, no matter who they serve."

"Or maybe they're just names. Huh?" Giron shook his head, smirking.

"Maybe." Bumpus grinned. "I could be reading into it more than it is."

"We may never know," Giron finally said, casting a long glance at the arrows laid before them.

But despite the uncertainty, Bumpus knew these tokens held answers they couldn't yet decipher.

Meanwhile, the aroma of spices, fresh bread and meat intensified. It was almost time to eat. Clay and Jaune burst into the room, laughing and jostling each other as they went. Clay gave Jaune a light shove, who stumbled with a grin before lunging back, grabbing Clay by the shoulders in a mock wrestling move. They paused, catching their breath and exchanging mischievous looks, their laughter echoing through the room.

"I'm hungry," Jaune said to Clay. "You think it'll be ready soon?"

"I don't know, but I'm going to try to steal a taste," Clay replied.

"She'll just shoo you away out of there," Cleet said entering the room and overhearing this part of the conversation. "You may even get smacked by a spoon," Cleet continued on to retrieve some cups in another room.

When Cleet left, Jaune and Clay went to try to sneak some samples. Bumpus looked over to Tassel. He was still sitting in his chair in a deep sleep. He smiled. But when he looked back to Giron, he had a more serious expression.

"I can't eat horse, Bumpus," Giron said.

"I understand, Giron. Maybe you can eat some of the bread and excuse yourself as not feeling well, as not to offend their hospitality. Afterall, you've had a trying past few days."

"I think I will follow that suggestion. And thinking about those bodies, I really am not feeling well."

Just then, Sama could be heard yelling at Clay and Jaune. "Get out, you scoundrels!" They came out running and laughing, with some small samples of food. Giron flopped into his chair.

"Ma, you out did yourself this time!" Clay yelled back.

"It's almost ready. Just wait a few more minutes and set the table," she shouted. She then could be heard telling Cleet to help bring out the dishes which he was already doing. The family began setting the table.

Sama then brought out the food. There was the same savory bread, vegetables, and gravy-covered meat.

Giron set his gaze upon the food before him. He then excused himself to the relieving room. They didn't pay him any attention and once again began eating without blessing their own food.

Bumpus took an extra moment to go through his normal ritual of asking Elyon to bless his meal before he partook. He already knew from experience that Sama could make almost anything taste good. He took a bite of the meat. It was indeed well-cooked and tender, as he had expected. "This is delicious. But then so is everything you prepare. You will have to share your secret with me one day."

"Thank you. Enjoy." Sama smiled.

Bumpus sopped some of the bread in his hand in the gravy and consumed it. He was more than halfway finished with his plate, but Giron had not returned yet. *Giron is taking a long time.* Bumpus' thoughts were interrupted by a snore from Tassel, who was still asleep and not fazed by the activity around him.

"You think we should wake him up?" Cleet asked.

"No, let him sleep, for now, Sama said. "He looks so comfortable. There will be plenty for him to eat when he does wake up." She then looked at Giron's empty chair. "Is Giron alright?"

"He did say he was not feeling well after returning from the lake," Bumpus said. "He has been through a lot these past few days. I better to check on him."

Cleet nodded.

"Let us know if there is anything we can do," Sama said.

Bumpus excused himself from the table. In doing so, he grabbed the piece of bread he was eating to take along the way.

He exited and went out to the relieving room, where Giron had apparently locked the door and barricaded himself. Bumpus knocked. "Giron, are you all right? Everyone is asking about you."

"Make an excuse for me. Tell them I'm not feeling well."

"You're bringing more attention to yourself than if you just stirred the food around a couple of times and went to bed."

"Elyon never meant for us to eat such things, Bumpus."

"I don't remember hearing that anywhere, Giron."

"Well, its common sense." Giron said as he gripped the edges of the bowl, his stomach twisting again as the nausea overtook him. *Maybe the ale that I drank from the two Hooni'i at the lake was bad.* The rank taste of fermented ale, mixed in with earlier rations of cake and berries, lingered in his nostrils, making it all worse.

He was grateful he did not try to eat the horse that was prepared for dinner. But the truth was, it wasn't just the food and drink that was making him sick. It was everything. The images of the past days haunted him: the blood, the cries, the fear. Two men Hooni'i dead by his own hand, two others lost to brutal ends by Zauphrii archers. He could hardly bear to think about it. And here he was, the supposed warrior and protector, brought low over a bowl.

He heard a knock on the door, then Bumpus's voice, calm but firm. "Giron, are you all right? Everyone's asking about you."

He swallowed, barely able to answer. "Make an excuse for me. Tell them I'm not feeling well."

"You're bringing more attention to yourself than if you just stirred the food around and went to bed," Bumpus replied, his tone carrying a hint of exasperation.

"Elyon never meant for us to eat such things, Bumpus," he muttered weakly, wishing for anything that might soothe his stomach.

"I don't remember hearing that anywhere, Giron," Bumpus chuckled softly.

"Well, it's common sense," Giron snapped, though his voice lacked conviction. "And I'm not faking it. I just puked. Maybe the two Hooni'i at the lake had rotten ale."

Bumpus chuckled again, resting a hand on his back. "Take your time, I'll get you some bread and water to settle your stomach. Then we can call it a night. Hopefully you will feel better."

As his stomach finally quieted, Giron slumped against the wall, half in shame, half in frustration. Just days ago, he was the Champion of the Race of the Warriors, full of pride and respect. And Lana, his beautiful and kind bride to be, had agreed to marry him. Everything should have felt right, perfect even. But now he was hunched over in the relieving room, his insides twisted with unease and doubt.

Giron glanced up at Bumpus, whose wild scheme had somehow swept him into danger, and something in him began to struggle. Bumpus had all his respect. But he'd heard Elder Doyle's warnings about Bumpus, dismissing them as unfounded or exaggerated. But now, the question gnawed at him. *Was Elder Doyle right? Is it meant for us to know the mysteries of the barriers? Shouldn't we stay away from them or suffer consequences that we cannot even imagine? In a few days, four Hooni'i are dead. Will there be more?*

Maybe Bumpus, with his talk of Elyon's Barriers possibly not holding, and the mysteries of those behind them, truly was dangerous. Maybe, when all was said and done, he'd tear apart everything that Giron held dear; their way of life, the peace they'd fought to build. The thought chilled him more than any fever could. But this was his, soon to be, father-in-law, whose daughter he was in love with. Giron's gut stirred again as he acknowledged the feeling that that something bad was going to happen, which they needed to be prepared for. *But what?*

He turned back to the bowl. Between breaths, he murmured Bumpus' name under his breath, repeating it like a warning to himself: "Glettlebottom… Bumpus Glettlebottom."

BUMPUS' DREAM

Bumpus brought Giron some bread and some water and he retired early to their room. They would be returning home and Bumpus had told Cleet he would return in a month or so to continue with his experiments. They agreed that Tassel could stay with them until he mended, and Tassel gratefully agreed.

When Bumpus entered the room, Giron was already asleep and appeared comfortable. Bumpus stayed up and reviewed some of his calculations. He still wanted to observe the barrier more closely. The idea of an iron plated covered boat popped into his mind, which would protect them from the fate of the unfortunate Hooni'i from earlier in the day. Of course, there would have to be adjustments to compensate for the additional weight and allow it to float. In the pursuing weeks, he would have to narrow down the variations of L 43 E-C for further tests. Once the barrier could be seen, he could determine its location around the land portions of the forest.

Bumpus squeezed his eyes shut and opened them again. Everything appeared bleary. He had stayed up later than he intended. The whole household had already retired to sleep. Bumpus hoped to do the same.

Exhausted, he laid down and let out a long sigh. His head melted into the pillow. He appreciated the tranquility of the moment. However, the faint, distant howl of a wolf interrupted his peace and solitude. It was as if the beast had waited until the exact moment Bumpus sunk into the pillow to cry out.

He did not hear anyone stir inside the house in response to the noise. He guessed Cleet's family was used to these forest sounds. It didn't seem to bother Giron either, who continued to snore over in the corner.

Bumpus rolled onto one side, then to the other. More wolves joined in the howling, creating an eerie chorus. He tossed back and forth. His tired eyes were now wide open. He stared at the ceiling. He knew he needed sleep, but sleep escaped him.

After a few moments of tossing and turning, Bumpus finally surrendered, letting his mind drift in time with the howling of the wolves. He closed his eyes and began to picture them, not as distant animals but as creatures close enough to touch. Each howl carried a presence of its own. He imagined their thick, musky scent, the gleam of their eyes and the rough warmth of their fur brushing against him.

He moved with them, feeling the chill of the night air. This chill invigorated him. He sensed the comfort of the pack around him. Their bodies nudged against his own as they moved into a fluid dance under the moonlight. As he trotted alongside of them, he could almost feel the soil under his paws, and the strength of his muscles. Some wolves playfully nudged each other. Others stood stoic, lifting their heads and joining together their howls in harmony. The sound was so beautiful he couldn't resist joining. He began to hum, then to sing, his own voice blending with the pack's. *I am one with the wolves,* he thought, feeling the thrill of unity. Together, they sang to the stars, their voices rising as one.

Then, suddenly, a flash of white caught his eye. Beyond the pack, three massive white lionesses emerged, their coats glowing like snow under starlight. Their golden eyes were fixed on the wolves with hostile intent. They prowled closer, readying to pounce. Bumpus felt a surge of tension run through the pack as an even larger lion emerged behind the lionesses, his white mane rippling as he prowled forward. His eyes narrowed toward the pack before he let out a thunderous roar that sent tremors through the night air.

Bumpus's heart lurched forward in fear. Without thinking, he bolted ahead with the pack. His feet pounded alongside them as they raced into the darkness. The wolves' song continued, though now it held a note of urgency. It was a frantic edge that echoed his own panic. The cold night wind stung his face as they sprinted toward a distant, towering mountain cloaked in snow. Bumpus recognized this mountain as the same mountain that was in Zauphrii territory.

At this time, they began to ascend off the ground. He felt the temperature drop further. His body shivered as the chill raced through his body. When they reached the base of the mountain, they rose higher.

Bumpus glanced down and observed the lionesses devouring the meat of an animal below. Bumpus wondered if the animal was one of the wolves from the pack, one of his newfound friends.

He felt himself being pulled upward toward the mountain by an unseen force. He looked around and realized he was alone.

Bumpus rose rapidly toward the top of the mountain. A bright light beckoned at the top, pulling him closer. He hurled towards it.

Then suddenly, Bumpus came to a stop. The suddenness of the change was startling. There was no longer a chill. The melodic singing continued but now from somewhere beyond him.

He looked down at his feet. He was standing on water. No, not water but glass: a sea of glass that was deep, sparkling and fluid. *It really seems like water, yet I am standing on it.*

Bumpus looked out and saw large arches covering the sky. The arches illuminated many colors. They surrounded what he somehow knew was a throne.

Elyon's throne, Elyon! I must be in Elyon's domain.

While holding his gaze upon this vision, he saw what seemed to be the likeness of a Hooni'i figure above the throne. The being was the color of amber from the waist up but as if made from a glowing metal. Fire seemed to burn all around and within Him. From the waist downward the being looked like he was consumed by fire with a reflecting prism of colors.

Singing voices boomed around the throne. The voices overlapped in melodies and notes Bumpus had never heard before, the most beautiful music he had ever experienced. Smoke filled the air. Bumpus began walking towards this vision.

Suddenly, a blindingly bright and winged creature, about seven times larger than he, soared over Bumpus and landed about twenty feet in front of him. The wind created by the creature roared and nearly blew him over. The creature looked directly at Bumpus and held out its hand for him to stop. Bumpus could no longer hear the melodic voices. It was as if this creature cut the voices off from his hearing.

The creature's size and majesty were startling enough, but Bumpus was not prepared for the intense gaze of the twelve eyes on its face. The reddish eyes were set in rows of four. Six huge wings of an orange reddish color spread from the creature's powerfully muscled body.

As he was considering the inside of one of its wings, Bumpus jumped back when dozens of eyes suddenly opened from inside the creature's wings. They blinked at him. As some would appear, others would close, and still others would reopen. Bumpus dared not attempt to estimate how many eyes were coming from this creature or why it had so many eyes. The creature spoke his name in a long, drawn-out echo: "Bumpus…"

The voice was like the rushing of many waters overlapping one another. Bumpus' body fell limply and he collapsed, as if the voice had physically struck him.

The creature set its gaze upon him intently. Each of its eyes swayed like pure fire that seemed to burn through Bumpus' body. The creature stood for a time and did not speak. Bumpus felt naked and exposed, as if in the intense purity of this creature's presence it knew everything about him. It could see everything about him. It felt everything about him.

He trembled uncontrollably.

The creature spoke again. "You are not allowed to approach, Bumpus." The words boomed slowly, as if drawn out syllable by syllable.

Bumpus shook even more. *It knows my name.* He chose his words carefully so as not to offend the creature. "Thank you. Y-You are worthy of honor, magnificent and burning one. I-I am honored to be in this place and in your presence, oh great one."

"Bumpus!" the creature cried out in a loud voice. The floor of glass shifted with violence.

Bumpus felt the purifying heat from the creature's many eyes searing his soul. The floor settled.

"Arise and do not bestow worship on me. I am a created being, like you," it thundered.

"Please, forgive me, I'm sorry."

"Bumpus!" the creature roared out again. "Nor should you seek my forgiveness!"

Bumpus' heart thudded. His mind screamed with fear. *Perhaps it's best if I remain quiet.* He finally rose, even though he couldn't stop trembling, and bowed again.

The creature raised one of its fingers and pointed off to the right toward what appeared to be an altar. Standing next to the altar was another being. This being was thankfully far less intimidating than the first. Its form was like a Hooni'i. It only had two eyes and four wings. It wore a long white robe. Its face shone as pure gold.

"Go, Bumpus," the first creature.

Bumpus turned and walked toward the altar.

The large creature then arose. When it did, it covered its feet with its lower wings and covered its face with its upper wings. With the powerful flap of its middle wings, it flew away toward the great throne. The sea of glass rumbled as the creature repeatedly cried out the word "Holy!"

Part of Bumpus was glad the creature had left. He couldn't stop himself from trembling. But now he was face-to-face with this other being watching his approach. This being had what appeared as a smooth flat stone in its hand.

A stone? What's he going to do, hit me with the stone for saying the wrong thing to the other creature?

The being didn't throw the stone at him but rather opened its hand and released it. The stone floated toward Bumpus in slow motion.

He stood mesmerized and unable to move. The stone finally touched his chest.

Bumpus found himself flat on his back. He lay there for a while. He looked around for the stone but could not find where it went.

Then to Bumpus' surprise, he heard a voice that was out of place with everything else.

"Hi ya, Bumpus."

Bumpus craned his neck backward only to see the grinning cheeky face of little Atu Doyle. "Atu?"

"You in dist dweem too, Bumpus?"

"Atu, what are you doing here?"

"Why yah hit me wit da wock, Bumpus?"

"I didn't hit you with a rock. He hit–"

"It otay, it didn't urt at tall."

"But how did you get here?"

"Do yah know where he went, da one wit da shiny golden belt around his chest? And da other one dat moves around a lot? Here and there, here and gone, shake, shake, shake." Atu laughed. "He got da wiggles."

"The wiggles? A golden belt?"

"Day say I could pway wit da white yions."

"No Atu, you must not play with the lions. They are dangerous and…"

"Yions!" Atu yelled out and then pointed. "I see um over. See ya ladder, Bumpus." Atu playfully ran away in the opposite direction.

"No, Atu! Stop! Come back!"

Bumpus looked back toward the being at the altar in hopes it would stop Atu from getting anywhere near the deadly lions, but instead he saw it had one of its hands buried in what appeared to be hot burning coals at the altar.

When the being took its hand out, its fingers glowed the same reddish orange as the coals. The being then floated toward Bumpus, its feet hovering off the glassy surface.

Bumpus didn't know what to be more terrified about, Atu getting devoured by lions or what this being was about to do to him.

The being then spoke in a firm, resonant tone. "Hear the words of Elyon. Troubled times are ahead, and Elyon will send the twenty-ninth lord to you. Do not be afraid. You must help him. Receive the mark."

The being held out his red-hot finger and placed it on Bumpus' forehead. He closed his eyes. To his surprise, he didn't feel any pain, not even the slightest touch from this being. He opened his eyes again and he was alone.

"Wait. The twenty-ninth lord? What mark? What are you talking about? Are you going to help Atu? I don't understand."

Bumpus suddenly found himself in midair again, falling back downward. As he plummeted, he could hear the being's voice echo, "The twenty-ninth Lord of the Zauphrii…"

The fall continued until he found himself standing upright in the forest. In the dim light of night, Bumpus caught sight of three powerful figures locked in fierce combat. Their swords clashed with blinding speed and raw power, each strike sending shockwaves through the air. The intensity of their movements, far beyond anything he'd witnessed in Hooni'i fighting, left him awestruck. One had long dark feathers for hair and the other two white. He watched in horror as the dark feathered figure slew the two white-feathered figures.

The dark-feathered figure then turned to Bumpus, pointing with a bloodstained sword, and then walked toward him.

Bumpus suddenly found he had a bow in his hand. He instinctively reached for an arrow in his quiver found one. Bumpus then looked up into the warrior's black eyes before it swung the sword down at him.

All Bumpus could do was close his eyes and yell out the name of Elyon.

When he opened his eyes again, he was sitting up in bed, squeezing his blanket between his fingers so hard his knuckles were white.

Giron was there, staring at him. Cleet and his wife ran into the doorway to see what was going on. Bumpus sagged back into his pillow, drenched with sweat.

"What happened?" Cleet asked.

"He sat up screaming." Giron touched Bumpus' shoulder. "Are you all right?"

"It's only a nightmare. I'm sorry I woke you all." Bumpus sighed. "I dreamed was about to get my head split open by what I guess was a Rauthlin."

"We need to hurry up and return home," Giron said, rubbing his eyes. "You have too much of this stuff on your mind."

"Yes, Giron, you're right. I'm sorry."

"You need a good strong ale to help you sleep, is what you need." Cleet folded his arms and frowned.

Bumpus smiled weakly. The rest of the details of his dream filled his head but he wasn't inclined to share. "I appreciate the offer, but I think I've already had plenty."

Cleet nodded. "Well, if you change your mind, let us know. Otherwise, try to rest."

"Will do," Bumpus said.

As Cleet and his wife left the room, Bumpus looked back at Giron who was staring back at him. "If you were going to have a nightmare, I would think it would have been about the Zauphrii, after what happened earlier," Giron said.

"Yes, Giron. This has been an eventful trip."

"Yes, it has been. Hopefully, it will be uneventful as we return home in the morning."

"You know, we'll have to tell Lana the truth about what happened. She will be full of questions."

"I know," Giron sighed as he laid back down. "That's not going to go over well."

"You can blame me. I got you into this."

"We'll see how it goes."

Bumpus laid back down into his pillow and closed his eyes. He would have to put aside the memory of the crazy dream filled singing wolves, white lions, and strange creatures. For the moment, he would try not to think about the Zauphrii or the Rauthlin.

But deep in his heart he knew his fixation on the barriers would not go away. *Help the Zauphrii? How is that even possible? Why would I do that?*

He knew he should have been more restless than ever. But for some reason, Bumpus felt a rush of peace coming over him that he could not explain. He rolled onto his side and fell fast asleep.

As Bumpus slept, unbeknownst to him, a four-winged creature stood concealed in the back of the room, invisible to the two Hooni'i. The creature knew the nights of Bumpus' comfort would be limited in the future.

The creature had done what it was sent to do. It had carried out Elyon's orders. Soon they would pay a visit to the Zauphrii camp. Shortly, the order will be given. Preparations had been made, and judgment would come.

As the creature continued to gaze at the two Hooni'i, its image swayed back and forth and wiggled from side to side. It disappeared from the room.

The time of the twenty-ninth lord was at hand.

THE ZAUPHRII
BURIAL OF LORD KRON

The silence was profound, broken only by the clomp of horses' hooves, the creak of a cartwheel, and the soft, relentless rhythm of thousands of footsteps. Lord Kron, the twenty-eighth Lord and leader of the Zauphrii, had died. He lay pale and regal on a fine white cushion, his feathered head resting among red petals, a dominant figure who had drifted away from the world where he once led.

Zerrah watched from a small hill, his gaze steady. Two white maned unicorns pulled the cart with solemn eyes that seemed to know the importance of this moment. They passed below him, looking briefly up his way. A slight wind tugged at Zerrah's own feathers, blowing across his face, but he didn't brush them aside. His muscles tensed, his pale, pupilless eyes narrowed as the procession moved below. In his mind, the outcry of past leaders echoed with every step of the mourners, each footfall like a drumbeat marking the march of time, of lineage, and of the inevitable future. *The twenty-eighth lord has passed*, he thought. *And I may be the twenty-ninth, if Elyon wills it.*

The priests would soon select the next Lord. There had already been spiritual trials and interviews, a rigorous evaluation of strength, knowledge, and wisdom. Zerrah felt confident. Not even General Abgron, Kron's son, commanded the same balance of strength and agility that Zerrah did. Although Abgron was respected, even admired, Zerrah felt he stood alone at the front, the clear choice. He could see it in the way Koo'rah, Zerrah's own daughter, had withdrawn, recognizing Zerrah's skill and position. *The choice is clear.*

The mourners began to slow, forming a circle around Kron's final resting place, their footsteps fell silent. Zerrah's gaze hardened. *The Zauphrii have been drilled long enough,* he thought. *It's time for battle. Elyon's vengeance awaits the Hooni'i and the Rauthlin.* He felt the rage beneath his calm exterior. *The Hooni'i are inferior creatures who had always struggled to follow Elyon's path. They deserved little more than the blunt force of Zauphrii justice. But the Rauthlin are the former kin who turned against their own blood. They deserved annihilation.*

As the salutes were given, and Lord Kron's body began to sink into the earth, Zerrah let out a silent vow to Elyon: *No mercy for the Rauthlin. Not for them.*

"My lord." The voice was quiet but carried an edge that pulled him from his thoughts. Koo'rah had joined him on the hill. Her tall form was steady, and her eyes were pupilless like all the Zauphrii. The two swords strapped across her back gleamed in the dimming light. She, too, bore the mark of readiness, which was a dagger strapped to her thigh. It was a testament to the time of war Elyon had promised them.

"It's done," she said firmly, her eyes fixed below. "Tomorrow begins the dawn of a new era."

"Every day holds purpose in Elyon's sight," Zerrah replied. "And what's this 'lord' business? I'm still a general until the priests make their decision. Until then, I'm no more than any other general."

She offered him a rare, sly smile. "We both know you'll be named Lord of the Zauphrii by week's end."

"Don't be so certain," he replied, lifting a brow. "Overconfidence is not the mark of a Zauphrii commander."

"In this, I am certain," she replied. "Let it be recorded in the annuals of time that I was the first to call you Lord of the Zauphrii." She glanced down at the scene below, her face resolute. "We are ready to follow you over the barrier."

He smirked. "You know, technically, I still outrank you, commander."

"Yes, General," she responded with a slight nod, acknowledging the proper salutation of rank.

For a moment, silence settled between them. Then Zerrah's expression grew more somber. "Abgron is favored by many, and you are more than capable of leading, as well. The priests may choose any one of us. Even you."

"You know I've withdrawn from the trials," Koo'rah answered, her voice firm. "It's futile. No one can match you. By the end of this week, you'll be lord."

Zerrah allowed her words to linger, taking in the field below, the mourners beginning to disperse as dusk approached. *The twenty-ninth*

Lord. He let the thought settle within him. "Have you truly considered the battles that await us, Koo'rah?"

"War and conquest," she replied with solemn certainty. "That's the prophecy."

"Yes. War and conquest, but also death and pain."

"And victory." She turned to him, her eyes gleaming with an edge and spoke the name that caused all of them bitterness. "And there is the matter of the Rauthlin."

Zerrah's jaw clenched, his gaze grew cold. "The Rauthlin," he repeated. "Judgement will be sure. Elyon's will, be done."

"Elyon's will, be done," Koo'rah affirmed, her tone mirroring his. They stood together, watching as the end of the procession faded from view.

As Zerrah looked down, he felt a wry sense of irony. Here he was, overlooking a burial, and yet, his mind was consumed not by mourning but by the promise of bloodshed. And he knew even Lord Kron's own son thought of the same.

His gaze continued to linger below, but after a time, he blinked himself back to the present, brushing aside his thoughts. He turned to Koo'rah, who was watching him patiently. With a nod, he gestured down the trail.

"It's time to head back," he said, his voice lighter now as he set off beside her. "Let's see if you mother kept any of those sweetened cakes for us, or if little Karama has gotten to them all first."

A subtle smile twitched at the corner of Koo'rah's mouth, a rare hint of emotion breaking through her usual composure. "She planned to make plenty. But if anyone's cleaned them out, it's probably Zon. He's been training hard lately and growing. He's one of our best archers now. Just this morning, he was excited about shooting one of the taunting Hooni'i down by the lake."

Zerrah smiled, a note of pride in his voice. "Yes, he's improved dramatically."

"He's been working with me on his swordsmanship too," Koo'rah added.

"Ah," Zerrah teased, twirling his finger in the air, "I hope you haven't encouraged him to do those spinning and flipping moves you love so much. He'll twist an ankle before he knows it!"

Koo'rah nodded. "Well, he might get a scrape or two. But he'll be ready if a flying Rauthlin swoops down on him."

Zerrah laughed. "Oh, so they've grown wings now?"

"Maybe evil has mutated further than we think. We'll soon find out, my lord."

Zerrah chuckled again but then grew thoughtful, his tone softening. "Speaking of which, you mentioned earlier something peculiar about the other Hooni'i at the lake. Zon and Taul didn't manage to intercept them with their arrows?"

Koo'rah glanced up at him, her expression turning serious. "I knew you were focused on more pressing matters, so I didn't bother you with it then. But yes, there was something strange about those Hooni'i."

"Strange how?" he asked while pausing mid-step and turning to her. Koo'rah hesitated, before they continued at a slower pace.

"These two were different. They appeared to be more cautious. They didn't engage directly, nor did they run away. They fell back, changing direction to avoid Zon and Taul's arrows. Once they were at a safe distance they stopped. They watched us." She looked away and stroked her chin. "It was as if they were studying us. And they weren't empty-handed either. They had instruments, strange objects, laid out along the shoreline."

Zerrah raised a brow. "Observing us?" He stopped walking entirely. *Could these Hooni'i be smarter than we thought? What were they doing?* "We may have underestimated them. If they're preparing, studying us, it's possible they're developing a new weapon."

He resumed walking, his gaze fixed ahead. "Once we're done with the final appointment, we need to convene with the generals and commanders. We must discuss this in detail."

Koo'rah nodded, falling into step beside him. "I assume a war council will be called before we cross the barrier, my lord?"

Zerrah smirked. "Well, Commander, we'll make sure Zon and Taul are in attendance. They should also give their input about what they had seen. We do not want to miss any detail."

Koo'rah's nodded. "When you are lord, there won't be any need for recommendations. Just give the order, my lord."

"All right, Commander," he said, his voice both warm and resolute. "We'll see how things fare with the priests."

A guard joined them and escorted them the rest of the way home. The pathway leading up to and around the home had been secured by warriors days before. Zerrah felt that the extra guards were not necessary for protection from a Zauphrii population that did not impose on one another because of celebrity status or rank. However, as leaders, he knew many Zauphrii held him and his daughter in high esteem. To have any semblance of normal life, it was necessary to maintain control to limit disruptions. As with Lord Kron, it would be even more so with the next Lord in succession.

Upon seeing the extra security, Koo'rah held her hand toward them. "You see, even Lord Kron's son orders your security in anticipation of what is to come."

"I'm sure it is the same for Abgron and the other generals as well," Zerrah replied.

"I know I'm not a general, but I don't have any extra security assigned to me other than what's under my command."

Zerrah smirked. "Well of course not. They are afraid to approach you. They fear you."

"I like to think that I am respected, not feared." She turned to one of the guards walking with them. "You, there. You aren't scared of me, are you?"

The guard looked over to her and back forward as he continued to walk ahead. Even though this guard was not under Koo'rah's command, it was obvious to Zerrah that he was contemplating how he should respond. Zerrah chuckled to himself. "No, Commander, I am not scared of you," the guard finally responded. "We all share the same objectives."

Koo'rah turned back to Zerrah and held her hand out toward the guard. "You see, he is not afraid of me," she said keeping a steady voice.

"He also said he shares the same objectives," Zerrah pointed out. "What happens when they have questions in their minds. The real question is when your orders and objectives become different in your warriors' minds and there are questions, will they follow your command out of fear, blind obedience, or trust?"

"It should be all of them, my lord. Healthy fear leads to proper reverence and respect. Obedience and trust go hand and hand. As we obey Elyon and trust in Him, we should also do so to our leaders."

"I have taught you well, Koo'rah. The next Lord's reign will bring many situations where all of that will be tested."

"The Zauphrii will be up for the challenge, my lord."

They soon spotted an old Zauphrii female ahead of them off to the side of the road. She leaned against a tiny cart drawn by a small horse. The horse was occupied by munching on the grass below him. The guards looked at each other and then one of them trotted out ahead to talk to her. Zerrah could see the guard going through the contents of the cart. The old Zauphrii said something back to the guard and held her hands out.

As they approached, the female stood up straight and bowed to the general and commander. "Sorry for all the disturbance, General. I didn't mean any harm. My name is Bana. I'm just an old Zauphrii trying to sale my knitted covers before it gets too late in the evening. I know many are breaking up from Lord Kron's burial, and I am late getting there. I was taking a shortcut. I have several coverings left."

Zerrah nodded. "I'm afraid the ceremony is already over, but there may be some that are lingering around the site. Do you mind if I have a look?"

"Not at all, General."

Zerrah looked at the guard, who shook his head. "It's several coverings, General, just as she said."

Bana and Zerrah walked over to see the merchandise with Koo'rah remained silent. Zerrah could feel her staring over their shoulders.

The coverings were knit in a variety of darker colors. They were nothing special, but he figured she was in need if she was hustling to sell her goods to a crowd at a burial.

While he was looking, Bana set her gaze upon him. "Is it true what they say about the barriers, General? Are they going to be brought down? Are we going to war?"

Zerrah glanced back at her and nodded. "Yes, it will be as you say. Elyon has said it will be during the next reign. The time will be soon."

"The Rauthlin are treasonous and must be dealt with," she said. "I thought I would die before I saw this day. But I prayed that I would live long enough to see the twenty-ninth lord cross over."

Zerrah was taken aback by her vehemence. *Even in one so old. But I have also shared these same thoughts since my youth.*

"The time of Elyon's wrath is at hand," Koo'rah interjected.

Everyone nodded in confirmation, including Zerrah. He held up one of the coverings. "How much?"

"Six pence, but I will give it to you, General, for four.

Zerrah reached into is satchel and retrieved some coins. "I'll buy the whole lot of them and pay the six pence each, so you don't have to trouble yourself chasing Zauphrii down below the hill." He gave her the coins.

Bana smiled with evident excitement and relief. "May Elyon bless you, General. You are both kind and generous."

Zerrah held out a couple toward Koo'rah. "Which one do you want, Koo'rah?" When she did not immediately respond, he held one of them up to her. "Take this one. I will give the others to Abia."

Koo'rah nodded and received it. "Mother will appreciate it."

Zerrah distributed the others between two of the guards to help carry them and they continued down the pathway.

As the pathway turned, Zerrah's home came into view. It stood solidly among the forested hills, a grand lodge of stone and timber that spoke of his high rank. Massive tree trunks framed the entry. Inside were polished wood and rugged furniture built to withstand generations, all reflecting the strength and honor of a high general's home.

When they entered, they were greeted by Abia, Zerrah's wife. Her beige dress was pulled in at the waist by a woven yellow belt. She wore a matching yellow scarf upon her head, as a headband, pulling back her feathers into soft flowing crown down to her shoulders. Abia was a Zauphrii of quiet strength, warmth and love. Her presence as steady and comforting always ushering in peace no matter what was going on.

She'd prepared a special meal of spiced meat, roasted vegetables, and plenty of sweet, honey cakes. The honey cakes were a tradition she enjoyed when her husband returned from his missions. She moved with ease, offering food and comfort to her family. She accepted Zerrah's small gifts with a tender smile. The evening unfolded with stories, laughter, and a strong sense of family, filling the lodge with warmth and unity.

Zerrah cherished this time, sensing that these comforting family evenings were going to change in the future.

Into the evening, he rested, knowing the next day would bring the final competition of combat. While doing so, Zerrah couldn't help but remember the expression on the old female's face desiring revenge against the Rauthlin. He recalled the footsteps of the horses before Lord Kron's procession and the united Zauphrii walking in sync. Even though he was not yet appointed, a different pressure of responsibility weighed upon him heavily. The footsteps in his mind continued and then suddenly ceased.

As he sat in his chair, he imagined all the Zauphrii population, including past lords, standing at attention looking at him for direction. He would be the one responsible for battling the enemy. He would be the one to carry out the burden of thousands of years. It would soon be time to retaliate for the high treason of the Great Rebellion. Order had to be re-established.

He looked out the window and let out a sigh. The season of the barriers was coming to an end.

TEST OF COMBAT

(APPOINTMENT OF THE 29ᵀᴴ LORD OF THE ZAUPHRII)

The capital city was alive with activity, a bustling sea of Zauphrii gathered in honor of the upcoming test of combat. Zerrah walked with his guards, taking in the scents of roasted meats, honeyed bread, and the earthy aroma of open fires drifting through the crowd. Laughter and conversation filled the air. Children darted through clusters of friends and families getting ready for the main event which would take place within the hour.

Zerrah's gaze traveled to the slope of the hill where Zauphrii were finding places to sit and watch the spectacle below. The combat grounds stretched wide and open, surrounded by ropes and wooden barriers to mark the fighting space. He could see the glint of steel in the afternoon light, where dulled swords awaited the combatants.

The rules were clear: each warrior would wield only one sword, rounded at the tip and dulled along the edges, ensuring that victory would come by skill, not bloodshed. There were no shields permitted, and each fighter was allowed three surrenders or "death blows" before they were eliminated. The stakes were high. Though the victor would not necessarily be appointed by the priests, this would be the last trial in a series of tests that would influence the final selection.

As he scanned the crowd, Zerrah could hear the murmured anticipation: would anyone truly challenge him, or would they submit and concede before the fight even began? Many had traveled far, hoping for a glimpse of the warriors who had become legends in the eyes of the Zauphrii; there was General Zerrah himself, strong and unwavering; Koo'rah, the formidable High Commander, both revered and mysterious; and the legendary General Abgron, son of Kron, a warrior whose skill in his youth was the stuff of songs were sung. Alongside them were other respected names like General Tedros, known for his cunning, and Commander Ajani, a seasoned tactician. Captain Zorion, too, had drawn attention, an agile and unpredictable fighter, one of Koo'rah's finest protégés, and a master of her intricate techniques.

Zerrah's gaze moved to the elevated platform where the five high priests sat. Arrayed in their ceremonial robes of many colors, they watched the gathering with unreadable expressions. The exception being the head priest adorned in a white robe with a grey shawl over his shoulders. Zerrah knew two of them, including the head priest, leaned toward Abgron, the longest serving general and who favored more traditional ways. But Levani, the fifth priest, was harder to read. He had kept his preferences carefully guarded during their recent interviews. In truth, Zerrah wondered if the priests had already decided on a successor, and if this contest was more a formality than a test.

The seeding had been announced, and Zerrah noted the matchups with interest. Tedros would face Ajani, and Zorion would go against

Aitan in the first round. Zerrah and Abgron, as the highest-ranking generals, would face the winners of these initial bouts. Zerrah's thoughts drifted toward the matches to come, considering his potential opponents and the tactics each might bring.

He glanced once more up at the priests, considering the war to come, wondering how heavily their choice would weigh on the combat. *Just because my skills may be superior to others, that doesn't make me the leader that Elyon needs. Elyon, have your way.*

Zerrah watched as the lower ranked participants rode out before the audience. This left the three generals who sat on their white unicorns, waiting for their introductions. Zerrah glanced over at Abgron and Tedros with great pride. *These are indeed two bold leaders. It has been an honor to serve with them.*

Abgron caught Zerrah's gaze and smiled back at him. "Look out, Zerrah. I may be getting up in age, but if you relax too much, I'm going to beat you today."

"Don't worry, General. I won't be lured into overconfidence by your age proclamation. I know what you can do." Zerrah nodded. "I respect you too much to relax."

"Abgron!" Tedros shouted. "You have to get by Aitan first, or worse yet, Zorion, with his twisting in the whirlwind fighting style."

Zerrah responded to both. "I've seen Zorion spar with Koo'rah. Beware of an immediate counterattack after an exaggerated acrobatic defensive move. It's an intentional setup. The move can catch you off guard. There will be no hesitation on his part when he counters."

"Thanks for the tip, Zerrah," General Abgron replied. "But you probably should have mentioned that to Commander Aitan before he went out."

"It's the old wise one who needs the advantage," Zerrah replied jokingly.

General Tedros was introduced. He turned to the others. "Good luck to you both. If I am not chosen, know that it will be a pleasure crossing over the barrier under one of your leaderships."

"As with I," Abgron responded.

"And I," Zerrah said.

Zerrah watched Tedros ride his unicorn around to the cheers of the crowd. Zerrah turned back to Abgron. He recalled how he received some of his early training from Lord Kron and later from Kron's son, Abgron. Abgron and Zerrah knew each other's styles very well. However, Abgron lost a step or two with age and Zerrah grew stronger and more skilled. He hoped Abgron would have an honorable showing, being that he was loved and respected by the Zauphrii population.

"General Zerrah, High General of Central Command."

The announcement boomed across the field, jolting Zerrah in his saddle. General Abgron put his right fist over his chest and bowed his head in salute. Zerrah did the same. He rode out to the roaring cheers of the crowd. As he looked around, he was overwhelmed at the sheer number of the Zauphrii in attendance. He passed the priests and saluted. They nodded back to him in unison. Zerrah glanced at his daughter. He could sense Koo'rah's tension as only a father could. She also saluted him. He saluted the remaining commanders who stood with her at attention, along with several administrators.

Abgron was announced, and the others waited for him to complete the same ritual to join them. No mention was given of this being the time of the 29th Lord, but all knew what was at stake. They dismounted and took their places in view of the circle of combat.

Zerrah leaned back, hands resting on his knees. He watched as Zorion limbered up, his arms swinging in controlled arcs, testing his reach and range. Opposite him, Commander Aitan gripped his chosen sword with a familiar confidence, slicing it through the air in practiced swings. Finally, they stepped forward and faced each other, the anticipation building until the referee signaled the start.

As the first clash of steel rang out, Zerrah's eyes shifted up briefly to Koo'rah. Zorion's fighting style was unmistakably hers, fluid, strategic, relentless. He pressed Aitan with a ferocity that was thrilling to watch, every movement driven by precision and speed. Zerrah could tell he was eager to showcase his skill, and the crowd responded with voices of admiration.

Steel met steel in a rapid succession of strikes, and at one point, Zorion closed the gap, lunging forward to press Aitan back.

But Aitan held his ground, deflecting Zorion's attack with a skillful parry and then, with a quick sidestep, shoved him out of range.

Zorion stumbled but quickly regained his balance, coming back in fast, his determination evident.

But his aggressiveness had left him vulnerable. Aitan, seizing the opening, swung his blade in a sweeping arc, landing a solid strike against Zorion's chest.

The referee gave the first nod to Aitan, marking a point, and the two fighters paused, catching their breath. Zorion's face was intense, but he showed no frustration. He raised his sword, signaling his readiness, and they prepared to engage once more.

Zerrah studied them carefully as the contest resumed, both warriors driving forward with an exchange of blows. He admired Zorion's agility, the speed of his movements. It was a clear testament to Koo'rah's training. Yet Aitan was experienced, adapting quickly to Zorion's relentless style, meeting each of his attacks with measured strength and patience.

At one point, Zorion dodged Aitan's swing with a falling twist spin.

He simultaneously kicked Aitan's feet out from under him.

Zorion swung down stopping his swing right in front of Aitan's head. The score went to Zorion. This was a great move that Zerrah foresaw, but Aitan apparently did not.

The crowd cheered.

Zorion had become more comfortable. His movements were fluid. It appeared to Zerrah that Zorion had discovered how to take advantage of Aitan's more focused and deliberate style and defend against his technical strengths. Zorion scored again in a similar fashion. Aitan had no answer. Zorion eventually won the match. Aitan was escorted away and sat in front by the priests. Zorion was escorted to his seat near Zerrah, where he received water and a wet towel to wipe his head.

Zerrah nodded to him as he took a drink. He acknowledged Zerrah in return.

In the next match was more physical with General Tedros taking an early lead by two. But it was not a dominant performance either. It could have easily been the other way around. However, Commander Ajani connected on a direct blow straight center puncturing Tedros' skin and injuring his rib. Tedros grimaced when trying to continue and raised his hand. The healers came out to examine him and determined he had broken a rib. If this were a life and death situation, he would continue, but under this circumstance he chose not to. Commander Ajani advanced to the next round and would face Zerrah.

After the half-hour break, Zerrah settled in to watch the next match between Zorion and Abgron with intense focus. Zerrah could tell that Zorion felt no intimidation. The younger warrior held his ground, ready to take on the legendary general without hesitation.

As the fight began, Zorion's quickness was immediately on display, darting in and out with light, rapid swings that forced Abgron to stay on the defensive. Abgron moved fluidly, dodging and parrying with minimal effort, almost as though he was studying Zorion rather than fighting him outright. Zerrah's eyes narrowed. Abgron is being careful, almost too careful, as though testing Zorion's reach and timing with every small shift of his stance.

Zorion seized an early opportunity, landing a quick strike on Abgron's side, earning him the first point. A round of cheers lifted from the crowd. Zerrah could see the young warrior's confidence grow, his attacks becoming more assertive. Yet, even as Zorion pressed his advantage,

Abgron was calm, his eyes never leaving his opponent, quietly observing each move.

It became clear to Zerrah that Abgron was piecing together a strategy, biding his time while he analyzed Zorion's rhythm. His posture remained relaxed and his footwork precise.

After a brief reprieve, the referee signaled for them to continue.

Zorion swung in again, a rapid series of strikes aiming for Abgron's chest.

But Abgron was ready. With a subtle shift, he deflected the blows one by one, letting the force of Zorion's momentum work against him.

Just as Zorion was overextended, Abgron seized his opening, bringing his blade down in a controlled but forceful strike that knocked Zorion off-balance.

The younger warrior stumbled, catching himself quickly and resetting, but it was clear he'd felt the power behind Abgron's counter.

As Zorion steadied himself, Zerrah noticed that Abgron's lips curved into a faint smile. It was the look of a warrior who understood exactly how to turn an opponent's strength against him. The clatter of the crowd increased with excitement. *This is over,* Zerrah predicted. *Abgron may not be as strong as he used to be, but he uses his mind and is a formidable foe.*

Zorion spun around and kicked Abgron to the side of his face. Zorion seemed surprised on his follow-through how quickly Abgron recovered and was suddenly close enough to elbow Zorion up under his chin with the butt of his sword.

Zorion crashed to the ground.

Abgron held his sword toward Zorion and scored the point.

Zorion rolled over, clutching his jaw. He spat blood.

Abgron waved over for the healers to come. It was a scary moment as everyone fell silent. Zorion laid flat. They finally sat him up and the crowd applauded in relief.

Zerrah clapped, too. *Tedros is down and now Zorion. He is a superior frontline warrior who will not be able to fight for a while.*

It was now Zerrah's turn to face Commander Ajani. *I know how to beat him. I must be aggressive and not give him the opportunity to believe he has a chance. I shall not give him an opportunity to think.*

When they got the nod, Zerrah swung his sword from right to left down on Ajani.

Ajani backed away but Zerrah sensed right away that Ajani had no defense to his strength.

One of Zerrah's downward swings had so much force Ajani almost lost his sword even though he blocked the strike and fell back to the ground.

Zerrah scored as he held the sword to Ajani's chest.

Ajani took a break to drink water and compose himself. Zerrah did not but waited where he was for him to return.

From that point on, Ajani tried to use speed and mobility to keep away from Zerrah. Unfortunately for Ajani, Zerrah proved swifter and more mobile than he was.

Zerrah did not want to let up. *I must not give Ajani even the thought that he can contend with me. Ajani is outmatched with skill, but I should still quickly finish this respect as a fellow general.*

Zerrah quickly parried swings and made contact to Ajani's body, signaling the referee to shout out a score each time. The match took only minutes. Zerrah had hardly needed to exert himself. Ajani was clearly outmatched from the start. Zerrah held back, avoiding any unnecessary blows, showing the restraint he'd honed over years of disciplined training. Despite the restraint, the crowd responded with eager cheers. When it was over, Commander Ajani sheathed his sword and approached, bowing with respect. "I appreciate you sparing me the humiliation of injury, Zerrah," he said with a wry smile, his voice carrying both sincerity and humor.

Zerrah returned the smile warmly, bowing his head in acknowledgment. "We all need to be ready to go when Elyon calls us forward, General." He hoped Ajani would sense his respect. To Zerrah, these matches were a display not only of strength but of the restraint each leader needed, even in times of war. Still, he knew that the crowd saw his swift victory as a testament to his skill, if not to his reputation for invincibility in their eyes.

Only the two top generals were left: the legendary General Abgron, son of Kron, and Zerrah himself. Zerrah was confident in his chances against Abgron, but he knew not to be overconfident. Abgron's strength was in his ability to anticipate and adapt, as he did with Zorion. *That's what makes him such a great general.*

If truth be told, Zerrah did want to be the twenty-ninth lord. But Abgron was worthy as well and Abgron had trained him. Zerrah dared not beat him too quickly and he dared not hurt him, out of genuine respect.

However, there may be no other way to defeat him. If Zerrah let his guard down, Abgron could hurt him. The one sword, no shield rule did not help either. It was not how either preferred to fight. Zerrah preferred no shield and two swords and Abgron preferred fighting with a shield. They had trained as such. Both had to adjust for this competition.

Everyone stood. The two high generals faced each other in the circle of combat to the applause of the crowd.

"Thanks for the tip about Zorion," Abron said. "I checked on him, they say he'll be perfectly fine in a week or so."

"That's not going to help you now, General. I didn't give you any tips on how to beat me," Zerrah replied.

"I helped train you. I know you well."

"And I know you well also, Abgron."

As the referee's nod was given, both wore smiles on their faces. Zerrah knew Abgron enjoyed the rush of combat as much as he did. The two circled around feeling out each other.

Abgron swung his sword. Zerrah blocked it and stepped back, then lunged toward him and made a backhand swipe.

Abgron blocked both with evident ease.

They both stepped back and circled each other again. Zerrah played to the crowd, wanting to extend the match out of respect for Abgron. The crowd stood to their feet and cheered.

They clashed blades.

Zerrah forced Abgron's sword downward, but Abgron brought it up in a backward motion toward Zerrah's shoulders.

Zerrah ducked and struck Abgron's chest with the palm of his hand, forcing Abgron to stumble away.

Zerrah knew he should strike at Abgron while he was off balance, ending the contest, but Zerrah didn't charge. He stepped back in defense waving his sword from side to side, and smirked. "If I didn't know any better, I would think you are trying to hurt me!" he shouted.

"Maybe just a little bit." Abgron shrugged. "I appreciate the love tap."

They both nodded to acknowledge that the time for games was over. They clutched their swords and circled each other once again.

Zerrah and Abgron exchanged several blows. It was clear to Zerrah that Abgron was doing his best to avoid direct blows from him, trying to come at him from various angles, but despite this strategy Zerrah was able to parry with forceful strength on one of Abgron's lunges, knocking him off balance. He followed through by slapping the flat part of his sword across Abgron's chest.

The score went to Zerrah.

The two rested for a few minutes before they re-engaged. The match was already longer than any other match of the day and there was only one score. They then engaged again.

After a few minutes, Abgron lunged at Zerrah with a downward swing. Zerrah dodged to his side and countered with a swing of his sword to Abgron's side.

Abgron hunched as Zerrah followed through with a quick thrust to his back. The thrust was light as Zerrah did not want to hurt him.

The second score went to Zerrah.

Zerrah held his sword out and grinned. "Almost there," he said.

"Not over yet," Abgron replied.

They both got the nod to continue.

Zerrah continued with a more passive approach. He bid his time waiting for an opening to attack. However, Abgron had adapted and become more aggressive with his attacks. Zerrah's approach backfired on him when he stumbled backward after one of Abgron's aggressive barrages. This allowed Abgron to swipe Zerrah across his side. It was scored for Abgron. *That would not have been but a scratch wound in battle. But I should have known better from our training together.*

The two took a break for a few minutes to drink and ready themselves again. Zerrah knew Abgron was able to handle his strength by his defensive angles and counters. *I can't fool around. I need to distract him somehow.*

After the break, the two nodded toward each other and began again.

Zerrah ducked as Abgron's sword sliced inches over his head. *If that had connected, that would have been a problem,* he thought. *He is trying to set me up. But I'm not going to let him.*

Abgron then did a similar swing, but this time Zerrah stepped in and punched Abgron across his chin before he could react, one hard enough to make Abgron stumble.

Zerrah then hit him on his side with his sword. It was fitting that it was a move that Abgron had taught him several times during training and one of which Zerrah had been the recipient. It was the final score for Zerrah. The referee signaled the point in Zerrah's favor and held his hand up to acknowledge him the victor.

Abgron hunched over and put his hand on his knee. He then rose and spat blood from his mouth.

"Are you okay?" Zerrah asked.

Abgron nodded and smiled at Zerrah glowingly. "You remembered. It's ironic that I was drawn into such a distraction. But you are the better of me Zerrah."

The crowd applauded and cheered as the two high generals bowed to each other in salute.

Zerrah shook his hand in the air. "You have a heavy chin, Abgron. Good match, my friend, maybe next time."

"The honor was mine. But know this, Zerrah: if you are selected, the next time I raise my sword, it will not be against one of our own." Abgron saluted him again before departing and taking a seat.

Zerrah turned and took a seat next to Ajani. Ajani gave him a pat on the back, along with several others who nodded or gave him their congratulations. But amid the crowd's celebration, Zerrah found himself looking up toward the priest's platform. To his surprise, the five priests had left without a word.

Ajani glanced over, noticing Zerrah's look. "Expecting them to say something?" he asked quietly.

Zerrah nodded. "I thought there'd be some announcement or something to acknowledge the victor of the test of combat. But it seems they've gone."

Ajani shrugged.

Just then, Koo'rah made her way over to him, her stride purposeful and eyes steady as always. She gave him a subtle smile. "Congratulations.

Abgron put up a better fight than I'd expected, but I knew you would prevail." "How is Zorion?"

"He will mend."

Others continued to give him accolades. But after several minutes had passed, Zerrah looked around. "What is next?"

"Was something else supposed to happen?" Ajani asked. "Or do we just all go home, now? Where are the priests?"

"They dismissed themselves into a tent," Koo'rah said. "I suppose we are to wait."

Ajani sat back and folded his arms. "Nobody is leaving. Only they can disperse the crowd," he replied. "Nobody is going anywhere."

Zerrah felt that the minutes dragged on for about an hour. The silence thickened as the crowd became a sea of hushed whispers and shuffling feet. At last, the tent's flap stirred, and the priests emerged. They strode forward, serene yet resolute, bearing an aura of finality. With a single raised hand, the head priest stilled the crowd, and a hush fell over the people, a silence that could have held the weight of an empire.

One of the priests beckoned over to Zerrah. "Zerrah, come forward and stand before us."

Zerrah stepped forward, his face stoic but his heart thudding in his chest.

The lead priest adjusted his gray shawl and regarded him with an intensity that seemed to bore into his very soul. "It is the will of Elyon," the priest began, his voice deep and resonant, "that we no longer delay what has been long awaited. Zerrah, the trials have proven you worthy not only in strength but in heart and mind. You have demonstrated the resolve and honor that Elyon demands of those who lead the Zauphrii."

Another priest, Levani, stepped forward, holding a cloak woven with symbols of leadership and legacy. They were symbols that spoke of sacrifice, duty, and power. He draped it over Zerrah's shoulders with reverence. The weight of the garment was palpable, settling upon him as a silent testament to the burden he was to bear.

"Today," the head priest continued, raising his hand for the Scepter of Lords, "we proclaim you the Zauphrii's leader, chosen by Elyon, destined to be our guide. By the authority vested in us, we crown you the twenty-ninth Lord of the Zauphrii. May you carry forth Elyon's justice, uphold the honor, and bring about the long-awaited destiny spoken of in the prophecies."

The priest's voice softened but held an edge of gravity. "In the months ahead, you will climb the Great Mountain of the High Priests to seek Elyon's guidance, that our paths might be made clear. But all the Zauphrii know what you are called to achieve. There will be justice for Elyon, and vengeance for the Zauphrii." Zerrah was overcome by seemingly the corporate drive by all. *Wrath will be poured out upon the Hooni'i,* Zerrah thought, *and Elyon's account against the Rauthlin will be settled for their rebellion.*

The crowd erupted in cheers, though some wept openly, overcome by the significance of the moment. Zerrah looked at Abia, who had been brought to his side, her presence grounding him as she reached for his hand.

As he raised the scepter, Zerrah felt the weight of the Zauphrii hopes and the coming storm. The cheers subsided, and for a moment there was an echo of silence reverberating a calm before the tide of war. It would be a war that the twenty-ninth lord would initiate.

BUMPUS AND GIRON BACK AT THE NORTHERN HOONI'I VILLAGE

"No! Absolutely not, no! You are not going back there!" Lana exclaimed.

Giron looked at her sheepishly.

Bumpus stood behind the table pretending to examine one of the Zauphriinian arrows. "Such care, such workmanship."

"Stop it, father. It's not funny!"

"I think she's mad, Bumpus."

"Yes, I'm mad!"

"Yes, Giron, this is what she does when she's mad. Get used to it."

"Yes, but she is still so beautiful," Giron replied in an apparent attempt to lighten Lana's anger.

"Beautifully mad," Bumpus said flippantly.

"Stop it!"

"Now, Lana, please calm down so we can talk this through," Bumpus said.

"Talk this through? Calm down?" Lana pointed her finger at her father. "You… you almost got my husband killed before I even married him. And you!" Lana snapped at Giron. "You went along with his madness. Why didn't you stop him? My father could have been killed!"

"I couldn't have stopped him anyway, Lana."

"And you both lied to me!"

Bumpus put the arrow down, hunched over and sighed. "You are right, Lana. We didn't disclose everything to you up front because…"

"It would make me mad, and you knew I would have had something to say about it?"

"Well, yes," Giron said.

"And now you are telling me you are going back there again after what happened?"

"Yes."

Lana huffed and folded her arms.

"We did tell you everything when we got back," Giron said.

"That doesn't count."

"Lana, at least give Giron a break. Didn't you say you wanted us to get to know each other better? He spent some good quality time with his future father-in-law." Bumpus chuckled.

"You can go have a few drinks together, play some games, not almost get murdered together by the Zauphrii!" Lana shook her head as if to plead with them. "Can you image what would have happened if both of you didn't come back to me? The two I love and care about more than anything in the world. Where would I be? What would I do? Don't you care about me? How can you do this? It doesn't matter to you I almost lost a father and a husband?"

"Well, you could always replace a husband," Bumpus replied.

"Thanks a lot, Bumpus," Giron said.

Lana rolled her eyes at them in exasperation.

"Lana, seriously, there is something bigger going on here," Bumpus said. "I think you are missing the importance…"

Lana stomped her foot on the ground. "I'm not missing the importance!"

Giron gestured at her for calmness. "We made it back okay."

"Okay? Look at the nasty cut on your arm. How did you get that again? Okay? And father, the arrow you are looking at. How did you come by it, huh?"

Giron glanced at Bumpus and chuckled. "She does have a point, and she didn't even mention the horse being served for dinner."

Lana put one of her hands on her hip and scowled back at Giron once more. "Oh, you think I'm playing around with you too, do you?"

"Lana, I know you have reason to be mad," Bumpus said. "But this is important. I'm convinced that Elyon's hand is pushing us to do this research."

"Oh, now blame Elyon," she said sarcastically. "So, Elyon told you to deceive me, to put yourselves in danger, and to go into a forbidden area without the approval of the elders?"

"Lana, please," Bumpus said. "Elyon protected us."

"He has always protected us by telling us to stay away from the boundary of the Zauphrii." Lana walked over and picked up one of the Zauphrii arrows on the table. She shook it toward her father. "Stay away!" She slammed it back down.

"But Lana, your father is about to crack the mystery of the invisible barriers. Aren't you moved even a little bit?"

"Why? It hasn't been a problem for thousands of years."

"I know but…"

"They want to kill us, Giron. They scare me," Lana said with tears in her eyes and a tremble in her voice. "They should scare you too."

"Now that really is the point, isn't it," Bumpus said. "It is my desire to protect us and all Hooni'i from them. Elyon put this in me. This I must do."

"Why is it always you, father? Nobody does what you do. Protection is already there. Elyon created the barriers."

"But for how long, Lana? Was it meant forever?" The three of them remained silent for a moment before Bumpus held up his hands in surrender and continued. "Lana, darling, something is going on. It's not normal. Apparently, their pattern of behavior has changed. We haven't heard of such increased activity at the barriers before. We must study them."

"And you are the keeper of Elyon's barriers?" Lana finally threw up her hands. "This is above you, father. You need to consult with the elders. If you don't go to them, I will."

Bumpus and Giron looked at each other. Bumpus begrudgingly nodded. "Okay, Lana, we will consult with the elders, but I must do what I must do. Giron can do what he wants to do."

Giron did not respond to Bumpus' comment other than to say, "Fine, we will consult with the elders, Lana."

"Okay, fine then," Lana replied.

"Fine," Bumpus said.

"I'll go and prepare some dinner even though you two don't deserve to eat." Lana gave Giron a cold stare and walked past him into the other room.

"Yeah, she's mad," Giron said.

"She'll get over it. We'll call on the elders for a meeting in the morning. I will ask Bracket to attend as well. We could use his insight. Maybe Lana is right. It may be time for us all to talk about the barriers and what we found out. But know this, Giron: I must go back and finish what I've started. I hope you'll come with me, but I understand if you don't."

"Let's just talk to the elders and go from there," Giron replied.

At that moment, Lana came back into the room to retrieve a towel she had left behind. She avoided eye contact.

Giron tried to get her attention. "Lana, precious, do you need some help? What are you making?"

"Your horse!" Lana then put her head up in the air and stomped back out of the room.

"Guess she's still mad," Giron said.

"Yes, I guess she is."

The two stood in silence for a few moments.

"I'll be back, Bumpus."

"Where are you going?"

Giron smiled nervously. "To check on my horse."

The meeting of the elders took place in a circular, stone-walled chamber inside Elder Grier's residence. A massive wooden table sat at the center. It was carved with intricate designs that depicted the Hooni'i's history and their covenant with Elyon. A single chandelier made of polished crystal hung overhead, with unlit candles available for lighting the room upon evening meetings.

However, it was midday. Outside, hundreds of Hooni'i had gathered. Their whispers filled the air with curiosity and unease. The soft murmur of the crowd filtered through the open windows. Somehow, word of Bumpus and Giron's encounter with the Zauphrii had spread, drawing the attention of the entire village.

At first, the elders asked Bracket to report his story to all who were present. He stood nervously, shifting his weight as he detailed their brush of death on the southern border at the hands of a Rauthlin assassin. When he finished, he stepped back, and all eyes turned to Bumpus and Giron to report regarding their experience at the northern border.

Bumpus cleared his throat and began. His voice was steady despite the tension in the room. Together with Giron, they recounted every detail. They reported their journey into the Forbidden Forest, the hospitality they received, and their confrontation with the Zauphrii across the lake.

When they finished, the room fell into an uneasy silence. The elders exchanged glances, their expressions grave.

Elder Doyle broke the silence. His sharp tone was accusatory. "I've already addressed my concerns with Bracket privately, but what's wrong with you two? Don't you know it's called the Forbidden Forest because it is forbidden? Bumpus, we talked about you not going back there years ago, and now you've dragged Giron into it too?"

Elder Grier interjected, his voice calm but firm. "Doyle, we've already discussed this. It's done. Let's focus on what's in front of us now."

"Did you bring the arrows?" Elder Frencrest asked, his eyes narrowing on Bumpus.

"Yes." Bumpus carefully unwrapped the arrows and the cylinder, placing them on the table for the elders to inspect. He handed one of the arrows to Elder Doyle.

Doyle examined it, turning it over in his hands. The intricate craftsmanship of the Zauphrii was undeniable, the arrowhead shimmering with an almost unnatural luster. He passed it to Elder Grier before fixing Bumpus with a strong gaze.

"Bumpus," Doyle began, his voice heavy with disapproval, "there comes a point where we simply must believe. If Elyon protected us by creating barriers, we should trust Him to do what He said He would do. The barriers were put up for a reason. There is no need to try to uncover their substance or learn about the populations beyond them. It is what it is and has been for thousands of years. Your actions risk planting seeds of doubt in Elyon and encouraging rebellious attitudes. Do you not see the danger? Hooni'i will be intrigued by what lies on the other side. They will lust after strange lands rather than appreciate what Elyon has already given us." He paused, his voice dropping to a near whisper. "Just like those Hooni'i who perished at the lake. They hated Elyon for not giving them their selfish desires, for what was not theirs to begin with."

"These are wise words, Doyle," Elder Grier said, his tone conciliatory. "It is clear that the Rauthlin and Zauphrii are instruments of Elyon's judgment. Those who venture outside His protection will perish. Surely, you understand this, Bumpus."

Bumpus gathered his thoughts before he responded. He took a deep breath and nodded. "My esteemed elders, is it not in the stories of Elyon we tell every year that the Hooni'i walked away from Elyon's guidance, and in the heat of many quarrels and fighting, the Hooni'i did evil to one another? We hated, coveted, cheated, and killed one another. We were made worthy of Elyon's wrath, which the Rauthlin and Zauphrii are apparently more than happy to carry out. Remember, even amongst ourselves, we have only been at peace with one another for a little over a decade."

He turned and looked at his audience, making sure he commanded their attention. "Is there still not hate, cheating, and murder among us? I'm sure you agree. It is strictly Elyon's mercy that put the barriers up to prevent us from total annihilation. But we have already stepped outside of His boundaries of protection. At some point, we just might be judged. Are we immune from judgment? At some point, won't Elyon require us to face what's really in our hearts? In the absence of the barriers, would we really trust Him?"

Bumpus wasn't expecting a response, but the contemplative gazes he got in return convinced him to keep going. "It is then and only then would we know for sure who is for Elyon and who is not. Nowhere in any of the stories of Elyon have I heard that the barriers endure forever. We have been in the season of His mercy for sure. Now, I don't know if anything could happen to the barriers in my lifetime. All I know is Elyon has put it in my heart to be concerned about it. He has given me insight and knowledge regarding them."

The Elders fell silent and seemed to contemplate what he had said. Elder Grier leaned over and whispered to Elder Frencrest.

"Well said, Bumpus," Giron whispered. "I didn't know all that was inside you. Maybe you should be an Elder."

Bumpus smirked. "There is something more to consider, my esteemed elders. It appears the Zauphrii are becoming more aggressive. Who knows what's going on in the South? From Bracket's testimony, we can glean more about the Rauthlin too. I recommend we coordinate with the other Hooni'i villages and gather intelligence. We must prepare for the unthinkable."

"What are you saying?" Bracket asked. "The unthinkable what, Bumpus? If the Rauthlin get across the barrier, we're all dead. They're evil!"

His voice shook and his body trembled in response. He lowered his head, apparently unable to meet anyone's eyes. Giron walked over and put his arm around Bracket's shoulders.

"Even if the barrier was removed, Elyon would protect His own," Elder Frencrest said.

"What happens if Elyon lifts both barriers at the same time? We will be stuck in the middle," Giron said.

"Now that's a thought," Bracket said under his breath.

"If that were to happen, who is to say the Rauthlin and Zauphrii won't kill each other and leave us alone?" Elder Frencrest asked.

"Wait a minute!" Elder Doyle exclaimed holding his hands up. "Wait just a minute. Have we already jumped to the conclusion that Bumpus is right about anything, and that Elyon won't just keep the barriers up for another ten thousand years?"

"No, I don't think anyone has jumped to conclusions about anything," Elder Grier replied. "But it may be wise to gather intelligence and exchange information with the other villages. I say this even though I agree it may cause those very concerns you shared earlier, Elder Doyle."

"I concur," Elder Frencrest said.

"All of you are crazy," Elder Doyle replied. "We could be putting Hooni'i in dangerous situations."

"Bumpus and Giron seem willing to take the risk," Elder Frencrest said. "Let's look at what we know so far," Bumpus said. "We know the Zauphrii are strong and skilled archers. They also have at least one female warrior of rank. We also know from Cleet's reports that the Zauphrii are beefing up patrols along the boundary. Soon, we will be able to know exactly where those lines are. And from Bracket's testimony, we know the Rauthlin who attacked them used the element of surprise. The Rauthlin also had to be extraordinarily strong to swing a sword with one arm and sever Bracket's friend's head." Bumpus glanced at Bracket, who still had his head bowed. "Sorry, Bracket."

"There is also the mystery of the metal rods, which I think may have something to do with measurement or marking of the barrier," Bumpus continued.

"I think we should allow Bumpus and Giron to go back to continue the experiments." Elder Grier deliberately pointed his finger at Bumpus and Giron. "However, you will take a troop of warriors with you and not take unnecessary risks. We will send a contingent to the lake communities to advise them. Meanwhile, we'll have Tam go with another troop to the southern villages to speak with them and gather information." He turned to Bracket. "And if Bracket is up to it, he can accompany Tam as he is more familiar with the area and Hooni'i there."

"I don't want to go anywhere near the boundary," Bracket snapped.

"You can stay back in one of the southern villages, far away from the boundary," Elder Grier said. "We understand if you are not up to it. Again, only if you are willing."

"I disagree with all of this," Elder Doyle said. "You now want to send my son?"

"Just to the southern villages, not to the boundary," Elder Grier replied. "He is of age. He can decide for himself."

Bumpus watched the exchange with Bracket with a growing sense of unease. He couldn't help but feel for Bracket and the horrors that he experienced at the southern border. Bumpus recognized the slight tremor in his hands and the shadow in his eyes. *Poor Bracket. He is still healing and should not be dragged into more turmoil. But I feel we are running out of time.*

When Elder Grier suggested Bracket might stay in the southern villages to aid Tam, Bumpus wanted to interrupt, but he knew his father already had. Bracket closed his eyes and grimaced for a moment. Bumpus could see the conflict warring within him.

Bracket finally opened his eyes and looked at Bumpus. "As long as I don't have to go close to the boundary. I suppose it will be alright."

Bumpus nodded slightly with approval, though his heart understood the step of bravery Bracket was taking to overcome his fears.

"So, it's done then," Elder Grier said. "Bumpus continue your experiments to the North. Giron, assemble a contingent of warriors to go with Bumpus for his protection."

Giron nodded and promptly stepped outside to give out orders to one of his subordinates.

As the meeting wrapped up, Bumpus's own future weighed heavily on him. He had a second trip to the Forbidden Forest to prepare for, and Lana would not be happy about it. She had longed for stability, a quiet life, a wedding, a home and a family. But those dreams would have to wait. In his mind, doubts continued to creep in that screamed instability and turmoil. What had begun as a personal obsession had now become an official mission, sanctioned by the elders. There was no turning back now.

He barely noticed the murmuring crowd as he stepped out of Elder Grier's residence. He was lost in thought, imagining the difficult conversation that awaited him with Lana. It was then that he felt a hand seize his arm. He stopped and turned to face Bracket, who had stopped him.

Bracket's eyes burned with intensity as he spoke. "Bumpus, I need you to understand. The one thing that stuck with me, more than anything else, was the Rauthlin's hatred; pure, dark hatred. It's hard to explain, but it was a deep, lustful anger."

Bumpus sighed and shook his head. "Elyon was right to create the barriers to keep this evil from us." He put his hand on Bracket's shoulder. "Despite what I said inside, I hope the barriers will never fail. I have no desire to confront the Rauthlin, or the Zauphrii for that matter, none whatsoever."

"Neither do I."

Bumpus smiled at Bracket warmly. "May Elyon guide and protect you with this commission. And may you never again encounter a Rauthlin."

Bracket smiled in return. "And Elyon's covering to you too, Bumpus. May He protect you from the wrath of the Zauphrii." He then looked deeply into Bumpus' eyes. "And the Rauthlin." Bracket turned and walked away into the crowd.

Bracket watched him walk away with a pang in his heart. *I am afraid, too, Bracket,* he confessed to himself. *May Elyon help us.*

THE RAUTHLIN
THE RISE OF ROG

I declare that all Rauthlin shall submit to me under the Shawktee banner. The Shawktee, the Awutanee and the Wyunaktee shall be one. By my will, Elyon's barriers will be broken and the Zauphrii and Hooni'i vanquished. I am Rog.

It was a warm day. The afternoon sun blazed in a pale-yellow sky. Lord Rog sat in the intricately carved wooden chair provided for him outside his tent. The canvas of the tent flapped gently in the warm breeze. His imposing figure cast a long shadow over the dusty ground. Below his right eye, etched deep into his pale face, was the tattooed emblem of the Shawktee creed. Angled crisscrossed blades with a downward sword between them. It was the bold mark of his Rauthlin clan. It stood as a reminder of his lineage and his ferocity.

Rog ran his fingers through the black feathers on his head. The motion was deliberate and meditative. The events of the past days churned in his mind. He pondered the drama of the past few days.

He had wearied from battles against the Awutanee forces, led by Lord Standist. Today, as expected, the Awutanee suffered badly at the hands of Rog. The Shawktee had proven superior and more disciplined.

It had been decades since the Shawktee were exiled from Rauthlin City by the Wyunaktee sect. Over time, they had clawed their way to survival and forged a new home in the unforgiving high plains by the edge of the great divide, near Hooni'i land. There, Rog had risen, carving order from chaos and molding the Shawktee into a force to be feared. Through sheer grit and cunning, they had survived relentless assaults from the two other Rauthlin factions. Their victories cemented Rog's name in awe throughout the territories.

The Shawktee land was on higher ground and was strategically easier to defend. Even Lord Styness, the arrogant king of the Wyunaktee, had grown tired of throwing his soldiers at Rog's unyielding walls. Instead, Styness turned his malice toward the Awutanee, leaving Rog to rule the "edge dwellers" without his intervention. The Awutanee desired to take Rauthlin City and also subdue the Shawktee. Such was the Rauthlin balance of power. But Rog wanted more. Rog was successful today, but he knew the Awutanee would be back. He clenched his jaw, pounded his fist onto the chair and cursed the name of Standist.

Rog gazed across the great divide toward the land of the Hooni'i and gripped the arms of the chair tightly. While he wasted time fighting the Awutanee, he really desired the land which held Elyon's disgusting breed, the Hooni'i.

Rog glanced at Auntar, the High Captain of the Shawktee Guard, who was standing nearby. Upon catching his eye, Auntar gave a signal to another who went running off into a nearby tent. The guard returned to Rog with a small cage. Inside the cage was a rodent. The guard bowed before Rog and offered him the cage.

The presence of the rodent had a calming effect on Rog. He stood and received it. "Ah yes, come here little one." Rog opened the cage and retrieved the rodent into his hand. The rodent squirmed within his clutch. Rog sat back down and continued in thought. He gripped the rodent firmly in his hand and stroked the back of its head with his thumb.

Rog dreamt of the day when he didn't have to war with other Rauthlin, but with the Hooni'i and Zauphrii. It was true the great divide prevented them from going over onto Hooni'i land. However, the Hooni'i could just come across the barrier without resistance. *Where was the justice in that? Of course, Elyon isn't just, which was why the Son of the Morning rebelled against Him in the first place.*

Rog considered the high unclimbable back mountains blocking the outskirts of Rauthlin land. He also considered the unnavigable seas. The Rauthlin condition reminded him of the lizard box he kept when he was a youth. As the lizard was trapped inside by the walls of the box, so too were the Rauthlin trapped. *Trapped like the rodent in his hand.*

Rog's anger rose.

The Hooni'i are vile creatures. Why did Elyon create them? Why does He protect them? Not many Hooni'i dared to cross over the barrier. But Rog was pleased when some stupid Hooni'i tried their luck and got caught. Those who were caught paid the price of a mutilating death at the hand of the fortunate Rauthlin who caught them.

He privately envied Druce, the blacksmith's son, who had recently honored Rog with two severed Hooni'i heads and a Hooni'i sword. Rog was so pleased he promoted Druce on the spot. Druce had matured into a great Shawktee warrior. His father, Bleen, had trained him well.

Notwithstanding this praise, Rog wished it were he who killed those Hooni'i at the Great Oak instead of Druce. Regardless, he was happy with the trophies. That was the way it was supposed to be, Rauthlin killing Hooni'i and… the Zauphrii.

When Rog introduced the Zauphrii into his mind, the grip tightened around the rodent's neck and skull.

The rodent squirmed.

Auntar returned. "My lord, High General Nook approaches."

Rog looked out and observed General Nook riding toward them from a distance. Rog nodded his acknowledgment to Auntar and waited for the general.

As always, the general was dressed in black leather military gear. He wore his ceremonial Shawktee headband tied under his distinct military helmet, the helmet that only he wore. He was the most trusted amongst a very few of Rog's confidants.

The general's ashen horse kicked up dust as the General snatched in its reins and forced it to an abrupt stop. The horse was known to be the general's favorite beast. The rare creature was freakishly muscular and larger than a regular horse, with flesh the color of a living corpse.

Rog knew these horses were few and difficult to tame. But when they were tamed, they became a Shawktee symbol of strength and status. They were second only to the swift dualicorns he preferred.

General Nook dismounted. A Shawktee guard took control of the horse. Nook approached Rog and bowed his knee. Rog nodded back but continued to stare off with the rodent still in his hand. General Nook looked to Auntar whose expression did not change. He turned back to Rog. "You sent for me, my lord?"

"This is such a waste of Rauthlin life, isn't it? Dear General, don't you want to kill the Hooni'i and the Zauphrii?"

-Everything about Rog's disposition continued to be measured and controlled. However, the rodent began to squeal, attempting to squirm away from Rog's grip.

"Yes, my lord," sneered the General ignoring the rodent.

Rog said nothing more but continued to ponder his thoughts. General Nook waited patiently.

"Hooni'i puke," Rog blurted as he narrowed his eyes. The rodent squealed and shook violently as Rog crushed its skull within his grip. He could feel the crushing of bone between his fingers. He could feel the convulsing of the warm furred body in his hand. This brought him pleasure. It felt good. Rog gazed forward as if his hand had acted independently.

General Nook waited until the jerking rodent fell silent. "What is your pleasure, my lord?"

Rog continued to hold the lifeless rodent in his hand and turned his attention back to the General. "Have they set up the extra measuring rods as instructed?"

"Yes, my lord. And Commander Druce has increased our stealth patrols at the divide near North Oak."

"Good. Make sure I am advised regarding any observed Hooni'i activity, no matter how small or insignificant. Any movement or change with the barrier needs to be reported to me. Bleen had reported with great confidence that the barrier at North Oak moved several inches."

"My lord, can we be sure about what the Blacksmith reported?"

Rog aimed a cold smile at Nook. He tossed the dead rodent to the ground. "I would hope that's the case, General. The Blacksmith was a great warrior at one time. He's still a combat trainer for the Shawktee. His family makes weapons and supplies us with many swords. We also just promoted his son, Druce." Rog nodded. "It would be unfortunate to have them terminated for Bleen's error in judgment."

"Yes, my lord, most unfortunate."

Rog looked back over the Rauthlin plain. "We'll need to gather the commanders together to plan against Standist's next attack. We embarrassed the Awutanee today.

"Indeed, we did, my lord."

"I expect Standist to be even more reckless the next time." Rog gestured. "That's all, for now, General."

"By your command." Nook bowed his head and excused himself.

Rog noticed Auntar had stood during their exchange with an icy cold indifference. The sacrifice of many years of battle was etched deeply in stark lines and scars on Auntar's hardened face. Behind his dull charcoal-colored eyes, Rog had no doubt rested visions of blood, murder, and mayhem, all done in the service of his master.

The present tussle with the Awutanee had lingered longer than expected. Rog knew they would be at the front for a while longer. A return home would not be forthcoming.

"Auntar." Rog beckoned for him. "I want you to personally deliver a message to my wife."

Auntar nodded and awaited instruction.

"Tell Darmonla that we shall be here for a while and not to worry. Remind her she and Daman are safe, and that Rog still lives." Rog then fell silent.

Auntar hesitated as if expecting more. No more came. He saluted and started to leave.

"Auntar…"

Auntar stopped and turned back. "Yes, my lord?"

"You've been with me a long time. You do not agree with my decision to prohibit Darmonla from fighting, correct?"

"It is not my place to agree or disagree, my lord."

"But what, Auntar? You may speak freely, at least for the moment."

Auntar slowly nodded. "My lord, she is trained and of the Shawktee creed of the highest order like you and I. Remember we all fought together before coming over to this plain. This is our way. If I were forbidden to fight by your side, and the pride of the Shawktee, I would rather see death."

"Yet you would still obey me."

"Of course I would, my lord."

"And so, will she. Being trained and being ready are two different things. My orders have well thought out reasonings behind them. My enemies would go after her to get to me. Do you understand?"

"Yes, my lord."

"And I sense I'm about to acquire some more enemies. But these will be enemies of a different kind."

Auntar gripped his sword and looked at his master. "Is something amiss I need to know about?"

"Standist will not take this last beating lightly. The Awutanee will soon be eliminated, or we will." Rog leaned closer to Auntar and smirked. "I don't plan on being the one eliminated. The Shawktee shall survive."

Auntar lightly grinned in return but dropped the expression just as quickly in favor of resuming his hardened expression.

Rog sat back up in his chair. "When we are successful, there will be some who remain secretly loyal to those we defeat. This will be an enemy of a different kind. They will honor the Shawktee to our faces, but plot against us behind our backs."

Auntar's blackened eyes narrowed. "We will destroy Standist and his army, my lord. Any disloyalty will be dealt with harshly."

"Yes indeed, Auntar, but know for these Rauthlin, the more power they gain, the more power they will lust for. They have no history with Rog, nor of the Shawktee creed."

Rog looked up to the sky and stroked his chin. "I have been thinking… Yes, I have decided. Besides the General, you are one of my most trusted and dependable warriors. I need Darmonla to be better prepared. She also needs to be reined in to be focused on what is to come. I am assigning her and Daman to your care. Keep her skills intact; gather others to spar with her. Arrange her guards and monitor her servants. She must understand the urgency of the situation. For the sake of the future Rauthlin Kingdom, I need her to be better than she is now. Bring in whom you need."

"My lord, you're not going to need me for Standist?"

"You're only a messenger's ride away, Auntar. So, gather who you need quickly. Inform her of the message and your assignment."

Auntar put his head down, breaking his rigid demeanor with a smirk. "Do I have permission to defend myself after I deliver the message?"

Rog smiled back at Auntar's humor. "Just deliver the message, Captain."

"Yes, my lord."

"You might want to make sure she is not armed, though."

Auntar bowed his head to give leave.

"Oh, and Auntar…" Rog nodded to the dead rodent on the ground. "Food for Darmonla's pet."

Auntar scooped up the dead rodent in his hand. He gave final salute and left. Another guard, who stationed himself by Rog's tent, jogged over and took up Auntar's post.

Rog sat back in his chair. He returned to his own thoughts and dreams—thoughts of Standist's next attack and dreams of Hooni'i and Zauphrii blood.

Commander Druce was as muscular as he was tall. He wore the typical Shawktee military clothing of black pants and a black leather vest. Although he was allowed to cut his shirt and have his vest sleeveless, which was comfortable to him and exposed his sizable arms. Druce knew the Hooni'i didn't know exactly where the barrier line was. They could not see the barrier as the Rauthlin could. Which was why his father's measurement of it was important.

His father, Bleen, was aging. His feathers were still black and body strong, but his face etched with the wrinkles of time. Even with his age, Bleen was still of great use to Rog and respected amongst the Shawktee. He had taught Druce the ways of stealth, which he in turn taught others under his command.

Bleen was also a great weaponsmith. In fact, making and repairing weapons was the family's main responsibility these days; Druce, who was the eldest living son, being the exception.

Druce was the commander of the rear patrol. Bleen's other two living sons were still relatively young. Even though many Rauthlin their age fought in Rog's armies, those two had been better utilized helping Bleen with the trade of making weapons.

Bleen had reported to Druce about the movement of the barrier at North Oak. Bleen did not know if something happened just in one spot or if indeed there were other movements elsewhere. His markers had been placed at different locations along the barrier of the Hooni'i.

It was the afternoon. Druce was to meet General Nook at his father's dwelling. While waiting, Druce joined his father and brothers to help get the latest order of weapons out in preparation for Lord Standist's next attack. Druce put some swords to the side, and he yelled out to his brother Mlug. Mlug was tall like his brother Druce but had a thinner stature. However, he shared Druce's tendencies of over aggressiveness. "Get those coals hotter!" Druce shouted. "We must finish these swords and center Rog's symbol on each one!"

"I'm working on it! Calm down!" Mlug shouted back.

Kawn, the youngest brother, sat shirtless, sanding one of the swords off to the corner. He was shorter than his brothers with a stout build. He took a pause and raised his brow at his brother's bantering.

"You won't be calm when the Awutanee comes and rips your limbs apart," Druce hollered.

"I don't care if you are a commander," Mlug snapped. "If you yell at me again, I'm going to cut your guts out and cook it over these coals!"

"Scrawny one, your head would be on the floor before you could even reach for a dagger."

"Knock it off!" Bleen said. "Just keep working!" Bleen's hammer came down hard on his creation.

The brothers sneered at each other and continued to work. Bleen did as well. The sword was fashioned with the specific detail Rog liked for his warriors. As he burned the symbol of Rog into the sword, he dipped the finished product in the barrel of water next to him. "In an hour, this one will be ready for buffering."

While Bleen inspected his creation, one of Druce's Shawktee came to them. He walked up to Druce and saluted. "Commander. General Nook has arrived outside of the camp and will be here soon."

"Very well," Druce replied, nodding toward his father in silent apology before stepping away to follow the Shawktee. *What could be so urgent that Rog sends the High General himself?* he wondered.

The Shawktee led Druce to where General Nook's massive horse was being tied to a post. The General himself was already striding toward them. Spotting him, Druce approached and saluted. "General."

"Commander," Nook acknowledged with a nod, thumping his fist to his chest in greeting. "Rog has called a meeting of commanders at the front. You were excluded because your work here is critical. I've come to brief you and deliver your orders personally."

"Yes, General," Druce responded, his tone firm with respect. "It is an honor for Lord Rog to send the High General himself to deliver this message."

"There is more to it, Commander. I'm checking on the weapons. Some of our warriors fight with their personal swords that lack the girth of Bleen's weapons. How is the order coming? We'll need them."

"All is well, General. Come and see. Bleen can give you a more accurate update." They both walked back to where Bleen and the brothers were diligently at work. Nook approached Bleen. The two smiled and greeted each other with an arm-to-arm greeting.

"Bleen, you are looking good."

"And you too, General. Everything is in order. Rog must have plenty of weapons to protect us from our short-sighted Rauthlin brothers who want to kill us, take our land, and possess our wives and little ones."

Nook nodded his approval. "Your family has always come through in time of need. Lord Rog considers you dependable and an asset to the Shawktee. I want to make sure you stay in Lord Rog's grace."

"As do I, General."

Druce noticed Nook's expression then became more serious. He nodded at Bleen and then turned his attention to Druce. He addressed them both. "I have an update regarding Standist. Our informants tell us Standist plans on committing his entire army in two to three days. All commands must be ready and be alert. We will move the population back here to the North. Order your captains here to prepare to receive them."

Nook reached for and examined one of the swords. He noted Rog's symbol with pride. "These weapons will help us. The symbol of Rog will give our warriors courage."

"Why would Lord Standist commit his whole army?" Bleen asked.

"Or most of it," Nook corrected. "He may leave a remnant back, but he is becoming desperate. His recent strategies have been reckless." He glanced over to Bleen's two younger sons, who had stopped what they were doing to listen to the General's report. "I'm afraid you and your sons should also arm yourselves. Everyone should be ready if the battle retreats here to the North. Either way, Rog needs all to be available."

Druce and his brothers looked intently at each other with great pride. He smiled at them knowingly in return. Bleen's eyes narrowed. His expression was stern.

"We'll be ready, General." Mlug held up one of the newly fashioned swords, his pride in his craftmanship evident to Druce in the way he stood straight. "We are of the clan of the Shawktee. We have Rog."

Druce felt his blood pumping within him. *Yes, brother, we are the Shawktee. Nobody defeats Rog.*

Darmonla moved with precision, her blade meeting the guard's in a rhythmic clash that echoed through the camp. She was a trained Shawktee warrior and the wife of Rog. She spared almost daily. It was meant to calm her, to channel the storm inside of her into the focus required of a Shawktee warrior. But the storm inside of her never stayed quiet for long. Her gaze flickered briefly to Daman, her son, as he stood with a guard, watching and learning the basics. *So young, yet already under the weight of what being Rog's son meant.*

Auntar approached them with a bag in his hand. When he approached, the sparring stopped. The guards saluted him with the thump of a fist to their chests, and Auntar returned the gesture.

Darmonla's heart quickened. *Why is Rog's High Captain here? Why isn't he with Rog? What could have happened?* Her mind betrayed her, as it often did, racing to every dire possibility. She fought to maintain her composure, though she knew how fragile that balance could be. Her voice cracked as she spoke. "Is all well, Auntar?"

"Yes, Darmonla, all is well," he replied, his tone steady, as if sensing her inner turmoil. "I have a message from Rog. May I have a moment with you?"

She was relieved, though it didn't quiet her suspicions entirely. Her brows furrowed as curiosity replaced fear. "It must be an important message if Rog sent his High Captain to deliver it personally." She turned to one of the guards. "Continue to take Daman through his basic drills while I speak with Auntar."

The guard bowed and turned to the child, leaving Darmonla to approach Auntar. Together, they walked a short distance away, her eyes studying him for any sign of bad news.

"All right, Auntar, what is it?" she asked. "What's your report?"

"Rog said not to worry. We'll be at the front lines for a while longer."

Her lip curled, a mixture of frustration and sarcasm bubbling to the surface. "Don't worry, Auntar? She jeered at him, her voice rising. "He says *don't worry!* The Awutanee have increased their attacks while we continue to bury our dead."

Auntar's expression remained composed. "He wanted me to remind you that you and Daman are safe. And Rog still lives."

"Yes, he lives," she shot back, her voice seething. "Rog loves to flirt with death while I sit here and watch from afar. He doesn't include me. I could help him. You know I could. Our clan has never played it safe, Auntar. I should be fighting by his side." Her voice cracked, anger and hurt intertwined. She cursed and kicked the ground hard, sending a spray of dirt into the air.

Auntar shifted slightly, his stance changed. It was subtle gesture, but enough for Darmonla to notice. *Is he bracing himself? Does he think I'm going to strike him?* The thought both amused and annoyed her. She let out a short laugh. "Do you think I'm going to hit you or something?"

"The thought did occur to me," he admitted, his tone dry.

"Maybe I should," she teased, a faint smirk tugging at her lips.

"I'd rather you not."

Her laugh broke free this time, dispelling some of the tension. But Auntar, ever the professional, stayed on task. He held out the bag he'd been carrying. "Rog asked me to give you this for your cantu."

Darmonla took the bag, her lips curling into a wry smile. "A peace offering from Lord Rog? How thoughtful." Peering inside, she found a freshly killed animal, its blood still staining the cloth. "Oh, how sweet. And he killed it already, so my cantu doesn't even have to trouble herself. I bet he enjoyed that."

Auntar said nothing, his silence was more telling than words.

Darmonla dropped the sarcasm, her gaze locking onto his. "But there's more, isn't there? Rog wouldn't have sent you all this way just to tell me not to worry and that he's alive." Her tone was steady now, but beneath the surface, her mind churned, preparing for whatever truth Auntar was about to reveal.

"Rog has assigned me to you."

Darmonla closed her eyes. She felt the pressure rise within her once again. She breathed rapidly and grinded her teeth together. When she opened her eyes again, Auntar had taken up a defensive stance again. She rolled her eyes. "What? Why?" The questions burst out of her, though her voice carried only the edge of the frustration she felt. Are you supposed to keep an eye on me? So, I won't slip away with the Shawktee to fight? I ought to you know. Fighting is what we do, Auntar. He won't even let me be one of his guards, under your command." *Am I not enough for him?* "Am I not as skilled and worthy as one of your guards?"

"Yes, you are, Darmonla. But no, he has something else in mind. He has ordered me to head your security and to work with you and Daman to improve your skills. He told me to use whatever resources and bring in whomever I need. He said I was to make sure you and Daman were prepared for combat, for defense, and for stealth. I have the authority to bring in Bleen himself if I see fit. I am taking charge of your security and your training now."

Darmonla stopped walking, placing a hand on her hip as she narrowed her eyes at him. "Rog sent his personal guard to tend to my security and to improve my skills?" she repeated, her voice low but sharp. *What is he really thinking?* She searched Auntar's face, but his expression was unreadable. "What's really going on here?"

"I'm not sure what he is thinking? But you know Rog's mind is always thinking ahead. I trust his orders and leadership."

His tone carried a pointed edge, almost a challenge. She could feel it. It was a statement, but also a question to her. *What about me? Do I trust his orders and leadership?* Darmonla lowered her head and sighed. "As do I, Auntar. As do I. It's just sometimes difficult to separate the leader Rog from my husband Rog."

"I do know Lord Standist is planning a massive attack on us. Druce is having his captains evacuate the population back to the north."

"As a last defense?" she asked, her voice now softer.

"Yes, Darmonla, as a last defense." Auntar then looked intently at her. "But we've been here before, haven't we? Rog has always gotten us out of it."

Darmonla nodded but didn't reply immediately. It was true, but it didn't make the weight of it any easier to bear. "It does seem we are always one step from destruction, doesn't it? We are always on edge."

"Yes, we are," Auntar agreed. "But my order to work with you goes beyond this immediate threat. We will not be defeated, Darmonla. He is consumed by thoughts beyond this. I can see it in his eyes. Part of his focus goes beyond the Awutanee, and even beyond the Wyunaktee and Rauthlin City." Auntar's gaze narrowed as though piercing through the layers of strategy and foresight. "He has been consumed lately about the Hooni'i."

"The Hooni'i?" Darmonla repeated, startled. *What do they have to do with this?* She felt her stomach tighten, unease creeping in. "While Standist's Awutanee are..." She cut herself off, exhaling slowly. "All right, Auntar. I'll submit to his will. I will submit to your continued training. But it would be a mistake to take my skills lightly."

"We have a long history, Darmonla. I will not go lightly on you."

Darmonla looked back over to Daman's sparring. "Daman is ready enough. He can handle more. When do we start?"

"Soon, Darmonla. But now, we'll have to assist Commander Druce. The evacuations are already underway."

Darmonla nodded, her mind already shifting toward action. *One step from the brink, perhaps. But we've survived before. And we will again.* "Very well, Auntar. I'll get Daman."

THE AWUTANEE LORD STANDIST'S ARMY GATHERS BEFORE ROG

Much of the Shawktee population had already been evacuated towards the upper hills and caves. Guarding them were battalions led by two of Druce's captains. Darmonla was sent to support these captains. They would be the last defense.

Even though Shawktee land was easily defensible from high ground, Standist's army did not try to hide their planned frontal attack. Past efforts had failed. With the number of defeats mounting for Standist, Rog guessed that there was possible decent in the enemy ranks. Rog sensed Lord Standist was losing control and needed a victory, and he needed it quickly.

Rog looked over the open plain where the Awutanee army had gathered. General Nook stood by his side. At Rog's feet lay another dead animal slaughtered to calm his nerves. He and Nook purposely stood out to be seen high up on the hill. It was a sign of strength and courage to his Shawktee.

The Awutanee army outnumbered them by about seven to one. *That means each of us will have to kill seven apiece,* thought Rog. To him, it looked like Standist's intention was simply an overpowering frontal assault with total disregard to the lives of his own warriors.

Standist is irrational and desperate. What a waste of an army.

Rog envisioned his sharpshooting archers easily taking out the front wave of the attack. Many of Awutanee warriors would be killed at the outset but eventually the sheer numbers would overpower Rog's front line. Rog's warriors would have to fall back to the second line and eventually be engaged in hand-to-hand combat. That's when Shawktee fatalities would mount.

There must be another way. If it comes to that, I will make them fight inch by inch. Hopefully, we can kill enough of them to even the odds and gain some advantage. Even from a distance, Rog sensed the anxiety of Standist's horsemen on the front line. It would be they who would embark on the initial suicide charge. The horsemen postures, meant to convey strength and readiness, wavered in subtle ways; warriors heads tipped slightly to allow nervous glances toward their commanders, fingers twitching on spear shafts, heads bowed occasionally in hurried prayers.

Further back in the camp, Rog saw movement that hinted at the chaos bubbling beneath the surface. A group of messengers darted between the central command tent and the reserve ranks, their hurried steps raising small clouds of dust. The commanders themselves stood clustered together, gesturing sharply. Even at this distance, Rog could tell there was no consensus among them.

There must be another way. He had to find a solution.

Rog's archers were in place and ready to rain down terror from every angle. *What a waste. It's the Wyunaktee, Lord Styness and Rauthlin City, who will be the benefactor of many Rauthlin corpses today.* However, a thought came to his mind, and he smiled to himself as his thoughts gained some traction.

Rog watched as two of Standist's generals approached. They rode black dualicorns and came under the flags of truce. This was customary when an army faced superior odds on the battlefield.

Rog turned to Nook. "How benevolent it is of them to give us an opportunity to surrender."

General Nook smirked. "Yes, after they are satisfied with cutting our throats."

Rog cursed the name of Standist and spat. "Take out a party to meet them. Let's hear what they have to say."

Nook bowed and then gave an order to one of the captains for an escort. Rog stood in place, a pillar of defiance, watching as Nook and his party met the two generals and began talking to them. One of the generals said something to Nook. It appeared to Rog that Nook was poorly restraining his agitation.

Nook left the group there and rode back up to Lord Rog. When he reached Rog, his eyes narrowed. He scowled as he bowed in salute. "They want to present the terms of your surrender in person."

Rog chuckled. "My dear General, did they get under your skin?"

"I don't trust them."

"You're not supposed to. You are the High General."

"The disrespect... the arrogance..."

Rog smiled. "This may be a good thing. I have an idea. Call them in. But for your comfort, order three Shawktee to join us in the tent should they decide to be dishonorable and break the flags of truce."

"Standist is desperate and capable of anything."

"He is also a stupid hothead. We can gain advantage because of his predictable foolishness."

Nook bowed and rode back out to meet the party once again.

Rog retired to his tent. He sat in his chair, which had been moved back inside. *If there was a time that I should pray, now would be that time.* He sat back in the chair and sighed. *But there is nobody to pray to but Elyon, and he has cursed us with the barrier.*

Rog, and, for the most part, the Shawktee clan, were not believers of the Rauthlin worship of the son of the morning, which was embedded in Rauthlin culture. Most Rauthlin outside of Rog's domain revered that name and the dark priests who profited by it. Dark priests might be shunned by Rog, but they were in large number in Rauthlin City under Lord Styness and very much so under Standist's domain. Rog figured if the savior of the Rauthlin was going to show, he would have done so already.

However, Rog recognized the utility of having unity around an idea, even a religious one. But Rog wanted to be the focal point of that idea. He was not going to share it with any dark priests, nor with Lord Standist. *Rog will deliver Rog.*

Three Shawktee guards entered the tent. Two took the place next to where Rog sat, one to the left and the other to the right. The third took a position within striking distance where the visitors would soon be standing.

Another Shawktee guard, who was posted outside the tent, showed himself through the opening. "My Lord, Standist's generals have arrived."

Rog nodded. "Show them in."

The Shawktee guard entered followed by the two generals and General Nook. Rog focused on them coldly.

Rog knew what any Rauthlin military leader would know, that the pending bloodbath would weaken the victor and make them easy prey to Lord Styness' ambition. Rog also had considered these generals were at wits' end with losing battles to him. He even sensed the possibility the generals might be questioning Standist's leadership. *Maybe I can flush out those doubts.*

They gave a slight nod to Rog and Rog nodded back, signaling them to speak. The first general unrolled a document and began to read aloud. "Under the Rauthlin flag of truce, Lord Standist offers the following terms to you and for your army's surrender: First, the immediate oath and allegiance of every Rauthlin under your command and authority, including all females, and young ones, under the penalty of death. Second, forfeit all lands under your control to Lord Standist. Third, Lord Standist will absolve all generals and captains under your command if they will give an oath, under the penalty of death, to obey and fight, along with their legions under the banner of Lord Standist. Fourth, Lord Standist, and all under his command promises to not harm, rape, steal or pillage Rauthlin under Rog's authority. Fifth and finally, Lord Standist will only require the dignified death of Rog, any wives, and offspring." The general rolled back up the document and tucked it into his vest.

Rog did not flinch or give any expression whatsoever during the reading of these demands. However, Nook gripped the hilt of his sword with white-knuckled intensity. Nook's chest heaved faster than before. Rog slightly tilted his head at the visitors. "Is that it?" He then looked at Nook. "Standist has become weak in his old age."

At Rog's remark, Nook's iron grip on his weapon loosened, and his shoulders dropped just a fraction. A faint smirk curled at the edge of Nook's lips before he quickly suppressed it."

Rog perceived the general to the far left stiffened almost imperceptibly, his jaw clenching. *Good,* Rog thought. But the messenger who had read the terms maintained his composure, his face as blank as parchment. Rog rose from his chair and approached the two generals. He locked gazes with each in turn. "Do you two have names?"

The first general, who had read the terms, hesitated at the question before he responded, "I am General Nash."

"General Braun," the other said. "We did not come here to be cordial and exchange pleasantries."

"It's clear you didn't." Rog stared at them. "General Nash. General Braun." Rog turned back to Nook and nodded in an approving fashion. "Fine Awutanee specimens wouldn't you say, General Nook?"

"If you say so, my lord."

Nook's response made Rog want to laugh. But he resisted the temptation. "It's a shame to waste such Rauthlin leadership on Standist's ineptitude. We Shawktee are superior, but only because of Standist's poor leadership."

General Braun eyed Rog with disdain but it was General Nash who answered. "I take it you're rejecting Lord Standist's proposal. What message should I give him in return?"

Rog held up his hand. "Hold on, General Nash. Hear my counterproposal and return this message instead to Lord Standist." He walked around them as he continued, "If we engage in this battle one thing is certain. Both armies will lose at least half or more of their forces. The victor will immediately be vulnerable before Lord Styness, who no doubt is lying in wait to attack whoever comes out on top. He will conquer and rule all harshly."

Rog glanced at the generals. They stood still, avoiding eye contact. "As I have said, I believe the Shawktee of Rog are superior to the Awutanee. I'm willing to prove it. Select five of the finest warriors of Standist for a fight to the death against four of my Shawktee and myself. Under the oath of the flags of truce, if one of the Shawktee is the last Rauthlin standing, I give oath all Standist's army will be fully absolved if they swear allegiance to us. However, if one of Standist is the last one standing, we agree to the terms of Standist as proposed." Rog smiled broadly. "You can send your best to kill me if you can."

The two generals looked at each other, apparently perplexed. At this hesitation, Rog put his hand on his chest in mocking gesture. "Surely you two aren't also convinced, as I, that we are your superior." He stepped closer to General Braun, watching his expression. "Or does the thought of killing me not appeal to you? Think of the honor to the one who can." Rog then looked back to General Nash. "Maybe it will appeal to your leader."

Both generals straightened up. "We will report your proposal to Lord Standist," Nash said. He bowed his head slightly, signaling their leave. Braun begrudgingly made the same gesture and the two soon left the tent.

Nook chuckled. Rog smiled at the outburst. "What are your thoughts, General?"

"My lord, you continue to amaze me," Nook said. "You have done what you have always done. You have given us the opportunity to even the odds. But I don't think they'll go for it. I think they see your wisdom regarding Styness and the Wyunaktee. A wasteful frontal attack probably does not appeal to their generals and commanders. I'm sure the generals want to preserve their Rauthlin. But I also don't think Standist will be happy about giving away what he believes is his advantage."

Rog raised his index finger. "But will his arrogance allow him to resist?" Rog turned a cold stare to the entrance of his tent. "We'll see. Meanwhile, continue to prepare for our defense as planned."

Nook started to dismiss himself, but Rog stopped him. "General, send swift messengers for Auntar and Druce to come up immediately, just in case our adversaries accept the challenge. Darmonla can continue to assist with the evacuation and securing the population in their stead. Let's hope it doesn't come to that."

Nook left Rog's presence to carry out his orders. Rog couldn't help wondering if Lord Standist would bite.

Hours passed. There was no response nor even a whimper from the Standist camp.

"They could be considering your proposal," Nook surmised.

Rog wasn't so sure. He crushed another rodent to help him stay calm. Meanwhile, Nook looked out at the entrance of the tent, then back to Rog. "Druce has arrived."

Rog nodded in return, as Nook stepped out to meet him. Rog then walked over to the corner of the tent and washed his hands in a basin. After he dried his hands on a towel, he walked outside to where Nook and Druce were talking.

When Druce saw Rog approach, he placed his fist over his chest and bowed. "My lord."

"Commander," Rog acknowledged.

Just then, Auntar rode up to them on his horse. He pulled the horse to a stop and dismounted. He approached in salute. "You have need of me, my lord? I am ready to do your bidding."

"How goes Darmonla and Daman these past days?" Rog asked.

"Their training goes well but was cut short with the evacuation preparations."

Rog held his hand out toward the gathering armies. "As you can see, Lord Standist has moved faster than we had originally expected."

Auntar nodded. He walked with Rog, Druce and Nook to look over the sloped enemy army below. "I understand the severity of the challenge you issued. Have they responded it?"

"Not yet. They must be arguing about it," Nook said.

"Or buying time to reevaluate their planned attack," Druce noted.

"They should reevaluate their planned attack," General Nook replied. "Either way, they still have the numbers to do us much damage."

"Maybe they need a little help with their decision," Rog said. He turned to Nook. "Take two of these Shawktee and come with me."

Nook signaled for the two Shawktee, Olog and Frogon, and they followed.

Druce and Auntar instinctively started to walk with him, but Rog held up a hand, indicating they stay put. Nook ordered two skilled Shawktee to go with them and the four of them proceeded to ride out toward Standist's army.

They came to a stop within one hundred feet of the army's front. Rog knew they were still considered to be under the flags of truce until after the final response was given. Rog commanded Nook and the Shawktee line up on their horses in a row. Rog rode out further in front to face Standist's army. He positioned himself in direct view of the command tent that bore the Awutanee flags, where he suspected Lord Standist was. He spoke out loudly.

"I am Rog, from the clan of the Shawktee. Lord of the Northern high plains." Rog paused to let his words soak in. He was addressing an enemy army, an act that was beyond any conceived battle etiquette. "I stand under the flags of truce without a response to our challenge. What's the matter, Standist? Has fear crept into the hearts of these great Rauthlin under your command? Are there not five brave Awutanee willing to accept the challenge and fight on your behalf? Then let me repeat the challenge for all to hear!"

No one moved on either side. Rog sat up high in his saddle and continued. "Select five of the finest warriors of Standist for a fight to the death against four of my Shawktee and myself. Under the oath of the flags of truce, if one of the Shawktee is the last Rauthlin standing, I give oath all Standist's army will be fully absolved if they swear allegiance to us. However, if one of Standist is the last one standing, we will submit to you."

Again, silence was the only response. Rog's horse shuffled beneath, and he pulled in the reins to keep himself facing forward. "Your generals know Lord Styness awaits a weakened surviving army of this battle," Rog said. "But if we abide by this challenge, Styness will find a united army marching on Rauthlin City! The only question is who will lead you there, Standist or Rog!"

Rog observed the attentiveness to his words and even a few nods. *Those in Standist's army who didn't know the details of the challenge before, know it now.* Rog thought Standist had made a great tactical error in allowing Rog to address his army.

Rog was attempting to rally the opposing army to himself. If discord existed in the Standist camp, Rog's goal was to cement it even more.

Lord Standist emerged from the command tent, a stark contrast to Rog in every way. Standist was older, his face carved with a strain and posture weighted by recent defeats. Rog, on the other hand, stood tall in his saddle, both strong and unshaken. His strength and charisma radiating like a fire that refused to dim. He was the leader who always found a way to outmaneuver, outthink, and ultimately defeat them on the battlefield. And now, here he was again offering not just conquest but a legitimate chance to lay siege to Rauthlin City, the jewel of Lord Styness' kingdom.

From the side of his camp, Standist stepped forward, his cloak whipping in the breeze as he pointed an accusing finger at Rog. "We accept your challenge!" his voice bellowing over the field. "The fight will be in one hour! That will be the appointed time of your death, Rog!"

Rog's eyes narrowed. A calm, predatory smile curled at the corner of his mouth. "So, we fight under the flags of truce?" he shouted back.

"Yes!" Standist snapped. "Under the flags of truce!"

Rog raised his sword high, its steel gleaming against the blue sky. "Then prepare your Awutanee," he declared. "The Shawktee will be ready."

Silence settled for a moment, as Rog held his sword aloft. The wind carried his words far beyond the gathering.

Standist scowled, as though trying to find a reply that wouldn't come. However, he returned an angry nod.

Rog then turned away with an air of confidence to prepare.

The armies closed in to surround the semi-level area where the fight was to take place. Standist sat with his generals. Standist was older and not the most skilled of the Awutanee. He chose his five participants.

Among the five selected from Standist were Generals Nash and Braun. General Nash and one other participant from Standist had shields.

Rog's participants would fight with two swords, no shields, as was the way of most Shawktee. To Nook's dismay, Rog selected Olog and

Frogon, along with Auntar, Druce and, of course, Rog himself. Nook approached Rog with a frown, his voice low but hard. "You didn't name me among the five. Why?"

Rog turned to him, calm as ever. "Because you have a greater purpose."

Nook scoffed. "A greater purpose than fighting at your side?"

"If we win, and I fall, someone will have to lead," Rog said firmly. "Someone strong enough to unite the Rauthlin and take them against Rauthlin City. That someone is you, Nook."

Nook's jaw tightened. "You'll survive this, my lord. You always survive."

Rog smiled faintly, a glimmer of respect in his eyes. "We must always plan ahead, Nook. If I go down, you must advance the Shawktee interest."

Nook looked away, his hands curling into fists. "I feel helpless."

"I need you ready to lead, not dead beside me," Rog said, his tone final. "Trust me, Nook. I'm counting on you above all others."

Nook nodded reluctantly.

The five Awutanee warriors strode forward with deliberate steps. Their eyes were locked onto their adversaries with expressions of grim resolve and quiet fury.

The five Shawktee, in stark contrast, moved forward like confident shadows. They were silent, and expressionless. Their faces were unreadable, as though carved from stone. They stood in a slight semi-circle, with Rog in front, with two Shawktee to Rog's right and Auntar and Druce to his left. Their swords glinted in their steady hands. Each of the Shawktee appeared calm, unshaken and unfeeling in the face of impending death.

All but Druce, who paced like a restless predator, his boots scuffing against the dirt as he prowled back and forth. His shoulders twitched with anticipation and his teeth clenched with excitement. His eyes burned like a maniac, a reflection of his apparent bloodlust.

The Awutanee warriors took note of him, their brows furrowing slightly as they tightened their grips on their swords.

I will have to chastise him about maintaining Shawktee etiquette in the face of our enemies, Rog thought.

Rog unsheathed his swords and stood ready. The other did so as well. Then they waited.

Druce narrowed his eyes and smiled.

The flags were dropped.

Rog raised his sword and charged. The clash began in a flurry of motion as the Shawktee strategy unfolded with calculated precision. On both ends of the line, the Shawktee warriors spun back sharply, slipping into the inside positions of their comrades. The shift was seamless leaving two Awutanee warriors on the outside suddenly exposed to being teamed up against by two Shawktee.

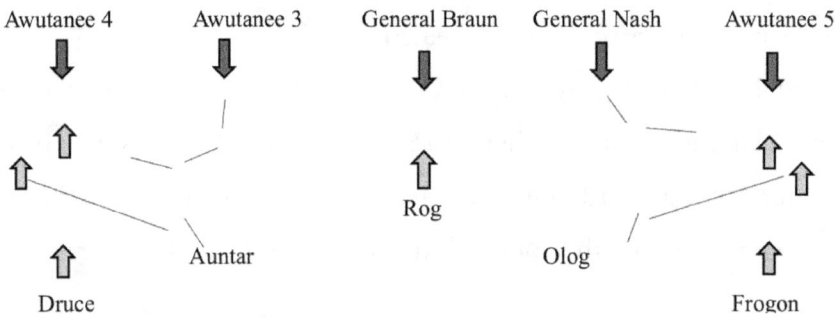

Auntar moved like a shadow, slipping behind Druce with silent grace. The Awutanee warrior charging along the outside had no time to react before Auntar struck. With a single fluid motion, he drove his blade deep, then pulled out his weapon and rolled off to meet the other Awutanee coming his way.

Druce followed through at the injured warrior, swinging his blade downward, ending his life. The body crumpled to the dirt, blood soaking into the earth.

In the same breath, Druce turned with blistering speed, his blade singing through the air, to assist Auntar with the remaining warrior on their side. The entire maneuver happened so quickly; it was over before the remaining Awutanee understood what had transpired. Confusion flickered in his eyes, Auntar was already in front of him again, back in his original position as if he had never left, driving forward with relentless fury.

The Awutanee now faced the impossible two Shawktee, blades flashing from different angles, each strike faster and harder than the last.

He fought to hold them back, under the relentless two-on-one assault. The Shawktee moved with a deadly rhythm. Druce's brutality balanced perfectly by Auntar's precision. The outcome was inevitable; the Awutanee warrior's fate was sealed.

On the other side, Frogon and Olog swung their swords high and low at the Awutanee warrior. When he reached to block Frogon's trust below his waist, Olog's sword punctured the Awutanee warrior's shoulder.

Frogon then met the approaching Nash and swung his sword.

Nash blocked the surprise blow with his shield and swung his sword at Frogon's head.

Frogon ducked as his sword clanged against Nash's. They continued to exchange blows.

But these dual maneuvers left Rog isolated in the middle with General Braun.

Rog swiped at Braun with both swords, driving him back.

Braun was able to dodge those blows and return his own strikes, though he couldn't stop his involuntary retreat.

-Meanwhile, General Nash kept Frogon in front of him engaged and appeared to be forcing him nearer to Braun, which Rog knew would only complicate their duel. Nash used his shield to angle Frogon's attack away from himself until his own sword came from behind the shield and struck a fatal blow through the Frogon's abdomen.

Nash hurried to Braun's side and joined him attacking Rog.

Braun, however, was giving Rog a significant challenge, pressing home his attacks with an aggressive flurry of strikes that Rog found more and more difficult to block with his swords.

A wide swing came only inches from Rog's face and would have surely cut his nose clean off had Rog not arched backward at the last second.

Rog let his fall carry him to the ground, then spun his leg in a wide circle and took Braun's legs out from under him. Rog then flipped to his feet.

Nash's thrust jabbed deep into the spot of dirt Rog had vacated a split second before.

-Both the Olog and the Awutanee to the left of Rog had injured each other. Olog had a puncture wound and was bleeding to his side. But the Awutanee warrior was injured more. His wounds were fatal as he fell to the ground clutching his side and writhing in pain. Olog then staggard toward Nash. Nash spun off the fight with Rog to intercept him.

Meanwhile Auntar suffered a gash to his right thigh and bled down his leg, but he didn't appear fazed by the wound and fought ferociously against the remaining Rauthlin to their side, with he and Druce forcing their opponents back.

Auntar pounced aggressively and swung low with his swords. but the Rauthlin blocked his slash. That gave Druce the opportunity to stab him in the neck. Blood splattered over Druce's face. He withdrew the sword and wiped blood away from his face with the back of his sword hand, smirking.

Druce and Auntar had handled the two Rauthlin on their side.

-Auntar turned to see the others fighting. He ran to help Rog. "Help Olog!" he shouted back to Druce.

Druce nodded and ran over to where General Nash and Olog circled each other. But before Druce got there, Nash rammed Olog to his face with his shield. Olog fell to the ground dazed.

Nash swung around with his shield just in time to meet Druce's blade, as if he knew the secondary attack was coming.

Auntar, on the other hand, was able to catch Braun unawares. Braun suddenly turned to meet him. With this distraction, Rog drove his sword deep into Braun's side.

Braun hunched over and cried out, blood gushing through his vest.

Rog withdrew his sword and kicked him to the ground.

As Braun fell, his sword flung away. He groveled and convulsed.

Rog and Auntar turned to look over at Druce and Nash engaged in combat. Out further, Olog lay on the ground struggling to get up. "Come on," Rog nodded to Auntar as they both ran over to assist Druce.

Nash was the only one from Standist's Rauthlin left. Nash pushed Druce backward and away from him with his shield.

Before Druce could strike back, he glimpsed movement to the side of him. Help was on the way. A faint, knowing smile tugged at the corner of his mouth.

As Rog and Auntar ran over to assist Druce, suddenly…

WOOSH…

Rog dodged a flying arrow which contacted his sword as he fell back out of the way.

"Argh!" came a shout from the crowd. It was Lord Standist. He had thrown down his bow, unsheathed a medium sized curved sword and charged at Rog. Rog rushed to his feet. "Stand back," he said holding his hand up to the others not to intervene.

Standist swung at Rog.

Rog stepped to the right and deflected the attempted blow, then thrusted his other sword into Lord Standist's side.

Lord Standist grabbed his side and cried out, as he rolled into the earth's dust.

General Nash and Druce broke apart, panting, and turned their attention to the sudden attack in disbelief. Both armies stood in silence. Olog scooted to his feet as well. Auntar walked up to and stood over

Lord Standist. "You shall die with dishonor," he said, his voice cold and final. He then gripped his sword with both hands and drove it downward into his chest. He held it there, unflinching, until life drained from the Awutanee leader's eyes. When the body fell still, Auntar pulled the blade free, blood trailing down its length. He turned and gave a curt nod to Rog.

Rog looked over to the others who were no longer engaging. Rog was shocked by Standist's actions. *Standist showed himself so dishonorably as to violate the flags of truce. This is a despicable act even for a worthless Awutanee like Standist.*

Where there should have been cheers from the Shawktee, there was silent grumbling because of the blatant dishonor of the Awutanee leader. Many Awutanee warriors put their heads down and shook their heads in shame. Nash was visibly angry. He threw down his sword and shield. He walked toward Rog and spoke in a loud voice. "Lord Rog, you have won. Standist had no honor. As High General, I pronounce all he has is now yours. I freely offer my life in exchange for his dishonor." He then kneeled before Rog, seemingly awaiting his fate.

Rog stepped closer, his boots grinding against the dirt, the sound heavy in the still air. He loomed over Nash saying nothing at first. Instead, his gaze drifted past him at the deflated Awutanee army that was once his rival. Rog's attention then returned to Nash, his expression momentarily unreadable. "Yes, General Nash," Rog said finally, his voice rising with authority for all to hear. "Your life is what I require—as one of my new generals."

Nash's head jerked up, surprise flickering in his eyes.

"Arise, General Nash," Rog commanded, his tone unyielding but with respect. "You have fought with honor. Gather your remaining generals and report to General Nook in my tent."

Rog spread his arms wide, his voice booming as it carried over the field to both armies. "It's time to prepare for battle!" he declared, a smile cutting across his face. "We have an appointment with Lord Styness and Rauthlin City. It's time for Rauthlin to be one!"

Cheers rippled through the soldiers on both sides, rising to roars of excitement.

The Awutanee army came forward, kneeled before Rog and submitted to Shawktee authority without any more bloodshed.

Rog knew word would quickly spread throughout the Rauthlin tribes. Lord Styness was all that stood in the way of complete unity.

No more retreating. No more regrouping. The Wyunaktee shall submit to me like the Awutanee. Rog knew it was the destiny of the Shawktee to lay siege to Rauthlin City.

He lifted his sword in front of his new army to thunderous cheers. *I will claim that unity by force or die in the effort.*

THE HOONI'I RETURN TO THE FORBIDDEN FOREST

Giron's troops camped out for the evening in front of Cleet's residence. There were forty of them, handpicked and trained under Giron's command. They wore light armor consisting of a breast plate and back plate fastened together and reinforced with stitched leather panels, offering both protection and mobility. At their sides hung short swords. A few carried long spears and bows.

They were focused and confident, understanding the breath of their mission. Throughout the night, they had illuminated the surrounding areas with bright long-burning torches that set up a barrier to possible night creatures wanting to wander into their camp. Though the air carried whispers of unease about the mysterious barrier, Giron's soldiers exuded calm and discipline. Bumpus had them tow a small boat on a land sled. The boat had been altered with covered plates of brass, arranged to his specifications. These plates covered the sides and doomed over it, shutting in those safely inside its shell. He was sure the boat could take the extra weight and had calculated the force of impact that the larger

Zauphrii arrows would have once it was hit, and rocking occurred. There were small openings and a space for the viewing cylinder between the plates.

The boat was loaded with its samples. Long ropes were linked on both sides of the boat to provide a safe escape if troops found it necessary to pull them back to safety. The troops were prepared to allow the boat to take hits, unless and until a rescue was needed.

What Bumpus needed to be done would only take five to ten minutes, depending on if his adaptations were as accurate as he thought.

When morning came, preparations moved quickly. Giron's troops gathered with practiced efficiency, but Bumpus' focus was drawn to the dozens of armed Hooni'i who had joined the group, clearly ready for a fight.

Bumpus shot a glance at Giron and shook his head. "Well, that was to be unexpected."

Giron folded his arms across his chest. "I' though we were clear that we would handle it."

The two watched as Clay and Jaune moved among the Hooni'i, wooden spears in hand and faces determined. From the porch, Sama stood with her hands on her hips shaking her head at them.

"*The folly the youth,*" Bumpus muttered. "I need this to go peacefully. If we march to the lake like we're storming a fortress, the Zauphrii will feel threatened and respond with violence. We need them to be docile for as long as we can."

"I'll handle this," Giron replied, his voice steady with that same confidence that seemed to anchor his entire troop. He turned toward the crowd, his deep bark carrying over the chatter. "Hooni'i! You've made your loyalty clear. No one questions it," Giron paced back and forth like he owned the ground beneath him. "But this isn't your fight, right now. Maybe that time will come. But today, we just observe. We do not need them to react to any appearance of aggression. You must stay back," he waved his finger in the direction of Clay and the crowd behind him. "Even our troops will hold back away from view and allow Bumpus to do what he needs to do."

The murmurs quieted, but Bumpus wasn't convinced. He stepped forward to add his own voice. "You'll do more good staying out of the way. This is important and we need to succeed." He held the palm of his hands out. "This is just a quiet look around, but we have taken precautions, as you can see. We appreciate your cooperation."

"Quiet doesn't seem to interest them," Giron muttered out of the side of his mouth, low enough for only Bumpus to hear.

Clay stepped forward with Jaune sulking behind him. "If you say so, Bumpus. We trust you. But all you have to do is send for us and we will be there. We are all willing to fight!"

Bumpus sighed and put his hand on Clay's shoulder. "I know you are. But this is not the time."

"I'll talk to them some more," Giron said putting his arms over Clay and Juane and walking them away.

Bumpus nodded and turned to check his supplies. When he did he saw Tassel approaching him, his forearm still tightly wrapped with setting sticks and a slight limp slowing his steps.

"You sure about this?" Bumpus asked, glancing at Tassel's arm.

Tassel grinned faintly. "I can sit in a boat, can't I? Besides, you need me," he nodded his head. "And I kind of owe you," he shrugged. "You and Giron can't watch everything alone."

Bumpus hesitated but finally nodded. "Fine. But you are sitting. No heroics."

Giron returned to them, looking satisfied. "They'll stay back, though they aren't happy about it. It seems the others have accepted to stay back as well."

"Good enough for me," Bumpus said as he and Tassel boarded their horses. He looked toward the road leading through the forest trees. "Here's hoping this is just a peaceful observation."

"Yes, Bumpus. Let's hope for peace," Giron said as he boarded his horse. He then slightly kicked the sides of Imperial and waved for his troops to head out behind him. Troops pulled forward the boat on a land sled with their horses as they all headed up the road to the lake of the Zauphrii. When they arrived, they took their positions away from the shore at what they believed to be of the edge of range for the Zauphrii archers, based on Bumpus's observations. Troops laid down the ropes.

It was then that Giron spotted Zauphrii warriors scrambling on the other side of the lake. He nudged Bumpus and nodded to Tassel. "Let's go." The three of them climbed in the boat and sat on the benches. The hollow sound of the plates echoed as the door was shut behind them. Bumpus secured it from the inside.

A group, under the cover of elongated shields, dragged the boat out to the lake. From inside, Bumpus felt the sudden change when the boat stopped scraping along the rocky shore and floated free into the lake.

Bumpus heard a distant horn from across the lake. This was followed by the rustling from their retreating troops who had dragged the boat out.

"That doesn't sound good," Giron said.

"We are ready for it," Bumpus said, tapping the inside wall of their protective enclosure.

"The worst-case scenario is happening already.

"No, it can get much worse," Bumpus responded.

"Are you sure these plates will hold?" Tassel asked.

"They better, or this will be a quick experiment," Bumpus answered. He examined the cylinder and slipped it into place through the designated opening.

Tassel sat silently for a moment and watched Giron row the oars which stuck out through the brass plates that sealed them inside. "We are going to have to sit here and just take it then?"

"Yep," Giron responded.

"We are in for a time, plus a hundred, I would say," Bumpus said.

"That's reassuring," Tassel replied sarcastically.

"No really, Tassel, plus at least a hundred, you want to take a look?"

Tassel received the cylinder from Bumpus and looked through it. His jaw dropped open.

"What is it?" Giron asked.

"They have more troops over there than we brought," Tassel said. "Maybe, double or more."

Giron shook his head. "How much further to the middle?"

Bumpus changed positions with Tassel and looked through the cylinder again. "We already passed the middle. Just keep rowing."

"You don't want to get too close," Giron said. "The closer you get the stronger the force from their arrows."

Bumpus ignored Giron and replaced the lens on the cylinder. He looked out again. "Yes, this looks good. A little farther… A little farther… prepare for impact!"

They all braced themselves. The impact of several large arrows bounced off the shielded plates. The boat rocked. A few of the arrows had enough force to lodge into the outer shell. Giron and Tassel jerked back at the impact as some of the large arrowhead tips penetrated inside.

"Keep rowing?" Giron asked.

"You can stop rowing. Just try to keep it steady as you can." Bumpus focused through the cylinder. "No, this lens is not quite right. Hand me the next one Tassel."

The boat rocked again from another barrage. Giron gripped the oars and held his position. He looked back at Bumpus and shook his head. Bumpus thought he muttered "Keep it as steady as I can, he says" under his breath.

Per Zerrah's orders, the Zauphrii had increased their patrol near the lake under Koo'rah's command. Koo'rah had secluded herself away from others to meditate. However, as she sat there against the trunk of a tree, all she could think about was the Hooni'i that dared to challenge them from over the lake. *Those Hooni'i are dangerous. Families can no longer enjoy the freedom of the lake because of them.*

Although the Hooni'i spewing vulgarity on the boat offshore was disturbing. It was the other two that apparently handled instruments and watched them from afar, that haunted her thoughts. *What were they up to? They must be planning something against us.* She reached for her satchel and retrieved a jagged stone the size of the palm of her hand. She then unsheathed her dagger and began sharpening it against the stone. *Zerrah will lead us over the barrier soon and we will rid ourselves of them.*

As she scraped her blade on the stone, a scout hurriedly rode his horse up to her.

What's happening now? She put the stone back in her satchel and stood.

He pulled in the reins and the horse stopped next to her. "Commander, the Hooni'i returned with troops and launched a covered boat on the lake. Our warriors are engaging them with arrow shots from the shore.

What is this? Koo'rah fumed. She narrowed her eyes and sheathed back her dagger. "Continue on to warn Zerrah! He is at Boulder Hill."

The scout nodded. He kicked the sides of the horse and continued to ride into the forest.

Koo'rah gathered her things and mounted her unicorn. She then forced her heels into its sides and raced toward the lake's shore, pondering how long they would have to wait until they could cross over and handle such insolence and disrespect from the Hooni'i.

When she arrived, she saw the archers had slowed their shooting. The boat was no longer moving toward them as reported. The Hooni'i troops on the opposite shore were back beyond the Zauphrii range.

She spotted Zorion, who appeared to be in some discomfort due to his broken jaw. He wore a tan leather brace on his chin that was strapped around his head. It changed the way he spoke. He talked through his teeth and it prevented him from raising his voice. He saluted her.

"Status," Koo'rah asked.

Zorion pointed back over to the other side of the lake. "Those troops are armed and positioned over there, as you see. They launched the covered boat, but it seems to be armored. Our arrows have for the most part bounced off it. Some have penetrated and are embedded to its sides. Once we fired on the boat it stopped. Somebody inside is working the oars sticking out to the sides. We're just shooting a few arrows at them every minute or so, now. We are also keeping an eye on those troops behind them."

"Save your arrows."

Zorion waved off the archers.

Koo'rah peered out over the lake and narrowed her eyes. *Are they planning to cross over and attack us? What are they doing? They've adapted from the previous encounter we had with them. These worms have created a floating fortress but for what purpose?* "The arrows just bounce off?" she asked again.

"Yes, Commander, for the most part."

"How long will it take to prepare fire arrows with sharper tips?"

"Several minutes at most to heat the fire. Adjusting the tips will take longer but we can do it."

"Never mind." Koo'rah walked out to the edge of the shoreline. The barrier discolored the air before her. She folded her arms. *Hooni'i degenerates.*

Zorion walked up and stood by her side waiting for her command. He looked at her and then back out toward the boat.

Koo'rah smirked. She saw movement in a space on the covered boat where a cylinder was protruding. She recognized the cylinder from their last encounter.

"Summon Zon and Taul over here," Koo'rah ordered. "Now."

The boat steadied. Giron locked the oars in place and waited. The bombardment had lessened and eventually stopped altogether.

"Better… Good…" Bumpus said. "Just one more. Tassel, hand me the last one again."

"What are they doing over there now?" Giron asked.

"They are just looking at us looking at them. And guess what?" Bumpus grinned. "We have a match. I can see it! Faintly, yes, but I can see the barrier."

"You can see it?" Tassel asked.

"You, did it?" Giron's eyes were wide.

"Let me see," Tassel asked. He looked through the lens. "I can see a clear line of discoloration straight across on both sides as far as I can see. Whoa, Bumpus, did you see that female Zauphrii on the shore with her arms folded?"

"The barrier, Tassel, the barrier," Giron said.

"Yes, but she is way more impressive. She doesn't look happy. I think you really ticked her off, Bumpus."

"You mean *we* ticked her off," Bumpus replied while scribbling in his journal.

Giron moved up to the cylinder to look. "Let me see." Tassel moved to the side so he could peer into it.

"You did it, Bumpus! You did it." Giron stared at Bumpus. "You really did it." He then went to reach for the cylinder again. "Ohhh!" he yelled out. Giron fell to the side as an arrow hit the protruding cylinder back inside the boat.

"You're lucky you didn't have your eye pressed up against it, aren't you," Bumpus said.

More arrows connected. One of them snapped one of the oars.

"Let's get out of here!" Bumpus shouted. "Pull up the flag for the troops to pull the ropes."

Tassel pulled the flag. The boat jerked and moved back toward the shore with increasing speed as horses on the other end pulled the ropes. They crunched down and held on tight. Bumpus thought he heard a voice yelling from the Zauphrii shore. Arrows thudded into the boat as it pulled away.

"We're moving too fast!" Giron yelled.

"What does that mean?" Tassel asked.

"It means we're going to hit the shore too fast. I don't know if the bottom can withstand the impact!"

"Awe, Bumpus!" Tassel cried.

The boat is not going to hold! Elyon help us! Bumpus stuffed his notebook inside his vest and held on to the bench. "Hold on!" he shouted. The boat slammed onto the shore. The dragging mount cracked. The vessel jumped and came down hard to its side, sending one of the armored plates flying off.

Giron dragged on the ground while he desperately held on to the bench he had previously been sitting on.

Bumpus grabbed Giron's shirt to try to pull him back in.

Hooni'i archers ran up closer, under the protection of shields, and shot back at the Zauphrii to draw fire away from them. Arrows whizzed by and clanked off shields, knocking some of the archers back. Bumpus could hear some of them cry out in pain. As the boat passed them, the warriors withdrew back to safety.

It wasn't until they were finally out of range that Giron let go. The boat slid to a bumpy rest and Giron rolled to a stop.

Bumpus took a deep breath and smiled. They had gotten what they needed even though they had lost the cylinder.

Giron sat up. He was scraped up and dirty. *Lana is not going to be happy if he's injured,* Bumpus thought. "You all right, Giron?"

"Yes, I think so." He wiped the caked-up dirt from his face.

Tassel laughed.

"Do you have what you need?" Giron asked.

Bumpus pulled out his journal and held it up. "Yes."

The captain of the warriors approached Giron and offered a hand to help him up. "Are you all right, sir?"

Giron stood up and brushed some of the dirt off his body. "Yes, I'll live. Anyone injured?"

"One dead and two injured who need attention. We are tending to them now."

Giron sighed. He put his head down. "It's been a long day. Let's get out of here and back to Cleet's place where we can better tend to them better."

The captain nodded.

Bumpus looked back over the lake. The Zauphrii warriors stood looking back at them, but the female warrior had been joined by another strong looking male. This Zauphrii was sitting on a beautiful white unicorn. He had ridden out in front of the others. There was no doubt this other Zauphrii was in charge. He glared at them from afar.

Even at this distance, Bumpus could feel the Zauphrii's seething anger. He sighed. "Yes, Giron. Let's get out of here and go to where it is safer."

Bumpus was pleased they they got what he needed. But it also raised the wrath of the Zauphrii across the lake. He was reminded how fragile life was and how weak he felt in trying to preserve it. And now, his actions have led to another Hooni'i death and the dismemberment of two others. *Elyon, I do not know what I am doing. I am weak and this is beyond me.* It was at that moment, he could see Grandel's face in his mind speaking to him softly, saying, *"In your weakness, Elyon is made strong. Trust him."*

They gathered what they safely could and left for Cleet's residence. Bumpus tried to show himself strong, but he was privately shaken. He struggled for peace within his mind. *Elyon, help me believe and trust in you. Give us strength. And whatever is coming, help us to be ready.*

RAUTHLIN PREPARE FOR BATTLE

Part of the price for the absorption of the Awutanee army was the inheritance of Standist's young widow, Reelema. For Rog, this was a political inconvenience.

Reelema came from well-respected Rauthlin leadership. In fact, her recent marriage to Standist, however short, was politically arranged to bolster Standist's popularity. Rog's acceptance of Reelema would seal the undying loyalty of many of the Awutanee who had been willing to lay down their lives for her. Because that loyalty existed, Rog knew it would be unwise to kill her.

However, he knew all too well, that Darmonla would perceive Reelema as a threat. Once Rauthlin City fell, Darmonla might even inherit a third rival if their queen survived. But all of this was just a clatter in Rog's mind. He would have to deal the problem of Reelema later. His focus was on the pending siege.

Rog stood at the head of the war table, a map of Rauthlin City, and its surrounding regions stretched across its surface. Candles flickered, their light casting long shadows over the faces of the two high generals:

Nook, representing the Shawktee and Nash, the Awutanee. The tension in the air was palpable as Rog broke the silence.

Rog nodded to Nash. "We are appreciative that Awutanee spies produced such a detailed map."

Nash nodded in return.

"We're moving against Rauthlin City," Rog began, his voice steady but commanding. "The eastern sea makes it a fortress, but if we're to cripple the Wyunaktee, we must also take Kantar to the west.

Nook leaned forward, his sharp eyes fixed on the map. "If Kantar falls, their supply lines collapse. But they'll see us coming. Styness isn't a fool."

"True," Rog admitted, tapping a finger on Kantar's location. "That's why Auntar will lead the attack on Kantar through the old territories of Standist and the Awutanee. We'll send a combined force of Shawktee and the Awutanee. That should keep them off balance."

"And my role?" Nash asked, his deep voice steady, though a flicker of curiosity danced in his eyes.

"You'll take the bulk of the Awutanee," Rog said, his finger tracing the path on the map. "Position yourself here, between Kantar and Rauthlin City. Your task is to cut them off entirely. No reinforcements, no supplies. When the time comes, you'll lead the charge against the Rauthlin City's west side."

Nook raised a brow. "And I assume you're giving me the front gates?"

"Exactly," Rog replied, his gaze shifting to the other general. "The Shawktee will lay siege to the gates and move around to the west wall. But you'll have an advantage. He looked up to Nash.

"Lord Standist was preparing for an assault on Rauthlin before we dealt with him," Nash said. "The Awutanee have battering rams, mobile fortresses, and ramps."

Rog turned back to Nook. "Use them."

Nook nodded, a hint of admiration in his tone. "I must acknowledge the resourcefulness of the Awutanee. Standist's preparations were thorough."

"But there's a problem," Rog continued, his expression darkening. "The Wyunaktee will expect this. Styness' generals aren't blind. Nash's charge from the west? Predicted. The siege at the gates? Predictable. We'll need an edge, something they don't see coming."

"What do you propose, then?" Nash asked, leaning in.

Rog's lips pressed into a thin line. "That's what we're here to figure out. I won't throw the Shawktee or Awutanee into a bloodbath without reason. If we're to succeed, we need more than brute force we need cunning."

The three stood in silence, the weight of the war pressing down on their shoulders. The map before them was not just lines and borders, it was a battlefield waiting to come alive with fire and steel. And Rog knew, more than anything, that the next move would determine the fate of them all. Rog's mind turned to thinking of other ways to bend the battle more to his liking. *We must strike at the heart of Lord Styness and his family. Are we not the Shawktee?*

General Nash pointed to a map of the city. "Look here, on the short shoreline is a point of entry. It's a door that leads out to the shoreline from inside. Standist didn't know how to exploit this weakness in the walls. The only way to get to it is either from inside or by sea. The sea is rough beyond a certain point and is not navigable by boat. However, a short distance offshore is not as bad. Small boats could be used but would be spotted easily. However, my lord, I believe we already have more than enough to be successful without this information."

"But it would be good to get inside before they know what's going on," General Nook said. "We can cause confusion by striking within during the outer siege."

Rog pondered his vision of the attack. Then an idea came to him. He looked up at his generals and smiled. "We can swim there."

"My lord?" Nash asked.

Nook laughed.

Rog's smile did not waver. "Think about it, General Nook. If the Wyunaktee expect us on land, they'll have no reason to guard the sea as closely. A contingent of Shawktee, trained and strong swimmers, could infiltrate their defenses unnoticed."

"Aye, my lord," Nook replied.

I'll admit, it's clever," Nash said. "Risky, but clever. But those are dangerous choppy waters."

"From what I know, it would only be not swimmable if we venture too far out from shore. We'll need Bleen to work out the logistics, but it can be done," Rog added, his voice regaining its authoritative tone. "Send for a messenger. I want Bleen, and Druce here by nightfall."

Nook nodded, already walking out of the tent to motion for a scribe to carry out the order.

While we wait, what of the rest of the strategy?" Nash asked. "You've spoken of the land forces, but this swim. What is the aim? To sabotage? To open the gates?"

Nook returned. "Yes, my lord. What are we trying to accomplish with the swim?"

"Maybe a bit of both," Rog said, turning his attention back to the map. "A small team could get inside the wall somehow and create chaos within the city. Open the gates, sabotage their supplies, or perhaps even take Lord Styness by surprise."

Nook's eyes gleamed with interest. "Striking a dagger into the heart of the Wyunaktee. I like it. But what about the frigid waters. A Rauthlin cannot survive them for long, even the strongest Shawktee."

"We'll account for that," Rog assured him. "Bleen can help us insulate the swimmers against the cold. We'll need to know the tides, currents near the city's edge by the sea here," he pointed to a specific location on the map with a wooden door that led into the city. "If we prepare properly, this could work."

Nook glanced at Rog with a smirk. "Swim to a door into Rauthlin City. It sounds mad, my lord. But maybe that's exactly what we need. They will not expect it."

Rog chuckled. "Madness or brilliance. Only time will tell."

The three continued to discuss the finer points of their plans. The conversation subsided and flowed between strategy and logistics until they finally broke for necessities.

Night had fallen a few hours later when Bleen, and his son Druce, arrived. The tent flap rustled as Bleen stepped inside, with Druce trailing behind him. The two generals, alerted to their arrival, also came into the tent as well.

Bleen's shoulders slumped under the weight of a dust-streaked cloak, and his boots left faint traces of dried mud on the floor. His face bore the weary, hollow-eyed look of someone who had spent hours in the saddle.

Druce, on the other hand, looked as he always did, unaffected by the environment and ready to do harm to his enemies.

Bleen pulled off his gloves slowly, flexing his stiff fingers as though the act of gripping reins for so long had left them aching.

"My lord," he said with a hoarse voice, bowing slightly. "I came as fast as I could."

"Bleen," Rog began, gesturing for him to join them at the map. "We have a unique opportunity, but it requires your expertise. I want to know if it's possible for a contingent of Shawktee to swim to Rauthlin City unnoticed."

Bleen raised his eyebrow but didn't scoff. Instead, he stepped forward, his eyes darting over the map. "It may be possible, my lord, but difficult. The water's freezing, and the currents can be treacherous. How many Shawktee are we talking about?"

"A small force," Rog replied. "Enough to infiltrate, open the side door and create chaos. If needed, even open the gates from the inside. But we'll need to protect them from the cold somehow."

"Furs soaked in oils can provide some insulation," Bleen suggested. "Though they'll slow the swimmers down. Maybe lighter clothing can be used." Bleen rubbed his chin. "The blue paste from Heron, that we make the blue oil, can be applied to the skin underneath light tied clothing." Bleen turned to Druce and nodded. "We have done that before, although it was for the appearance of stealth." He looked back at Rog. "I need to think this through."

"Stealth is good." Rog said, "We need to be undetected as much as we can."

Nook spoke up. "And what of the swimmers themselves? Are they trained for this kind of mission?"

"They will be," Druce replied firmly. We haven't done anything on this scale, but Bleen has trained a team of us in ways that we can go underwater with a breathing tube."

"Yes, my lord," Bleen said. "It is possible. We will find a way."

"Make it so, Bleen, you'll oversee the preparations. Let's talk about what we are doing and the timing of it."

The group spent the next few hours ironing out the details, how to prepare the swimmers, the fastening of a breathing tube for the swimmers, how to time the attack with the larger siege, and how to account for contingencies.

"Can we be ready within three days?" Rog asked Bleen. "We must attack in the dark under the cloak of the morning fog."

"We will make it so, my lord," Bleen replied. "Each Shawktee will be responsible for their breathing tube. We'll coordinate and give instruction."

"We need to allow for some adjustments after coming out of the water on the the shore. It may take a few minutes to be ready to fight. But if all goes well, we'll have the element of surprise."

"He's right, Lord Rog," Bleen smirked. "It will be fun, as long as we can get that door open and get inside"

"Hopefully, the potential breach that the Awutanee found has not been corrected," Rog said.

"Trust me, it hasn't," Nash said. "Nothing has changed for decades."

"General Nook will distract them and draw their attention," Rog said pointing to the front of the City's main gates. "He will give us the time we need."

"How long do you think we can survive with the paste in the cold water?" Druce asked.

"Probably about twenty or thirty minutes at the most," Bleen responded. "After that, the chill of the waters will start to affect our bodies."

"Then we'll have to make the swim in fifteen," Druce replied.

"How many can we deploy?" Rog asked.

"I can have about two hundred able swimmers which are strong enough to make the swim and fight," Druce replied. He looked at Bleen. "Sorry, Father."

"It's all right. I know my limitations," Bleen replied.

"Two hundred will be more than enough," Rog said. "That's including you and I, Druce. Since I have never done this before, I trust that you can help me get up to speed."

"We can tie a loose rope between Druce and you to keep you on track," Bleen said. "We will brief you on the rest."

Rog nodded his approval.

"Once again, it will be an honor to go into battle by your side, my lord," Druce said.

"We will prepare the Shawktee and gather the paste," Bleen added.

"Excellent," Rog said. "Then we leave tomorrow for Rauthlin City."

He dismissed them from his tent, leaving him inside to gather his thoughts. He walked over to a table and poured himself a cup of ale from a clay jug, then sat in his chair.

After a time, Auntar came by and peeked inside. Rog beckoned him to enter.

Auntar bowed. "All is in order, my lord. We are ready to march toward Kantar."

"Very good. Soon the Rauthlin will be united. Victory will be ours and the Shawktee will be vindicated."

"This is a great time to be alive, my lord. Our ancestors dreamt of this moment." Auntar glanced at Rog. "May I indulge you with a request, my lord?"

Rog waved his hand and gave a short nod.

"You have placed me over Darmonla and Daman. Darmonla is restless for glory, and it is my belief that Daman should see up close what a battle looks like." Auntar shifted his stance.

Something's bothering him, Rog thought.

"Darmonla presumes you will instruct her to stay back."

That's exactly what I had in mind.

"May I suggest that they go with General Nook's contingent? That way, she can stay back with Daman to give him instruction and perspective while still feeling she is part of the siege."

I know her ways all too well, Rog thought. "And what will prevent her from leaving Daman with a guard and running up to fight at the front?"

"Nothing, my lord. But there is no better training than real engagement. That engagement can be limited. But if she is involved just enough to whet her appetite, and be responsible for Daman's experience, I'm hoping her maternal instincts of protection will kick in." Auntar paced across the tent. "At least, I believe they would, my lord."

Maybe, Auntar is right. The uniting of the Rauthlin will be a historic moment. This may be an acceptable compromise for her to feel included in the battle.

Do you think it too risky?" Auntar asked.

"No, no, very well. I will have them join with the General. I'll talk to her." Rog poured Auntar a drink into a nearby cup. He handed it to him. "Here's to the unity of the Rauthlin."

"For unity, my lord."

They both nodded and took a drink.

"Under Shawktee rule, of course," Rog continued with a nod holding up the mug.

"Of course," Auntar replied. He then drained the rest of his ale. "For now, I'll take care of the attack on Kantar." He sat his cup down and saluted. "I look forward to joining you for a drink in Lord Styness' palace."

Rog also sat his mug down and clasped Auntar's arm with determined acknowledgment. "We have waited a long time for this, Auntar. Yes, we shall have that special drink soon."

Auntar nodded. He then bowed in salute and turned to leave. As he did, he spoke out. "To victory, my lord."

"Yes, Auntar, to victory," Rog replied. He then watched as Auntar exited the tent.

Having learned that the Awutanee threat was no more and that they would be on the offensive toward Rauthlin City allowed Darmonla and Daman to returned to their tent. Darmonla sat in a black leather chair with her pet cantu sitting comfortably in her lap. The cantu cooed as she petted its fur. Ferra, her servant, sat adjacent to her sowing one of Daman's cloaks that had a tear in it.

Several feet in front of them, a guard watched young Daman dutifully go through his fighting stances and drills with his sword. Daman was dressed in a full Shawktee uniform which included his black headband. A red Shawktee symbol was centered on the headband.

"Keep your head up!" the guard barked. "You're too extended with your thrust. Do you want to die quickly? Do it again."

Daman took a deep breath and began the drill again. Darmonla looked up to him. *He makes a face like he's frustrated but he is determined.* She smiled with pride as Daman repeated the drills.

"Lord Rog approaches," another guard called out.

Daman and his sparring partner stopped and glanced at Darmonla.

"Please continue." Darmonla nodded to Ferra, and she put the cloak down and came to her. Darmonla handed the cantu over to Ferra to take away just in case Rog was stressed and got any ideas. The cantu growled in protest at the sudden disruption of her comfort.

Darmonla stood and brushed off her lap.

Ferra helped her straighten up some of her feathers with the one free hand she had, having the cantu in the other. She smiled and nodded approval to Darmonla. She then rushed out with the cantu.

Darmonla sat back down and tried to appear calm, although, inside her thoughts were churning. She had already rehearsed what she was going to say. She wasn't going to stay back and sit around when the state of the Rauthlin nation was going to be determined within a few days. *I will emphasize my own loyalty and secure my participation in the pending battle.* That much she had resolved. She refused to be sidelined like a mere ornamental wife, no matter how others wanted to perceive her. She had earned her place among the Shawktee and was no stranger to blood or conflict. *I have fought in battles before,* she thought fiercely. *I can do so again.*

Secondly, and more infuriating, she was irate over the whispers about the political inheritance of Standist's young wife, Reelema. The Rauthlin Awutanee was known to be as beautiful as she was witty. *She could not be experienced in the ways of war. Even so, would she rival me in the eyes of the Shawktee?* She gnashed her teeth together. *Reelema,* Darmonla thought bitterly, the name tasting like burnt ash in her mouth. *What does she know of sacrifice? Of loyalty?* Darmonla's fists clenched unconsciously in her lap.

And Rog… Her thoughts stilled momentarily before knotting up tighter. *What are his intentions for her?* She didn't trust how closely her husband was tied to this political arrangement. She had always prided herself on understanding Rog's ambitions, even when she didn't agree with them. But now, she had her doubts. She felt vulnerable.

Her temper flared again. *Perhaps that's what Rog wants. Perhaps he thinks I've grown too complacent. And what will happen to the Wyunaktee queen when*

Rauthlin City falls? She could almost hear his voice reproaching her, telling her she was letting emotion cloud her reason. It infuriated her further.

And yet despite all her frustrations, she couldn't deny the deeper ache pulling at her. She loved her husband and missed him. The times of him being away from her had begun to wear her down in ways she hated to admit.

She straightened in her seat, her spine rigid with newfound resolve. The time for brooding was over. Whatever simmered between Rog, Reelema, and the state of the Shawktee, one thing was clear. Darmonla would not be a passive observer. *I will fight for my place. I will fight for myself.*

A part of her still hoped Rog would look at her as he once did, not just as his wife, but as his equal, someone he trusted, someone he *needed* by his side. *If he cannot see that, I will make him see.*

Rog entered. The Shawktee guard and Daman stood at attention and saluted. Rog was clearly proud at the sight of his young son in full Shawktee gear. Darmonla stood and slightly bowed her head. She then looked back up, nervously searching Rog's eyes for confirmation of his continued desire for her.

Rog saluted back and nodded at Daman with a smile on his face, "Continue on, young Shawktee." Daman's little chest seemed to poke out even more. Daman then proceeded with his drills as before. Rog watched his son a few moments more and walked up to Darmonla.

At the sight of Rog approaching, Darmonla lost her thoughts of protest and decided to soften her arguments. The desire for her husband filled her heart.

Rog stopped to admire her. He took a long deep breath. "Darmonla, weeks away from you have been difficult."

"My lord. It has been difficult for me as well. I hate being away from you this long." Darmonla's heartbeat rapidly inside her. She looked over to the guard and Daman. "Please take him outside while Lord Rog and speak in private."

Rog nodded his confirmation.

The guard saluted and he and Daman went outside to continue Daman's training

Darmonla turned back to her husband. "May I embrace you, my lord?"

"I am your husband. You need not ask. I long for your embrace."

Darmonla kissed him and embraced him tightly.

Rog ran his hand through the shiny dark feathers on her head.

Darmonla closed her eyes to his touch. "I am pleased Lord Rog still desires me after inheriting Standist's young widow. Will she also share in your embrace?"

Rog parted back some and chuckled. "Ah, so you have already heard then. No, Darmonla. She will not have that expectation. I have not met her yet, but there is profound respect and loyalty amongst the Awutanee for her. We must be careful. Unfortunately, the turn of events with Standist did not allow for her imminent termination. Perhaps an unfortunate accident can be arranged when the time is right. But for now, we must focus on uniting the Rauthlin. We must secure the appearance of her loyalty, at least for the time being."

Darmonla understood the politics, although she didn't like it. Nevertheless, she was relieved by Rog's answer and continued to press. "And the Wyunaktee, Styness' wife and children? Will you not inherit them as well after the victory in Rauthlin City?"

Rog let out a sigh that sounded like a steady growl. His gaze flicked briefly to her before settling on a spot just past her shoulder. "It is not my plan to have them survive our siege. I have a plan to get inside behind the lines. Hopefully, the issue will be resolved."

Darmonla's eyes narrowed slightly, and she tilted her head as though studying him. "And what is your plan for me, my lord? You have held me back all this time. Will you deny me glory by your side?"

Rog's lips pressed together as he turned his head slightly toward her, though he didn't meet her eyes right away. "You do not hesitate with your questions, Darmonla. Can we not even enjoy our moment together?"

"I have much on my mind, my lord. You understand what it means for me to fight. I was a warrior when you met me. Am I not still Shawktee?"

Rog's jaw tensed, a flicker of something, regret perhaps passing across his face.

"Yes. You remind me continually. But you are also the wife of Rog and the mother of Daman."

"You can only do so much to protect me, Rog. I am what I am. Let me be. Please, do not leave me behind this time." She stepped back and put her head down slightly, "my lord."

Rog sighed. His shoulders slumped as though the weight of both their worlds pressed down on him. He turned and walked over to the opening of the tent. He looked outside where the guard continued to give Daman instructions. The distant clamor of steel against steel carried faintly from outside.

"Do you think Daman is ready to see the carnage of battle?"

"One can never be ready. One must just experience it."

Rog did not respond right away, nor did he take his gaze away from his son. Finally, he turned back to her. "Okay, Darmonla. You can ride with General Nook's contingent."

Darmonla perked up at this response, seeking the hope of opportunity to prove herself worthy.

"Bring Daman and the guard with you. However, you must stay back and not be part of any initial charge of the warriors. You may participate with a clean-up crew when we are victorious." He raised his brow toward her. "Do you understand?"

I can submit to this. Darmonla thought. *It's not totally what I wanted, but at least I'm not going to be left behind this time.* "I understand, my lord."

"Of course, you must defend yourself as the circumstance dictates."

"Yes. Of course, my lord," she replied with a grin.

"And Daman…"

"Daman will handle it. He has your blood in him." Darmonla walked over and held his arm gently. She pressed herself to his side. "My lord, I have another request."

Rog turned his head to her.

"Please do me the honor, when victory is at hand, I request to participate in assuring elimination of Styness' wife and their heirs." She looked up, batted her eyes, and smiled. "We can't have them threatening the reign of the Shawktee and the future of Rog."

"Or the future of Darmonla, you mean." Rog laughed out loud. "That's wonderful, my love. Delicious."

He gently touched her cheek with his hand. He leaned over and kissed her. "You excite me. It will please me very much for you to have opportunity to slay them if the circumstance dictates as such."

"By your command, my lord," Darmonla responded with a coy expression. Rog kissed her again. Darmonla then eagerly looked into Rog's eyes with anticipation and desire. "When do we leave?"

Rog held her in his arms and whispered, "Tomorrow my love, tomorrow. But tonight is ours. Tomorrow, will have to wait."

Days passed. Rog's army had reached the outskirts of Rauthlin City and prepared for the attack. They had camped through the night and now it was hours before daylight. The sprawling encampment of Rog's army blanketed the plains before Rauthlin City. It was a ghostly sea of shadows in the pre-dawn fog. Campfires flickered dimly throughout the camp; their glow muted by the dense mist.

Rauthlin City loomed ahead. Its massive walls created an appearance of a huge silhouette block with torches wavering on top. These lights flickered weakly, too feeble to push back the encroaching darkness.

Within the encampment, Rog's army stirred quietly with disciplined activity. The Awutanee siege engines stood ready, outside of striking distance from an aerial attack. Towering wooden constructions adorned with iron reinforcements, their wheels and frames slick with dew. Catapults, battering rams, and towers built to breach the city's defenses awaited their moment to be unleashed. Three separate brigades began to form leading across the front of the city, with the calvary, ground warriors and archers.

Darmonla sat on a dualicorn and held in its reins. The horse jerked its head back and grunted. The chill of the night air kept Darmonla alert. The ocean sea blew in her face. She peered out at the burning lights flickering on the walls of City ahead of her. Daman sat on another horse next to her with his assigned guard.

General Nook had ridden back and forth through the ranks barking out orders. For Daman's benefit, Darmonla and the guard tried to keep pace with the General as much as they could without getting in the way.

Nook now stopped his horse next to Daman and nodded. He looked at him and breathed out the cool morning air. "Wonderful morning for a battle isn't it, young Daman?"

"Yes, it is, General," Daman responded.

Nook then turned to receive report from a nearby captain.

While he did, Daman yawned toward his mother and rubbed his eyes. "It's a wonderful morning, but it's still dark."

"Yes, Daman, it's still dark," Darmonla said. "Darkness and fog will give us advantage in this battle."

"But we won't be able to see them. How is that an advantage?"

"We know where we are going. They must react to us."

"But they know we are here and know we are coming for them," Daman replied.

"But there is also a lot they do not know."

"Aren't we going to attack the city? I heard we have the numbers to do it and our Shawktee are better fighters."

"You are learning, Daman, and asking the right questions," the guard interjected. "Your father would be proud of you. Yes, we are going to attack the city, but it's how we do it that will limit casualties to our warriors…" The guard looked back toward the city, "…and increases theirs."

"How many do you think will die?"

"Hopefully, it will be more of them than us. But ultimately the survival of the Clan of Shawktee depends upon our success today. It's important that you understand how important this day is."

Daman nodded in return.

Darmonla smiled at this exchange. She held it dear to her heart. *It is good that he is here. He is learning a lot. It will make him stronger when he comes of age and leads like his father.*

Nook came back to them and waved. . "Come. Let's see how Rog and Bleen are doing with their preparations at the ocean's shore."

Darmonla raised her brow. *What could Rog and Bleen be doing?* She knew Rog had something special planned with Bleen for the attack but did not know exactly what they were doing. She was focused on her own role and her son who looked toward his mother with excitement in his eyes. They both acknowledged him and followed the General into the fog.

The morning fog was thick. Thousands of Rog's Shawktee and Rauthlin gathered facing the city.

Although Rauthlin City was somewhat protected by its walls and barricades, Styness positioned some of troops around and in front of the city to face the coming opposition.

Rog considered this a bad tactical position. *Their strength lies within the walls of the city.* He didn't know if this was out of arrogance or just over confidence.

Maybe it was pure stupidity.

Nevertheless, the Wyunaktee apparently would meet them head on, rather than secure themselves behind the walls . They would try to prevent them from even reaching the city. Another possibility was that it was an act of desperation, and it was already conceded that they would not be able to stop Rog's armies from controlling the city.

It was apparent that Styness was not going to let Rog's army just walk up to the city with their rams, barricade breakers, and constructions.

It was reported that Styness also had a smaller contingent of troops to the west of the city, as he had been made aware more of Rog's army was to the west in between there and Kantar.

Nook's army was readying for the attack with the night fog as their cover. Meanwhile, two hundred of Rog's Shawktee sat with Bleen by the shore. They prepared their bodies and treated their extra outer garments and hoods with thin layers of blue paste.

Nook rode up to Rog with Darmonla and the guard with him. "My lord, the conditions are sufficient to start the siege while we still have the covering of the fog and darkness.

"Excellent, General," Rog responded as another Rauthlin helped rub the dark blue paste on his back and chest.

Darmonla grimaced at the vision of her husband.

Daman eyes were opened wide. He smiled broadly at his father.

Rog smeared paste on his face and returned the smile to his son. Bleen had come to Rog's side. They watched as Rog put on and tied down his outer garments. "Let him down," Rog said. "Daman, come here."

Daman was helped off the horse. "Father, what are you doing?"

"Yes, my lord," Darmonla said looking at him intently. "What are you doing?"

"When Nook is attacking the city from the front, we will have another attack to the west gate of the city," Rog said pointing to the west. "While the Wyunaktee are occupied with the battle, we are going to sneak around to the sea under the night fog." Rog then pointed to the crashing current. "Remember what I told you about stealth training? We will swim underwater with our breathing tubes sticking out. We are going to swim over there to the side of the city. We will get inside behind the enemy lines. Once inside we will pick them off secretly. They will be confused that we are already in the city and will know all is lost."

Daman looked between Rog and Bleen. "What about the paste?"

"It will help insulate them from the cold waters during the swim," Bleen said.

Darmonla folded her arms and shook her head.

Daman nodded. "How can I help?"

"Come," Rog said. "You can help us prepare some of the Shawktee with the paste."

Darmonla smirked. She signaled to Daman's guard to follow them. He dismounted his horse and took up his position.

At that moment, a messenger suddenly rode up to Nook. They all stopped to hear what the rider had to say. "General! We have just received word that Auntar and General Nash's armies have already initiated their attack on Kantar. A contingent of Nash's warriors are moving this way to join the charge of the city's west wall."

"It's too soon," Nook responded. "The rams are not in place to help them yet. They were supposed to attack after we had already engaged. They were supposed to wait just before the morning light."

Nook turned to Rog, who was standing there with the others. "Those coming this way to the west wall, many will be killed."

Rog felt his anger rise as he considered the deviation from what was planned. He closed his eyes and took a deep breath. *Something must have happened in Kantar.* He then opened his eyes and nodded to Nook. "Styness' generals must have gone on the offensive at Kantar," Rog replied. "We must be on guard for similar aggressiveness here too. We must attack before we are attacked."

Nook turned back to the messenger. "How much time until Nash gets here?"

"Maybe fifteen to twenty minutes," the messenger said. "But I'm guessing."

"Alert the ranks to prepare to move out now!" Rog said. "Bleen, let's hurry! Daman, come with me."

Nook looked at Darmonla on her dualicorn. "My lord. May I send Darmonla to deliver the message?"

Rog nodded.

Nook waved his hand to Darmonla. "Ride swiftly to the far end to inform the Commander of the far brigade that Captain Kombul must not wait to branch off to the west wall. Nash will be exposed with his approach. Have them move forward, now! I'll ride to the front." He turned back to the messenger. "Ride on and have them sound the alarms! We move to attack. Go!"

Nook and the messenger pulled their reins and rode off into the darkness.

Darmonla glanced out at Daman, who ran toward Bleen and Rog to help the other Shawktee swimmers get prepared. "Have Daman stay with Bleen when they part!" she shouted to the guard. "Bring him back to me when you can."

The guard saluted.

Rog nodded to her in assurance. Remember what we agreed to. After you deliver the message, fall back behind the ranks.

She saluted him. She then turned her dualicorn and rode off in haste into the night fog.

Several minutes had passed. Nash's warriors began to appear out of the fog charging toward the west side of Rauthlin City. It was too late to intercept them or slow them down.

Meanwhile, Nook's army plodded forward at the front with their rams and constructions. Supporting ramps plopped down over ditches. Warriors pressed forward holding up large shields. They pushed forward with the anticipation of the pending carnage. As the fog continued to roll in from the sea, the alarms from both camps echoed into the night air.

The siege of Rauthlin City had begun.

THE SIEGE OF
RAUTHLIN CITY

Out of the thick night fog, the first wave of Nash's Awutanee appeared on their horses. Then, like a rain of thunder, the whistle of darting arrows pierced through the fog without warning, finding flesh and littering the earth around them. Horses shrieked and toppled, throwing their riders to the ground. Awutanee warriors cursed and shouted in confusion, scrambling to shield themselves from the unseen onslaught. Riders frantically tried to regroup, shouting for orders that could not be heard over the noise of neighs and screams.

For those riding behind, the fallen had created a maneuvering nightmare. Horses cut around and jumped over them. The arrows kept coming. But so did the Awutanee.

Nash's horse was struck twice but he continued to push the horse forward to its limit. In the disarray the wounded horse stumbled. Time slowed as Nash was hurled from his saddle. He felt the wind of arrows fly by before he crashed and rolled forward in the dirt.

More arrows jetted by him and landed to the left and the right of him. The horse was no longer of use. He tried to ignore the pain to his ribs and hip from the fall. He winched and retrieved his shield.

Something has gone wrong. Where are the Shawktee? My message must not have gotten through in time.

Whatever the case, Nash was determined to press forward on foot. He was not alone. One of his Awutanee warriors rushed past him both on horseback and on foot. He unsheathed his sword and yelled out to his fellow warriors to press ahead. As they continued, several of his warriors were hit with arrows. Some staggered forward and others crashed to the ground in anguish.

He had taken only a few steps when a rider's horse jumped high over another and fell awkwardly. Nash tumbled aside. Its rider was thrown to the ground. The rider angrily rose to his feet and limped a few steps. He grasped his sword and, when he noticed Nash, offered a sharp salute.

Nash nodded in return and they both pressed forward.

Nash heard horns sound off from behind the walls. The steady stream of arrows was cut off. The Awutanee had reached Styness' ground troops and were cutting through their ranks. Through the fog, Nash could hear the enemy shouting as they rushed forward. Swords and shields clanged in a rising cacophony of battle.

A Wyunaktee warrior charged straight at him. Nash rammed him in the face with his shield. The Wyunaktee stumbled about, disoriented, blood streaming from his nose, before one of Nash's warriors ran him through with a sword.

More warriors had appeared from behind Nash, each bearing Shawktee headbands and battle dress. Tattoos adorned their cheeks.

Nash grinned. *Our new Shawktee allies have joined us.*

Another Wyunaktee hurled himself at him.

Nash stepped out of the path of his swinging sword and slashed his own blade deep across the Wyunaktee's chest, then shoved another out the way with his shield. When that Wyunaktee stumbled back, a Shawktee suddenly appeared from out of the fray and drove his sword into his back. The Shawktee did not linger over his kill but withdrew the sword in time to engage with the next Wyunaktee that appeared.

Nash pushed forward, as more of Rog's Shawktee joined the fray. Their battle cries pierced the fog, a fierce contrast to the chaos that had engulfed the west wall. It was then that Nash began to see the full scale of the carnage. He maneuvered around fallen bodies, both the Awutanee and the Wyunaktee. Twisted forms lay sprawled in the blood-soaked mud, their lifeless eyes staring into the void. Horses lay where they had fallen, their riders tangled beneath them, crushed or pierced by arrows some still crying in agony.

But amidst the grim scene, Nash noticed something else. More of his warriors were pressing forward, their numbers swelling as the Shawktee continued to pour in. Nash's keen eyes caught the disarray in Styness' ranks. His enemy's archers were retreating from their positions, their bows abandoned as they scrambled to escape the Shawktee onslaught. Wyunaktee ground troops, overwhelmed and outflanked, tried to form a defensive line but were cut down before they could regroup. The front of the west wall had become a slaughterhouse.

Morning was breaking. The pinks and purples of dawn suffused the midnight blue sky. Some of Nook's troops had arrived with rams and were crashing them upon the Westside gates. Ladders rose against the walls of the city. Warriors began their ascent.

As Nash approached the wall, one of the nearby climbing Shawktee was shot down and fell to his death. Nash watched as more were shot by archers as they attempted to climb to the top.

"Archers!" yelled out one of the Shawktee captains. Shawktee archers hurried forward and sent volleys to the top of the citadel walls. They were joined by the Awutanee.

The Wyunaktee archers shifted their fire from those on the ladder to the ground fire coming up to them. Some Wyunaktee on top attempted to push the ladders away, but it was difficult because of the angle and weight of the ladders.

The second a Wyunaktee appeared on the wall, he was shot at from ground archers.

The Shawktee and Awutanee continued to climb. It became apparent that the west side would soon be taken. Nash was joined by others, eagerly waiting for one of the west gates to be broken in. Their warriors were routing the remaining Wyunaktee ground troops.

Nash surveyed the battlefield, his eyes scanning for his commanders amidst the morning fog and carnage. *We must stay focused. The city is within our grasp.* His thoughts raced as he calculated the next move. *We must send word to Nook. He needs to know we're about to breach the west wall.*

He turned sharply, spotting one of his commanders. "Get messengers to General Nook!" Nash bellowed, his voice cutting through the din of the battlefield. "Tell him we're about to enter! We need his reinforcements ready to secure the streets!"

As Nash turned back toward the gates, the pounding of the battering ram echoed in his ears. It was a massive, hulking construct of darkened oak, reinforced with iron bands. Its head had several thick triangular points that castoff chunks of the wood of the gates with each crash. The ram was suspended by thick chains attached to a wheeled frame, which creaked under its immense weight. Each swing of the ram sent a shudder through the air. The relentless rhythm of wood against iron was like a heartbeat, driving them closer to their prize.

With a splintering crash, one of the thick iron hinges gave way, sending it clattering to the ground with a deafening boom. Nash's heart pounded as he saw the gap widening. *This is it. The walls that have defied us for years are falling.* He clenched his fists, as the next swing of the ram smashed through, creating a jagged opening in the once-imposing barrier.

A grin spread across his face. *Under Standist, I only dreamed of this. But under Rog, it's about to become reality.* Nash tightened his grip on the hilt of his sword. *The west city gate has been breached. Soon, the Rauthlin will be one.*

"Get ready to charge!" he hollered. "The city will soon be ours!"

"Incoming! Shields up!" shouted one of Nook's commanders, his voice cutting through the chaos of falling Wyunaktee arrows. The Shawktee main forces continued to push relentlessly toward the city's main gate, their advance undeterred by the bombardment of arrows clattering off their raised shields. Nook's archers, stationed behind the advancing shield wall, returned fire in precise, disciplined volleys. Many arrows found their marks among the Wyunaktee on top of the walls, while others plunged into the ranks of ground troops amassing for a countercharge at the city's front.

Nook stood at the center of his command, his sharp gaze sweeping over the battlefield. *They're gearing up for a frontal assault. Foolish.* His lips curled into a grim smile. *They should have stayed behind their walls, fortified their positions. But they've handed us the advantage. The Shawktee are right to rule over these Rauthlin. Both the Awutanee and Wyunaktee were cursed with pour leadership.*

He bellowed out to the archers. "Archers, aim low! We need to break their charge before it begins!" His orders were swiftly carried out. The next volley struck the advancing Wyunaktee ground troops and threw their ranks into disarray.

The Shawktee counter-defense was methodical, almost mechanical in its efficiency. Shields locked, weapons poised, they pressed forward like an unrelenting tide, forcing the Wyunaktee to cede ground. Nook allowed himself a moment of satisfaction as he saw the enemy faltering. *We're breaking them. The rams and siege towers will reach the walls unimpeded at this rate.*

Suddenly, the Wyunaktee warriors surged from their scattered ranks and launched a desperate frontal assault on Nook's advancing forces. Swords clashed, shields splintered, and the battlefield erupted into a violent melee of hand-to-hand combat.

Nook's confidence was unshaken. *They're desperate now. Our warriors are superior and thrive in hand-to-hand combat. This is exactly what we wanted.* "Stay tight and advance!" he roared, raising his sword high. "Let them feel the blades of the Shawktee!"

Shawktee voices roared as the Shawktee ran out to meet them.

The Wyunaktee warriors fought with determination, but for every foot of ground they gained, the Shawktee reclaimed it five times over. The Shawktee were in their element, their training and battle-tested resilience shining in the chaos of close combat.

It was clear to Nook that the Wyunaktee's strategy would not be successful. *Yes, they should have stayed behind their walls,* Nook thought, his smirk returning. *But instead, they've delivered themselves to us on this killing field.* He raised his voice again, issuing fresh orders. "Press forward, we break them here!" he shouted. "And get those towers and rams to the front!"

Toward the back edge of Nook's moving army, paste-covered Shawktee moved forward, waiting for the signal to break off in the dark fog to the sea. At the appointed time, Druce held up his arm and passed on short chirping whistles to his fellow Shawktee. Their dark figures ran quietly into the swaying waves of chilling waters. They waded in slowly, at first, limiting their splashes despite the waves.

Each Shawktee affixed their breathing tube firmly in their mouths. One by one they submerged themselves under the water.

Through the fog, Darmonla spotted the commander on his horse giving orders to several ground Shawktee under his command. They all turned to her as she approached. She pulled the reigns of the dualicorn and stopped before them. She spoke without saluting. "Rog commanded to sound the alarms and move out now! Nash is approaching the west side of the city earlier than planned."

The Commander turned to those around him. "Go, now. Sound the alarms!" He then saluted her and rode off.

She saw Shawktee gather in packs around her and move forward. She looked toward the city. Battering rams and towers were pushed forward by packs of warriors ahead of her. She could hear their shouts as they guided the structures forward over the terrain. The smell of warfare was in the air mixed with the morning fog. She rode out further toward the city toward a group of archers. Darmonla's heart pounded with excitement. She was in the fray and rode behind them.

"Shields up!"

Enemy arrows filled the air. They clanked against the shields and thumped into the ground. She could feel the arrows streaking around her. Some Shawktee cried out. Meanwhile, an arrow thumped into the flesh of her horse's neck. The horse jerked backward and neighed. Blood ran down from the horse's neck and covered Darmonla's arm as she tried to steady it.

All she could do was duck behind the mane of her horse and hope she was not hit.

The horse stumbled. Darmonla attempted to pull the reins back but she strained against the animal's throes. It bucked so badly she had to dismount.

More arrows showered them. Darmonla cursed while ducking again, this time behind the teetering horse, using it as a shield. Two more arrows thudded into its hide, and it dragged her a few feet as she held onto the reins.

The horse then jerked away from her, tearing the reins from her grasp and throwing her off her feet. It then wobbled and then collapsed.

Darmonla looked back toward a forward moving tower construction. She made a dash for the advancing warriors moving it, which also acted as their shield. More arrows whizzed by. As she slid behind the rolling tower.

Darmonla thanked the warriors who had covered her. She pulled out her sword. She had nowhere to go but forward with the advancing construction. Their role was to get the tower to the wall. Now, by default, it was her role also.

She cursed again under her breath. *Rog is not going to be pleased with me. This is worse than him swimming in the choppy water of the cold sea.*

Rog watched several Shawktee swimmers go into the water ahead of them. Meanwhile, Druce and Rog were tied loosely to each other, several feet apart, around the waist. They nodded at each other and entered the choppy chilling water behind the first pack of swimmers.

Rog could feel its frigidness against his body. *Did Bleen make a mistake about the paste insulating us? Well, I suppose it doesn't matter. We are committed.* Rog placed the prepared breathing tube in his mouth and submerged himself with the others. As he swam, he came to realize it would be much colder without the paste.

He peeked above water every couple of minutes to make sure his bearings were correct, while also tugging on the rope guiding him where he was supposed to do. If any of the warriors deviated too much, they could drift off too far and be sucked in by the unforgiving current. Occasionally, he bumped into another swimmer. That was also to be expected.

Rog felt the thump of his own heartbeat. The sound of his breath resonated through the tube.

Rog knew from the timing he would soon reach the point where they would turn inland to shore. He peaked his head out more frequently to hear. Listening was important as visibility was difficult beyond several feet.

When he put his head up, he didn't hear anything but some splashing and his own heartbeat. Druce had not risen yet; his rope tugged Rog on. He submerged himself again and kept swimming.

He came up again. He heard the low whistles of the front Shawktee. He submerged and swam ahead with the others.

Rog popped his head up again. This time Druce emerged, too, but he almost bumped into a Shawktee who was suddenly right in front of him, treading water. The Shawktee looked at him expressionlessly, then nodded to shore. They turned and started to swim to the shoreline.

Rog's anticipation raised another notch. They counted on being unnoticed. They all knew that if discovered, they would be exposed to archers who could easily pick them off. He kept swimming.

His legs touched bottom and knew within the next couple of strokes he would be able to stand. As soon as he could, Rog waded to the shore with the others.

He looked around him with pride at the silhouettes of Shawktee coming up out of the water in the night fog. They moved uncontested to the short shoreline of the eastern wall. On the shoreline, Druce cut loose the rope. They disrobed their outer insulated garments and acclimated themselves.

A small opening, on the bottom of the wall, big enough for a Rauthlin to slide through, appeared ahead. A bolted door to the outside was also nearby. *Our informants were correct*, Rog thought.

Druce and three other Shawktee slid through the opening while Rog and the others waited spread out against the wall. The remainder continued to discard their hoods and ready their weapons. Rog did the same. He shook the excess water from his black-feathered head and tightly gripped a sword in each hand.

A Shawktee slid back out from the opening and signaled it was okay for Rog to enter. As he did, the Shawktee also signaled for five more to follow. That signaled to Rog that all was not secure. Some clean-up was needed before they unbolted the door. Rog crawled through with his swords out in front of him. He came up in a storage area surrounded by several stacked barrels. He stayed low, listening intently. From the distance came a dissonance that brought a slow, satisfied grin to his face. The rumbling of frantic voices echoed punctuated by the shrill blasts of horns sounding alarms. Shouts overlapped and merged into an indistinct roar, thick with fear and confusion. It was pleasing to hear.

They're panicking, Rog thought, his lips curling into a predatory smile. *They weren't ready for this. They thought their walls would keep us out, but their city is already ours.*

Two Wyunaktee bodies had been dragged behind the barrels where they were. Rog scooted himself to Druce, keeping low behind the stacks of barrels. Just beyond them, some Wyunaktee warriors rummaged through crates near the bolted door, their attention focused on their search. Druce caught Rog's eye, his expression tense but steady. He then glanced behind Rog and signaled for five Shawktee to enter. The warriors scooted themselves in and crouched in readiness. Druce then pointed to the door and raised three fingers, to signal three targets.

The Shawktee retrieved their daggers and with practiced precision, slipped into the shadows, their movements fluid and deliberate. There was no sound beyond a brief rustling and some muffled grunts. Their final breaths stifled before they could call for help.

As this was happening, Druce leaned over and spoke with Rog in a low whisper. "My lord, according to the plans, Styness' palace is in that direction," he pointed. "These parallel side streets should lead us there."

Rog nodded with a smile.

Just then, shouts were heard that the Shawktee had reached the outer walls of the city.

"Let's hurry while we still have the fog," Druce said. "The morning light is starting to come in."

"Remember. We take out everyone we encounter along the way," Rog said. "Everyone."

"Understood," Druce replied. He passed the information to a lead Shawktee warrior.

By then, Shawktee had dragged the newly disposed bodies toward them and out of the way. Others assisted in unbolting and opening the door. The Shawktee came in and veered to the left and to the right to meet up with their leads. Then with organized precision, the Shawktee crept through the morning fog toward the palace. With swords drawn, their dark silhouettes moved down the narrow side streets.

They approached their destiny.

Rog could taste victory.

Some of the moving tower constructions were designed whereby they could scale the wall under the cover of it. A number of these constructions were already ablaze because of multiple hits from fiery arrows. The construction that Darmonla was with had a few burning arrows stuck in it, but the construction was not threatened to be consumed by fire yet.

In the heat of battle, Darmonla and her fellow Shawktee warriors protected the path and pressed forward. Hand-to-hand combat was now all around her. Her heart raced as surrounding Shawktee unsheathed and readied their swords. Darmonla did the same. A few attacking Rauthlin came close, and one took a swing at her with his sword.

Darmonla's sword met his as another Shawktee ran him through.

They refocused and continued to push the construction ahead and made way to remove obstructions and clear the way for the ground ramps to be laid over ditches.

Darmonla looked up as they were nearing the wall. Other towers and ladders were in place. Shawktee warriors entered the towers and climbed. Their rams slammed at the front gates.

The gates began to give in. Darmonla grinned. *I was supposed to hang back. But now the morning's blood is on my hands. They will accept me now. They will fully consider me with the respect I deserve. This is our triumph. This is my triumph.*

But she knew her personal triumph would only be complete when Queen Doma and her children were dead. At that turning moment, nothing else mattered.

Meanwhile, Shawktee rams pounded the gates relentlessly. Planks gave way. The enemy had abandoned the city wall. Shawktee swarmed up the wall uninhibited on ladders.

Darmonla felt a rush of satisfaction with Queen Doma on her mind. *We are going in.*

Rog and his Shawktee rushed down the city street. When they encountered enemy Rauthlin along the way, whichever warrior leading would break off to battle them and the next Shawktee in line would move to the front. It did not matter who they encountered—warriors, citizens, females, young ones, all met the same fate. At that point, the objective was no longer to remain unseen but was to act with swift surprise and keep moving.

A female and child came into Rog's path. Rog cut them both down without hesitation. He then fell back in line. He kept moving. He wondered why they were there in the first place and hadn't fled earlier. However, it didn't matter. They were in the way of his objective. Rog felt no remorse. *We must establish terror and fear over the population to establish our rule over them. Then we can demand their loyalty.*

The morning light broke. Rog considered that his warriors, under Nook, would soon start pouring in. But by then the palace would already be theirs.

He saw the palace through the fog as he approached. The gates were abandoned. Warriors fled. Rog heard more shouts announcing the invaders' presence. "They're inside the city," someone screamed.

Rog did not flinch when an archer, shooting at close range, hit a nearby Shawktee. Before the archer could steady another arrow, two other Shawktee killed him on the spot.

Rog's forces reached the palace gates and swarmed through like a deadly swarm of venomous insects. They maneuvered efficiently and killed Wyunaktee citizens at will. Rog acknowledged one of the commanders and called him over. "Take thirty warriors to secure the interior. Kill anyone that moves. More warriors will be fleeing the walls to retreat to the palace. But they must keep going by. We'll let Nook and Nash take chase. Right now, I want Styness!" He smiled. "Hoist our flags!"

"Yes, my lord," the Commander replied and trotted away to bark orders to a team of warriors.

Rog looked up. His team had draped Rog's flag over the palace gates, its fabric still damp and dripping from the underwater infiltration.

Rog listened as horns blared throughout the city, signaling the walls had been breached. The remainder of the Wyunaktee army was in complete disarray. Nook's Shawktee poured inside the city gates.

One of the Shawktee approached him. "My lord. This way. The palace is secured."

Rog followed Shawktee inside the palace after a group had fought through and secured inside. This was a well-executed slaughter. Another Shawktee approached Rog with a wry smirk. He held out his hand and bowed. "My lord, the skirmishes inside the palace have ceased. The throne room is this way."

Rog took a deep breath and nodded. "Don't relax yet," he called out to the others. "Search room to room and find Styness. If you find him bring him to me. Kill everyone else. No survivors."

Rog followed the Shawktee into the great hall. Three other Shawktee stood at attention. Two thrones sat slightly elevated, one bigger than the other—the thrones of Lord Styness and Queen Doma.

He must be here. He would have fled the wall when our entry was imminent. He certainly should have come here.

Another Shawktee emerged from the side area of the thrones. "My lord, all is secure."

Rog smiled. He pictured himself and Darmonla sitting on those chairs soon enough. He walked past several dead Rauthlin bodies, some

Shawktee and some Wyunaktee, ignoring them until he saw a familiar face. He paused and shook his head. "Poor Mlug, Commander Druce's brother. He was a good young Shawktee." Rog glanced at one of his guards. "Have a scout inform Druce his brother died honorably in the throne room of Styness. There is always some bitterness with victory."

He turned and held his arms out toward the thrones. "But it's victory nonetheless, our victory. Now, the Rauthlin will be united under the banner of the Shawktee."

"My lord, would you like to try the throne on for size?" one of his men asked. His fellow warriors grinned.

"No, I will not sit until I know Lord Styness is dead." *They are proud, and rightly so, but our triumph is incomplete.* He walked over and placed his hand on the shoulder of one of the Shawktee. "We'll set up in here. Let's secure the palace and wait for our armies."

Rog then walked around the great hall. He smiled at the sight of his still soggy shoes leaving thick, muddy prints on the polished brown tiles that led up to the two thrones. The walls were covered with various red tapestries with ancient Rauthlin designs and references to previous Wyunaktee leaders. There were references in the design to the Son of the Morning and his resistance to Elyon, along with the religion of their Dark Priest.

I'm going to have to change some things here. This will be a testament to the Shawktee way and what we desire. Rog stopped and considered the large oval table that extended away from the thrones. He imagined that there were many dining parties and large meetings that took place there, *including meetings about Lord Rog, no doubt.*

A messenger rushed into the hall. He came to Rog and saluted. "My lord, Commander Druce requests your presence outside. Styness has been captured. His two sons have been killed by his side. Styness is gravely injured, and Druce doesn't think he will survive being moved."

Rog beamed. "Looks like that chair won't be cold for too long." He turned back to the messenger and waved his hand. "Lead the way."

They trotted out of the great hall and headed outside. Rog became more and more excited with every step he took. They ran briskly through the front gate where Shawktee guards were posted.

The morning light shone through the fog. Styness' warriors had turned away from the palace as they ran into Rog's Shawktee. They only had one direction to go, out the back of the city and into the lower hills. Rog knew Nash's warriors would be in pursuit to head them off.

They found a group standing over an injured Rauthlin. Druce walked out to him in salute. However, he paused for a moment, his face was twisted with rage. His chest heaved. "I received the report about Mlug, my lord."

"I am sorry about your brother, Commander. Please know that he fought with honor in Styness' palace. They delivered to us the Wyunaktee thrones. It now belongs to the Shawktee. We have achieved our objective. He has done great honor to your father Bleen and will be so remembered."

"Thank you, my lord." Druce seemed to gather himself. "Mlug will be remembered as a hero in our household."

"As well as with the stories we tell about what we accomplished here," Rog replied understanding the numerous sacrifices that his family had made for the Shawktee.

Druce then motioned over to a fallen and injured Wyunaktee and spoke in a low voice. "Please forgive us. He was injured before we knew who he was. It's Lord Styness. We backed off of him immediately when we found out. Those are two of his sons lying over there," Druce pointed.

Rog looked at the two decapitated Wyunaktee. He looked back at Druce. "Your work, I see."

"Yes, my lord. I got word of Mlug, and they were the next to present themselves. Their heads are over there," Druce said pointing several feet away. He avoided eye contact and nodded toward Styness. "He is still alive, but barely."

Rog didn't know if he should be pleased with Druce or upset. It was for Rog alone to have that honor if the situation arose. However, he guessed Druce was entitled to some leniency for losing his brother, and Rog was in a good mood. *Druce is one of my best commanders. He has done well.* "Thank you, Commander."

Druce bowed his head, "My lord. It is for you to finish this."

Rog saluted him, which he meant as a gesture of honor under the circumstances. Rog then walked over to Styness. As he was doing so, Nook's Shawktee warriors, and riders on horseback, started to appear. Rog kneeled over Lord Styness.

Styness appeared weak. He was breathing fast and bleeding from his side. Rog leaned close and spoke into his ear. "Hello, Styness."

Lord Styness kept his eyes closed but turned his head slightly toward Rog.

Rog savored the pleasure of the moment. "Open your eyes to your lord. I am Rog. You should have surrendered power when you had the chance."

Helpless, Lord Styness looked up at Rog, whose face was inches away from his own.

"I have taken control of your palace. The city is mine. The Wyunaktee belong to me, now." Rog sneered. "Your sons are dead. Their heads are somewhere in the dirt being trampled over by Shawktee horses." Rog inched even closer. "Now, I will seize your throne, kill your wife, and restore the honor of the Clan of the Shawktee. I will blot out the seed of Styness."

Styness gnashed his teeth and glared at Rog.

Rog positioned himself over Styness and slowly forced his knee into Styness' groin. "Now you will die by my hand." Rog then seized Styness' throat and began choking him.

Styness gained what little strength he had to clutch Rog's arms in defense but was still too weak. Rog knew his hatred burned greater than Styness' fear.

Rog bashed Styness' head into the ground. He continued even after Styness' lifeless arms fell to his side.

He spat on Styness' body and stood. He pulled out both his swords and held them in the air for those around him to see, then looked around at the gathering crowd. "I am Rog! I am Rog!" He then held his arms out and looked up to the sky.

Rog closed his eyes with satisfaction. He took a deep breath and exhaled before reopening his eyes and gazing at his fellow Shawktee. "Today, Rauthlin are again one. The dishonor to Clan of the Shawktee has been vindicated! I am Rog!"

"Lord Rog!" Druce shouted, holding up his sword.

"Rog!" another yelled, and then another until all chanted his name in the morning fog.

Rog couldn't believe he had attained that which was unthinkable weeks ago—absorbing Awutanee territories, conquering the Wyunaktee armies, and seizing control of Rauthlin City and Kantar. He had vindicated the banishment of the Shawktee and united all the Rauthlin under one banner.

My banner, he thought. *The banner of Rog.*

Darmonla pushed through the splintered remains of the gate. Her steps were quickened by the roar of charging Shawktee around her. The fog was letting up. As she passed, she looked at the remnants of the gate swinging limply off its broken hinges.

"To the west!" bellowed the commander from his horse, his voice cutting through the chaos. He pointed his sword toward one side of the citadel. "Our warriors need reinforcement to the west! Move, now!"

Darmonla caught her breath and set her gaze toward the west side. The faint sound of clashing steel and cries of battle echoed from that direction.

"Fall in! We'll cut the Wyunaktee off before they can escape," the commander barked, pointing toward the stony escape route the fleeing warriors were aiming for.

Those with horses surged ahead galloping toward the fleeing enemy. Darmonla scanned the chaos around her, desperate to find a steed of her own. Her chance came when an Awutanee warrior, on horseback, attempted to corner two Wyunaktee fighters near a crumbling section of the wall. She instinctively ran toward them.

The Awutanee warrior fought with reckless determination, his blade arcing downward in a desperate, brutal strike. His sword found flesh, piercing the side of one of the Wyunaktee with a sickening crunch. The wounded fighter crumpled to the ground, gasping for breath as blood seeped into the dirt.

However, the remaining Wyunaktee shifted to the other side, and in a blur of motion, sliced cleanly across the Awutanee warrior's back.

The Awutanee let out a guttural cry. His body jerked violently as the force of the blow knocked him off balance. His grip on the reins loosened, and the horse, startled by the chaos, reared up, throwing him from the saddle.

He crashed to the ground and his sword flung. Dust rose around him. He groaned in pain as he grasped for his sword.

Darmonla arrived just as the Wyunaktee raised his sword high, poised to deliver a killing blow to the injured Awutanee. Without hesitation, cried out and lunged forward with her sword raised, her movements swift and deliberate.

The Wyunaktee turned too late. Darmonla's blade pierced his side. The force of her strike knocked him off balance. He collapsed in a heap, his sword clattering to the ground.

Darmonla turned her attention to the injured Awutanee, who struggled to sit up against the jagged stones of the wall. She crouched beside him, her voice steady but urgent. "Stay here and hold on. Reinforcements are on the way, they'll help you."

The warrior, his face twisted in pain, gave a weak nod.

"I am Darmonla. I need your horse," Darmonla added, her tone direct.

The Awutanee eyes opened wide at the revelation he was saved by the queen of the Shawktee. He nodded and gave a weak salute by raising his fist to his chest.

Darmonla rose, mounted the horse with practiced ease, and urged it forward.

As she rode, the sounds of battle faded into a quieting stillness of a city on the brink of collapse. She glanced around at the smoldering buildings and scattered bodies of warriors and some Wyunaktee citizens.

Her heart raced with exhilaration. *The city has fallen. Rog's plan worked and I am part of it. The Shawktee will respect me as I have fought with them in battle. Soon, I'll be queen of all.*

The thought strengthened her resolve. She gripped the reins tighter, her expression hardening. *I must tell Rog how I fought alongside the Shawktee for victory. But that's not enough. I need to prove my worth to him, and to the kingdom. The Wyunaktee must submit to me. The Awutanee must submit to me. Reelema and Doma must die.*

With that, she rode at a faster pace, her focus sharpening on the path ahead. *But right now, I must find Doma.*

Ahead, several riders galloped through the chaos, shouting commands to rally pursuit of the fleeing Wyunaktee. Their raised voices urged those on foot to rejoin the surging wave of Rog's forces. In the distance, the streets were choked with fleeing figures, both the Wyunaktee warriors and its terrified citizens. They ran together in a frantic, disorganized mass, desperate to escape the advancing tide of Rog's fighters.

Darmonla slowed her pace. Her gaze narrowed as she spotted one of the Shawktee High Commanders, she recognized as High Commander Rulion. Unlike the riders and foot soldiers engaged in the pursuit, Rulion sat motionless atop his horse, observing the chaos with cold calculation.

Darmonla called out and drew her horse to a halt before him.

Rulion saluted her in return. "Darmonla, I am pleased to see you are uninjured. I saw how you got caught in the attack outside the city gates."

"This is a great day, High Commander."

"Yes, a great day. I just received word that Rog and the Shawktee have already taken the palace. Lord Styness is dead."

"And his family?" Darmonla asked excitedly.

Rulion looked at Darmonla inquisitively. "Two of his sons died fighting at his side. Right now, it's just a matter of seeking out one of their high-level officials to authorize their surrender."

"We must find Queen Doma first."

Rulion raised a brow. "Find Doma first?"

"She and the seed of Styness are a threat to the Clan of the Shawktee and the Throne of Rog. My understanding is Doma has a couple of young children as well. Lord Rog authorized me to assist with any clean-up efforts. He expects us to handle this situation."

"I see," he nodded. Rulion then bowed to Darmonla. "Then I am at your disposal. What is your wish?"

"Gather all the females with children and hold them for me to question. We also need to get a Wyunaktee informant who would exchange his life for pointing them out. We don't know for sure what they look like."

He again bowed to Darmonla's authority.

"I presume Rog is also well and uninjured as you did not mention to the contrary."

"Of course. He is, after all, Lord Rog," he smiled.

Just then, Rulion's sharp gaze caught sight of a rider weaving through the chaos, clearly heading in their direction. He straightened in his saddle and raised a hand. "You, there! Report!"

The subordinate rider brought his horse to a stop before them, saluting briefly, but when he noticed Darmonla, he bowed in his saddle. He then turned back to the Commander. "Commander," the warrior began, his voice was deliberate and steady. "We've cut off many of those fleeing to the rear of the city. Most of the resistance there has been crushed. We've already slain dozens."

Rulion's expression remained impassive, but his silence urged the rider to continue.

"Many are hiding in the homes toward the back," the warrior added, his tone heavier now. "Families, females and their children among them.

Surrender seems imminent." He hesitated, then leaned slightly forward. "Your orders, Commander? Should we… continue the slaughter?"

The words hung in the air, as Rulion glanced momentarily at Darmonla before turning back to answer.

"Go door to door and drag them out," he ordered. Take Darmonla with you. She will oversee that decision. She has specific orders from Lord Rog."

"Yes, Commander,"

"We also need an informant," Darmonla repeated.

"We captured some of their warriors who are still alive for now. They were escorting some of the fleeing Wyunaktee."

"Escorts?" Darmonla asked, "For the common public? Were they scattered or with a select group?"

"I believe with a select group, but I'm unsure."

"Again, Darmonla will be in charge," Rulion said. "It is imperative we find Queen Doma and her two remaining children. Move swiftly, before the alarms of surrender are sounded off. After that point, it may become a little more complicated."

The warrior looked to Darmonla for instruction.

"Then let's go there," she said.

The warrior saluted and they both rode off swiftly.

When Darmonla arrived near the rear gate of the city, she observed hundreds of female detainees. They were gathered in defined areas with their children with dozens of disarmed Wyunaktee warriors among them.

The Shawktee took charge of this assignment. The Awutanee were ordered elsewhere. Darmonla's presence brought a few smiles to the Shawktee warriors' faces. She was dirty and in bloodstained Shawktee gear. She had fought just like they fought and now she was a symbol of Shawktee pride and triumph.

A Shawktee approached her and saluted as Darmonla took in the scene. "We are at your command."

Darmonla nodded at him and continued to assess the situation.

"How would you like to proceed?" the Shawktee asked.

"Which one is Doma?" she asked.

The Shawktee joined her in scanning the crowd. "Even fleeing, she and the children would have had a special guardian," Darmonla explained. "Look around for pockets where disarmed male warriors appear to be covering a female or child more than normal. Separate them by force. And get me an informant."

"More than normal?" a young Shawktee asked quietly. The other Shawktee gave him a stern look and the two left to pass the word.

Darmonla paced her horse back and forth around the outside of the crowd. The Shawktee guards separated around sixty females with children from this group. The Shawktee guards paid close attention to any of the detained warrior reactions when they did this and so noted it. As this was happening, she spoke to one of the Shawktee leaders nearby. "The Wyunaktee are not familiar with the hardness of the Shawktee creed. It's time to introduce them to our way. We'll find her."

At that moment, two Shawktee guards approached Darmonla, escorting a captured Wyunaktee warrior. He was lean but powerfully built. Yet now, his posture spoke of surrender. His eyes were downcast, and his face was darkened by defeat. As he shuffled closer, his shoulders slumped, each step a beckon of Wyunaktee failure.

"We briefly interrogated selected warriors and were not able to find one who would point out Doma. We can continue and be more persuasive, but this one seems talkative enough. He remained silent regarding Doma, but he seems willing to submit to Rog."

Darmonla looked down at the detained Rauthlin from her horse. Her gaze sharpened, catching the subtle shift in the warrior's expression as he glanced up, just briefly, before looking away. She could feel he was on the edge of a change in loyalty, teetering toward betrayal.

"So, you would submit to Rog. Yet, you will not tell us which one is Doma?"

The warrior remained silent. His silence told her that Doma was indeed amongst the detainees.

She lifted her head and shouted out to the crowd. "If you don't know by now, I am Darmonla, wife of Rog, of the Clan of the Shawktee. Lord Styness and his two older sons are dead. You are now under our rule. You may have the opportunity to swear allegiance to Rog or have an honorable death according to the Rauthlin way. All we require to settle the matter is Doma and her remaining children. Step forward and point them out to us. Your lives will be spared."

Darmonla inspected the crowds for their reaction. There was none. *Such loyalty is honorable. But they will submit to me after she is dead.* "Very well. If Doma is not given to us, we will begin the executions—Starting with the children."

Darmonla pointed into the crowd. "Round up ten children," she commanded the Shawktee.

The guards complied, prying the young ones from the arms of their sobbing mothers who kicked and slapped rather than standing by. Shawktee slew several warriors who moved to assist these mothers.

The informant, who was held by the two Shawktee next to Darmonla, jerked as if to also come to their defense but then made no other move.

Darmonla waited until order was restored. "Have them kneel."

The Shawktee holding them did as commanded and held their daggers ready, waiting to strike the killing blows.

"Doma, please!" one woman cried out. "Not my child!"

Darmonla smiled to herself in response. *Ah, that confirms it. This one knows she is here.* "Bring that woman forward," she said, pointing.

The Shawktee guards dragged the mother forward, her feet stumbling as they forced her into the open. Darmonla eyed her coldly as they pushed the mother forward in front of her. Darmonla smiled down from her horse. "Mother," Darmonla said, her tone deceptively calm. "Let's end the bloodshed. Where are they?"

The mother wept and looked into the eyes of her frightened daughter, whose wide eyes darted between Darmonla and her mother, her tears welling under the firm hold of the Shawktee warrior holding her.

The mother's body shook with every sob. With a quivering breath, the mother looked up at Darmonla, her eyes filled with desperation. But then her expression hardened. She pressed her lips together and bowed her head, from the judgment above. Though her body trembled, she said nothing.

Darmonla sighed and shook her head, both disappointed and impressed.

"I'll tell you," the would be informant warrior said in a raised voice. "Just spare the others."

Darmonla smiled approvingly and dismounted. "Untie him." She walked up to him and narrowed her eyes. "Now, point them out."

The warrior put his head down and walked to the right of the crowd. He pointed to a female Wyunaktee clinging to a young female child. He then pointed to a young male child standing nearby, his posture rigid, his fists clenched.

The Wyunaktee female straightened up. "I am Doma, Queen of Rauthlin City and Kantar."

"Former Queen." Darmonla could feel her heartbeat within her with excitement. "Well, former queen, present yourself and family for execution."

Darmonla unsheathed her sword. Doma walked forward with her daughter beside her.

Doma's young son was brought forward but flailed his arms and dragged his feet. He withdrew a hidden dagger, let out a loud yell, and charged toward Darmonla. A nearby Shawktee gave him a hard kick in his stomach, and he tumbled to the ground. Another Shawktee then stepped on his back, while the other took away the dagger.

The son shows more fire than his mother, the supposed queen. Darmonla scowled. She tapped her sword under Doma's chin so Doma could look up at her directly and view her executioner. "This is for the banishment of the Clan of Shawktee and your threat to Rog and to me."

She drove her sword through Doma's chest and then did the same to the daughter before either had time to scream.

"Mother!" the son cried out. He squirmed under the foot of the Shawktee, to warrior's apparent amusement.

"Give him his dagger back," Darmonla said. "This is how he chooses to die. Too bad. He could have made a decent Shawktee."

The son cursed Darmonla. The Shawktee holding him let him up. The other Shawktee threw the dagger on the ground before him. "I would never serve Rog or you!" the son yelled. "I would rather die for the honor of my father and my mother!"

"As you wish." Darmonla waved to him to pick up the dagger.

He picked it up and charged at her again, howling at the top of his lungs.

She simply sidestepped him and ran him through with her sword. He crumpled to the ground, lifeless.

Darmonla tilted her head. She dragged her sword across his body, wiping the blade free of his blood.

She then calmly approached the trembling mother whose daughter was still being held for execution. She sheathed her sword and fixed her gaze upon her. "Because you did not betray Doma your queen, even with the threat to your child, you and the children shall live, as long as you now pledge yourself to the throne of Rog and to me."

The mother nervously nodded and bowed in submission. She turned to the others, apparently looking to see if they would take the same pledge. Most, except for several male warriors, also knelt in front of Darmonla. Those that didn't were separated to be executed later.

Darmonla turned away and waved her hand. "I am satisfied. Release the children them back to their mothers."

The Shawktee took their hands off the captive children, and they ran back to their mothers, who cried out in joy and kissed their young ones.

Darmonla walked up to the informant. She glared at him coldly. "If you could betray Doma, your queen, you could just as easily betray me. Therefore, your services will not be needed in the Kingdom of Rog."

She gestured to the Shawktee standing next to the informant. He took his dagger and slit the informant's throat. The informant clutched his neck and collapsed. They watched as he convulsed and bled to his death.

Darmonla mounted her horse, feeling as if a great weight was lifted from her shoulders. She took a long deep breath and nodded to the Shawktee warrior next to her. "Now then, I think my work here is done. Long live Rog."

The Shawktee bowed in unison to their queen and saluted her. She then pulled on the reins of her horse and rode back toward the palace.

AFTER THE SIEGE

Rog and Darmonla rested together in the palace. Commanders organized the burial of bodies, tended to the wounded, and put to death those refusing to pledge loyalty to Rog. Rog had wiped much of the paste off him while Darmonla fell into a comfortable sleep. Because of their exhaustion, they had not changed out of their fighting gear. Darmonla had allowed Daman to go with his guard to be educated and absorb the non-glorified consequences of a battle.

Rog arose from his slumber to reports from Auntar that Kantar was secure. The death toll was far greater in Rauthlin City than in Kantar. Kantar also had a greater number of Wyunaktee now making their blood pledge to Rog.

Rog was used to military rule. However, he knew that over the next few weeks he would have to go through the tedious task of appointing governors and administrators who he trusted. These were positions most of his Shawktee would rather not do. Rog knew he would have to make use of former Awutanee personnel, and even some former Wyunaktee personnel. The Shawktee would have to transition to the tedious governmental affairs of large, structured cities.

Rog was already thinking about what he would do without having battles to fight. *Maybe there will be pockets of resistance to keep us occupied. Maybe Bleen and others can finally turn their full attention to the barriers.*

He called for a meeting of the high generals and commanders for the following day in the throne room. Although Rog's battle plans for conquest were very precise, his plans for governing after the fact were limited. A viable government had to be set up quickly.

Rog rolled out a map of the previous Awutanee territory and studied, frowning slightly as he perused the landscape.

Nook entered. The guards stood at attention and saluted his arrival. He walked up to Rog with a broad smile on his face and bowed. "Long live Lord Rog, supreme leader of the Rauthlin Kingdom."

Rog lifted his head. *I like the way his accolades sound.* He gestured at the map. "Yes, General, and now it's time to govern."

"Your continued leadership and wisdom are all we need. "You sent for me, my lord?"

"Is Nash on his way?"

"I was not with him. I presume he will be here shortly after receiving the message."

"Good. I would like to talk to both of you prior to the meeting tomorrow. We might need to explore if there are any worthy Wyunaktee administrators?"

"We are still in the process of separating those who pledge loyalty and those who prefer execution. I'll order them to start interviewing any loyalist to see if any would be to your liking." Nook shook his head.

"But I believe we might have better luck with the survivors from Kantar. Maybe Auntar will have a better idea of some potential administrators."

"Yes, administrators who can be trusted," Rog replied sarcastically.

Nook smirked as he walked around the table. "So, my lord, how was your swim?"

"Quite refreshing, General. Thank you for asking. I must give my regards to Bleen and the properties of the paste. I'm thinking about implementing this training for all Shawktee."

Nook laughed. "You didn't leave much for us to do at the palace."

"Just as planned, General."

Nook eyed the table where the map had been scrolled open. "Ah, the new map of the Kingdom of Rog."

"Indeed it is. Although, again, we must appoint governors and administrators. Our military leadership must keep them in line," Rog said. "We must deploy our original Rauthlin and Shawktee strategically."

"Yes, my lord. I see your concern. Nook straightened his posture, his eyes blinking momentarily to the map sprawled out before them. The Awutanee already have a form of government in place that pledged loyalty to you. Maybe we can take advantage of that structure. Tweak it here and there."

"Yes, but they had a governance who is not used to my wishes, nor the way of the Shawktee." Rog's hand tightened on the edge of the table. "Conflict will arise."

"A Rauthlin who dares to have conflict with Rog will be executed." Nook's voice was firm. His gaze was unwavering, as if daring the room itself to defy the statement.

"There have been many Rauthlin who have chosen death today, General." Rog's tone was low, almost reflective.

"And Rog has risen above them all. Long live Rog," Nook bowed his head slightly, his motion precise, deliberate.

"Okay, General. It is right to celebrate for the moment," Rog said, his mouth twitching with a slight smile. "Tomorrow, we have some work to do. Advise me when General Nash arrives and bring him to my chamber." Rog chuckled. "My chamber, I like the way that sounds."

"Your chamber, my lord?"

"Yes, down the great hall then to the right, General," Rog pointed.

Nook saluted and left the throne room.

Rog spent the next few minutes mulling over the map before him, until shouts of triumph from outside caught his attention. He crossed to the window and looked out.

A large gathering of Rauthlin followed a female riding on a beautiful black dualicorn. She was young, very polished-looking and dressed in a black fitted outfit. The horse seemed to prance as it approached the palace. General Nash rode his horse just behind her. Many shouted cheers and followed in behind them.

The commotion eventually caused Darmonla to awaken from her rest as well. She walked up and joined Rog at the window. "What is all the commotion about, my lord?"

"I'm not sure. But I'm sure I don't like it."

Rog saw Nook standing in front of the palace waiting for the visitor. Five Shawktee stood both to his right and to his left.

Rog's eye twitched. He clenched his fists

"Reelema. Standist's wife," Darmonla replied in disgust. "The Awutanee. What kind of treason is this?"

Reelema, and the following crowd, stopped in front of Nook. She halted gracefully in front of him. Her smile was radiant yet measured, as if carefully crafted to disarm. "Greetings, General. I am Reelema, wife by gift of the Son of the Morning to the supreme leader of all Rauthlin!" She spoke with gentle authority and confidence, as an adored queen introducing herself to her subjects, projecting her voice loud enough for the crowd behind her to hear.

She turned her dualicorn with an elegant fanfare. She extended her arm toward the crowd, her fingers elegantly spreading as if presenting a great treasure. "Lord Rog!" she shouted, her voice full of pride. When she shouted Rog's name, the gathering crowd repeated Rog's name in praise.

Nook and the Shawktee remained unmoved.

Reelema turned her horse back around and spoke to Nook in a lower voice that Rog and Darmonla could not hear.

From above, Nook's irritation was plain. His jaw was clenched, a muscle ticking just beneath his cheekbone. His brow furrowed deeply, and he exhaled through his nose, the force of it visible even at a distance. His gaze then drifted upward, locking briefly with Rog's. His eyes were shadowed with frustration.

Reelema also looked up toward Rog at the same time to see how he would react.

The Awutanee now challenges us through this crafty female? Reelema has played this well, Rog thought. *I do not want to disrupt the Awutanee's euphoria of unity under my banner. We will bide our time. I can gradually implement Shawktee rule and eliminate their traditions. She can be dealt with later. I must be patient.*

He raised his hand, palm open, and rotated it gently in a downward arc, a gesture of restraint and acknowledgment. Then, with a slight incline of his head, he nodded toward Nook, the motion slow and deliberate, carrying the weight of his authority.

Nook grimaced. He turned back around to face Reelema. After a moment of hesitation, Nook slightly bowed. The Shawktee next to him followed his lead and did the same.

Rog smirked, watching the reaction of the adoring Rauthlin warriors. "It appears the Kingdom of Rog already has divided loyalties." Rog held out his hand for Darmonla to join him. "Let's go down and meet her, shall we?"

With hesitation, Darmonla gripped his hand. The two of them walked down the stairs and outside to the front of the palace.

Darmonla tried to compose herself to repress the burning rage she felt. The Shawktee stepped back to make room for them. She and Rog took up positions next to Nook.

Darmonla became even more self-conscious upon seeing Reelema up close. She became conscientious of her own bloodstained clothing, nowhere near as lovely as what this polished and attractive young Rauthlin wore. She watched Reelema dismount her dualicorn and prostrate herself before Rog. Darmonla's eyes widened. *She's prostrating herself before my husband.* She felt panic..

"My lord, you are blessed and ordained by the Son of the Morning to rule over us," Reelema said, pitching her voice loudly so everyone could hear "I am but a symbol of pledge to what you have inherited from the Awutanee territories. All that we are and all that we have, even to our very spirit and soul, we submit to you." She looked up at Rog. "I submit to you, my lord, my very breath and my very soul, Lord Rog of the Clan of Shawktee."

Darmonla's hands twitched. She was horrified. Then she was furious.

But then Nash and all the gathered Awutanee knelt before Rog. The Shawktee near Rog looked toward one another and began kneeling as well. Darmonla begrudgingly knelt, not wanting to be the only one not doing it. It was begrudging not because of any disrespect for Rog, but because Reelema was the one who initiated it.

"Then come, Reelema." Rog's face was a blank mask, devoid of emotion. "Stand with us as a symbol of Rauthlin loyalty and unity."

All arose. The crowd cheered. Reelema took a place on the opposite side of Rog from Darmonla. Rog spoke to Reelema without looking at her, keeping her volume well below that of the cheers. "Well played, Reelema. We obviously underestimated your gifted talent of manipulation."

Reelema continued to smile to the crowd. "I wouldn't want my lord to be tempted to terminate me without fully understanding my usefulness."

Darmonla, who was also looking straight ahead and waving to the crowd, replied, "Oh, I think I understand your usefulness all too well. I am very tempted."

Reelema did not look at Darmonla or acknowledge her presence. However, she addressed Rog in response. "Darmonla's justice toward Queen Doma has been noted, my lord."

If Rog weren't between us, I would show this rat my justice. Darmonla fantasized running her through with a sword but then dismissed the image. *Doma's death was merciful, but hers will not be.*

Rog's voice interrupted Darmonla's thoughts. "Then I give my congratulations. You have made yourself nonexpendable." Rog turned his head toward her and raised a brow. "For the moment. We will discuss your role later."

He faced one of the guards. "Please have preparations made for appropriate rooms for Reelema and her servants."

"Thank you, my lord." Reelema gestured to her entourage. "And thank you for honoring your agreement under the flags of truce by not harming me."

Rog let out what sounded like a steady gurgling sigh through clench teeth. "You're welcome."

Darmonla understood the delicacy of the situation for Rog. These were battle tested non-Shawktee Rauthlin warriors swearing allegiance to him. Darmonla could tell he was holding back his own rage. *He will probably need to kill something soon to calm his nerves.*

She tried to figure out what happened to such a great day of promise. It was a day that elevated respect for her with the Shawktee Clan.

However, with this intrusion, her insecurity was heightened. She was becoming more resentful by the minute. Yes, she knew Rog probably wanted to kill Reelema too, but that wasn't the point. To Rog, Reelema was an inconvenience. But to Darmonla, she was a threat. Reelema was young and beautiful. She rode in on a prancing dualicorn. She wore a black tailored outfit that emphasized her shapely figure. She used these traits for seductive manipulation, which she was apparently good at, to influence the entire Rauthlin Kingdom.

But despite all of this, what bothered Darmonla the most was that Reelema possessed that certain threatening feminine quality she had no words for, but which every female knew. To make matters worse, she had charismatic power; power which rivaled hers and could eventually turn the affection of Rog.

Reelema must go. No. She must die. She must die painfully.

A LIGHT FLICKERS OUT

AT THE NORTHERN VILLAGE

Weeks had slipped by since their return from the Forbidden Forest. Bumpus had buried himself in his work, fine-tuning the lenses that would reveal the hidden barriers. His mind shifted to Grandel. Lana had been visiting Grandel regularly and kept him updated to her wellbeing. Bumpus had yet to speak with her himself. Yet the urge to share his findings, and hear her thoughts, had been quietly building. At last, he resolved to seek her out the first thing in the morning, as Grandel liked to get up early to pray. *This would be a good time to see her because I could use guidance and prayers right now.*

The following morning, he rose early and made his trek over to her house. The sun was only beginning to press light into the sky when Bumpus reached Grandel's home. When he reached to knock, the air was still, too still for his liking. There was no smoke from the chimney and no scent of herbs carried on the wind. He frowned.

He rapped twice on the door. "Grandel?" he called, waiting for the familiar shuffle of feet or the light laugh that always followed. However, there was only silence.

He tried the latch and found it unlocked, as always. The door creaked open. The quiet inside greeted him coldly. The fire was out. Her chair by the window sat empty, as a beam of morning light shone upon it. The blanket she'd been knitting lay folded neatly on the seat. His heart fluttered. "Grandel?" he said again, stepping in.

He found her in bed, lying on her side, facing the window. One hand rested on her chest, the other beneath her cheek. She looked peaceful. As if she had only just fallen asleep.

But he knew: He knew before he touched her hand. Before he whispered her name again, softer this time. Before the finality of her stillness gripped him like ice. He knew.

Bumpus sat heavily in the chair beside her bed. His fingers trembled as he took her hand into his. It was cool. Her skin, even in death, felt like love and kindness.

He stared at her as his eyes watered. "You slipped away in the morning, like you always said you would," he whispered. He shook his head. Grief welled in him. I was not the kind that came with loud sobs. It was the quiet, crushing kind. *Oh Grandel, I really needed to receive your wisdom and prayers. But even now, I know that you had prayed for me.* There would be no final advice, nor any parting wisdom. Just stillness...

He sat with her for a long time. Then, without realizing it, he found himself kneeling at the side of her bed, just as she had prayed over him so many times. The words didn't come easily, but they came.

"Elyon... she's Yours now. Thank You for the time she gave us. Thank You for her wisdom... for her laugh... for every time she told me what I didn't want to hear." He paused, voice cracking. "I don't know how to do this without her."

A breeze pushed the curtain slightly, letting in more light, seemingly being stirred by unseen hands. Bumpus stood slowly, wiping his eyes. "I'll keep pushing forward," he said quietly. "I'll keep pushing forward."

The walk home was longer than it should have been.

When he returned, Lana was already outside gathering herbs from their garden. She looked up, smiling but upon seeing him, her face changed. She put the basket down and hurried to him. "Father?" she asked, gripping his arm. "What is it?"

He didn't answer right away other than handing her the blanket.

Lana pressed it to her chest. Her lips parted, and her eyes filled fast. "No," she said sadly.

"She went quietly," he spoke lowly. "In her bed. Like she always wanted."

Lana nodded with tears slipping silently down her face. She hugged him. They stood like that for a long while, neither trying to stop the sorrow from coming.

The following day after Grandel's passing, the village had gathered on the eastern hill, where the pines gave way to a plush meadow. It was the resting place of many of the Northern Village Hooni'i.

Bumpus stood with Lana, both dressed in simple earth-toned garments. Grandel had once told him not to fuss when her time came. "Wrap me in a proper cloth," she'd said, "and plant me next to my husband where I can keep an eye on the horizon."

And so, they did. Her body was laid in a shroud of clean linen, embroidered with old symbols of Elyon's light. A few villagers brought flowers from the hills and herbs from their windowsills.

Lana stepped forward and read aloud a short blessing. Her voice wavered, but she carried it through.

When it was Bumpus' turn, he stepped up and looked down at the wrapped body of the widow who had been a second mother to him. His voice was quiet and careful. "She prayed for us," he said. "All of us. Even when we didn't know it. Even when we didn't ask. She gave us what she had. Her sweet wisdom, her loving patience and her best recipes. She listened, and somehow, she always knew what to say." He paused and blinked hard. "And sometimes she didn't say anything at all. She just sat with you until your own words caught up to you," he smiled. "I'll miss that most of all."

Lana reached out and took his hand.

"I guess I had always expected her to outlive us all." He paused and looked over to where she was put to rest. "She was never afraid of the end," Bumpus continued. "She called it going home. Elyon, receive her."

He stepped back, and one by one, those that gathered placed a stone on the grave. Each one being smooth and hand-picked tokens of remembrance. When it was done, and the last shovelful of soil was laid over her, Bumpus lingered at the foot of the grave. He held the folded blanket under his arm. The widow who guided him as a mentor, and to trust Elyon, was laid to rest.

That night, some of them went over to the widow's house one last time. The house was as she had left it, tidy, warm and simple. They had lit a fire in the hearth in her honor. It crackled gently, as if trying to mimic her presence. They exchanged a few stories and warm memories. But after the evening had run its course, all had left, including Lana who had gone back home to rest. But Bumpus stayed behind a little longer.

He sat in Grandel's old chair. He absently ran his hand over the armrest, feeling the worn grooves her fingers had made over the years. His other hand still clutched the folded blanket.

It was only when he stood to place the blanket on her bed that he noticed something tucked beneath the cushion of the chair. It was a piece of paper neatly folded and tied with a thin strip of yarn. It was a note with his name written on the front in her careful, slanted hand.

His breath caught as he sank slowly back into the chair and opened it.

Bumpus,

If you're reading this, then my time has come, and Elyon has called me home.

Don't cry for me, dear one. I have lived long, and I have seen so much good in my years. Just like your mother, you held a special place in my heart. I have prayed for you often.

But I know your heart is troubled. You've felt it, haven't you? That tug. That ache that things are not as they seem. That something stirs beyond the Barriers.

That tug is not madness. It's not rebellion. It is Elyon. He is speaking to you.

The questions you've been too afraid to ask, the thoughts you've hidden away, the dreams that wake you in the middle of the night, all of it is part of His calling.

Difficult days are ahead, harder than you know. The kind of days that will try to unmake even the strongest Hooni'i. You may want to run from it. You may want to bury your head, pretend none of it is happening. But you cannot. Because you were born for this.

Old Hooni'i lore says your name, Bumpus, means "watchful one." As a child, you always thought it silly. I never did. Elyon placed that name on you for a reason.

You are a guardian, a questioner and a keeper of things that others have forgotten. And when the storm breaks, because it will break, it will be your voice that steadies others. Your hands that lift them.

That which Elyon has put in your heart to study and develop, do it!

Do not doubt your worth and do not let fear rule you. You do not walk alone, Trust Elyon's guidance.

I have prayed for you often and now I entrust you to the One who made you.

May His fire guide you always.

With all my love,
Grandel

Bumpus sat still for a long time with the letter resting in his hands. He felt the ache of losing his mentor, but something heavier pressed on him. It was the weight of the world. He rubbed his eyes. After a while, he set his jaw and slowly straightened his shoulders. He carefully folded the letter and tucked it into his pocket.

Bumpus signed. *I hear you,* he thought. *Elyon, help me.*

He rose and walked to the door. But before leaving, he turned to take in the room one last time.

Then, Bumpus returned home.

It had been weeks since Grandel died, yet Bumpus still felt her presence. The feeling was not sadness, but a focused sense of purpose.

The Rauthlin, Bumpus thought. *What are they like? Would they be more of a threat to us than the Zauphrii? Why did they side against Elyon in the great rebellion?*

Bumpus was back in his study adding measurements of distance to maps based on reports from the Southern and Northern barriers. He had picked up a slight cold and was sipping on the herbal drink Lana had prepared for him. He took long sips. The warm drink felt soothing to his parched throat. He was appreciative of the drink but was irritated at the inconveniences of the viral intrusion.

Communication had opened to the Forbidden Forest inhabitants, as well as to the Hooni'i of the Southern Villages. Bumpus supplied them with his special lenses to spy, gather information and report to the various village councils.

Not everyone in the Northern Village was pleased with the cooperation of what they considered anti-Elyon communities and populations. This was especially true of Elder Doyle. However, all shared the same fear regarding the populations beyond. Bumpus thought it ironic that at one time his obsession had been his and his alone. Now it appeared everyone was influenced by it. *My obsession is now the Hooni'i obsession.*

There came a knock at his door. Bumpus ceased writing on his map. "Yes?"

Lana poked her head inside. "Father, Elder Doyle is here to see you."

Bumpus wiped his nose with the rag he had in his other hand. "All right, Lana, you can have him come on back. Thanks."

Lana nodded and went to get him.

Doyle hurried into the room. He scowled. "This has gotten out of hand, Bumpus. Giron is taking teams of Hooni'i to the Grafa forest for warrior drills and Tam and Girard are now recruiting babies!"

Bumpus chuckled. "Babies, Doyle? Really?"

"Well, they look like babies. They are too young."

"You must have forgotten how young I was when you recruited me years ago."

"That was different. We were at war."

"I would rather we be prepared and not have to fight than have to fight and not be prepared."

"Oh, enough with the rhetoric, Bumpus. This is different, and you know it. You know how I feel. We have the barriers in place. Believe it or not, there is a contingent from among the Southern Village Councils who are talking about crossing over and engaging the Rauthlin. Ridiculous!

Suicide! My son came back from the Southern Villages and pretty much barricaded himself in his room. This pandemonium must stop. You are the only one who can do something about it."

Bumpus blew his nose into the rag. He then gently folded it and stuffed it in his front pocket. "I'm sorry about Bracket. I know all of this has been tough on him, but what exactly do you want me to do about it?

"Talk to the Hooni'i. Tell them the invisible has been made visible by the grace of Elyon and your discovery is to help us get closer to Him. Preach the message that the barriers are visible and it's proof Elyon is protecting us. He has made the boundaries visible, so we know where our limits are so not to be harmed." Elder Doyle took a gentler, more measured tone. "The Hooni'i need reassuring. They no longer have peace of mind."

Bumpus was amazed at how the same set of facts could be seen in two totally different ways, or likely more than two. Bumpus hoped Elder Doyle's approach to it was the correct one. It was a more comfortable approach.

I wonder what the Zauphrii and the Rauthlin think about the barriers? Surely, they perceive it as a hindrance, just like the Forbidden Forests people. He considered that Elder Doyle was not completely wrong about his perspective. It was how one viewed the facts that were important, but that view could be delicately manipulated. He figured that was Doyle's role as Elder, to make sense of it all.

"All I can do is tell them the truth," Bumpus said, leaning back in his chair and rubbing the bridge of his nose. "They are going to draw their own conclusions about it, whether it brings us peace of mind or not. Yes, being able to see the barriers is by His grace. My hope is this discovery does help Hooni'i get closer to Him. But why He revealed it to us now is yet to be determined."

"This craziness is not healthy. It's divisive," Elder Doyle replied, waving his arms and pacing a short line across the room.

"Yet Hooni'i are becoming united from the South to the Lake communities, to the Northern village all the way to the Forbidden Forest, or should I say the Northern Forest, now. Yes, Hooni'i unity."

"This is our opportunity to influence them back toward Elyon." Doyle stopped pacing and turned to face Bumpus, his brow furrowed deeply. "I'll admit, some are taking it seriously and praying more, but for the most part it's pandemonium."

"The barriers show us for sure He is." Bumpus tapped the table lightly with his fingers. "However, I think at this point Elyon has already revealed Himself enough. Either Hooni'i will be so influenced or not."

"But influenced how, Bumpus? Doyle jabbed a finger toward him, his voice rising. "With panic, fear, anger, covetousness, hatred, and selfishness? These are the traits of the spirit of war. We are not even fighting a war."

"Courage, bravery, sacrifice, perseverance, tenacity and strength also comes with war as well," Bumpus countered, leaning forward, his palms flat on the table.

"As does pain, loss, and death, Bumpus," he said sternly. "It should not be glorified. I think that is what's happening."

Bumpus sat back with a resigned sigh and held his hand up. "Hypothetically, if Elyon allows them to get through the barriers, we will only have one choice, and we would have to accept everything that goes along with it to survive."

"Again, Bumpus, that's a hypothetical," he waved his hand dismissively. "What proof do you have anything remotely like that is going to happen? The answer is nothing, and you should say so."

"We are still studying the barriers and their populations' behavior. Both the Zauphrii and the Rauthlin's behavior has become different. It seems like they are in preparation for a war themselves."

"Yes, like what we are doing," Doyle threw his arms wide in exasperation. "Maybe it's we Hooni'i who antagonized them to this, Bumpus. Even if it wasn't the case before, it is now. Hooni'i should have just stayed away from the barriers."

"Well, that didn't happen and here we are, Elder Doyle," Bumpus exhaled sharply and shook his head. "What shall we do then? Walk over to the Rauthlin, give them a hug, and say we're sorry?"

"Ayi!" Elder Doyle threw his hands up, again pacing the floor.

Bumpus took a deep breath and clasped his hands together, visibly calming himself. "The elders can put whatever spin on this as they want."

"Our opinion doesn't mean much outside of our Northern Village. Yours does. Besides, the elders are not on one accord about what to do, either."

"Well, Elder Doyle, respectfully, I will continue my work and you Elders can get together and decide how to spin it." Bumpus coughed and cleared his throat.

Elder Doyle shook his head. "Bumpus, Bumpus, Bumpus." His eyes then caught an image in the corner of the room. He walked over to the corner and bent over for a closer look. Elder Doyle's face became pale. He looked back toward Bumpus and pointed to the object on the floor. "Is that what I think it is?"

Bumpus again took out his rag and wiped his nose.

"I thought we agreed. Are you insane, and in the house?"

"It's safe," Bumpus said pointing to the object flippantly. "I plan on renewing experiments far away where it can cause no harm."

Elder Doyle closed his eyes and shook his head. He opened his eyes again and glared back at the object. "Who else knows about this?"

"Giron, Tam, maybe Girard."

"What am I supposed to tell Elder Frencrest and Elder Grier?"

"At this time, nothing, I hope. But I guess you'll have to decide." Bumpus coughed into the rag.

Elder Doyle threw his hands down and started to walk out of the room. "Yes, you're mad. Maybe you are even more dangerous than the Rauthlin!" He stopped at the door and pointed back his finger. "Keep quiet about this and do it way out on the edges of Grafa for Elyon's sake." He then looked down to the ground and back up to Bumpus again, then strode for the door. "Keep me updated. And take care of that cough!"

The door slammed behind him.

"Okay, Doyle, I will," he said. "I will."

Bumpus was alone with the object in the corner of the room. He walked over and picked it up. While he did, he considered the blue oil inside. He gazed upon it intently. *It's such a small and harmless looking object and yet so deadly, so painful.*

Bumpus' eyes welled and he let out a long sigh. It had been about eighteen years since he had last considered this object. Droplets of sweat formed on his forehead. His heart raced. He couldn't tell if he was getting a fever, or it was the stress of responsibility pressed upon his shoulders. He patted his forehead with the rag in his hand.

Bumpus gathered his resolve and continued to stare. He knew what needed to be done. *I must focus. It's time to put my fears behind me. Our lives may depend upon it.*

End of Book I

The saga continues in Book II: Get your copy of
RESCINDING BARRIERS